Courage for the Flying Nightingales

Vicki Beeby writes historical fiction about the friendships and loves of service women brought together by the Second World War.

Her first job was as a civil engineer on a sewage treatment project, so things could only improve from there. Since then, she has worked as a maths teacher and education consultant before turning freelance to give herself more time to write.

In her free time, when she can drag herself away from reading, she enjoys walking and travelling to far-off places by train. She lives in Shropshire in a house that doesn't contain nearly enough bookshelves.

Also by Vicki Beeby

The Women's Auxiliary Air Force

The Ops Room Girls
Christmas with the Ops Room Girls
Victory for the Ops Room Girls

The Wrens

A New Start for the Wrens
A Wrens' Wartime Christmas
Hopeful Hearts for the Wrens

Bomber Command Girls

The Girls of Bomber Command
A Wedding for the Bomber Girls
Christmas for the Bomber Girls
High Hopes for the Bomber Girls

The Flying Nightingales

Courage for the Flying Nightingales

VICKI BEEBY

Courage *for the* Flying Nightingales

CANELO

First published in the United Kingdom in 2026 by

Canelo, an imprint of
Canelo Digital Publishing Limited,
20 Vauxhall Bridge Road,
London SW1V 2SA
United Kingdom

A Penguin Random House Company
The authorised representative in the EEA is Dorling Kindersley Verlag GmbH.
Arnulfstr. 124, 80636 Munich, Germany

Copyright © Victoria Beeby 2026

The moral right of Victoria Beeby writing as Vicki Beeby to be identified as the creator of this work has been asserted in accordance with the Copyright, Designs and Patents Act, 1988.

All rights reserved. No part of this publication may be reproduced or transmitted in any form or by any means, electronic or mechanical, including photocopy, recording, or any information storage and retrieval system, without permission in writing from the publisher.

No part of this book may be used or reproduced in any manner for the purpose of training artificial intelligence technologies or systems. In accordance with Article 4(3) of the DSM Directive 2019/790, Canelo expressly reserves this work from the text and data mining exception.

A CIP catalogue record for this book is available from the British Library.

ISBN 978 1 83598 320 1

This book is a work of fiction. Names, characters, businesses, organizations, places and events are either the product of the author's imagination or are used fictitiously. Any resemblance to actual persons, living or dead, events or locales is entirely coincidental.

Cover design by Lisa Brewster

Printed and bound in Great Britain by Clays Ltd, Elcograf S.p.A.

Look for more great books at
www.canelo.co | www.dk.com

For my family:

Mum

Duncan, Jana & Emma

Chris, Katka & Elena

Chapter One

March 1942

An air of excitement greeted Ruby Morris when she trudged into her sleeping hut. Her two best friends were huddled around the stove, one red and one brown head close together, so engrossed in their conversation that they didn't appear to have noticed her arrival.

'I'm going for it,' Holly Hardwick, her friend and fellow nursing orderly was saying. A lock of red hair fell over her eyes and she pushed it aside. 'What about you?'

Meg Fairweather's eyes shone. 'Try and stop me. This will make everyone back home sit up and take notice.'

Ruby closed the door behind her, and the slam made Meg glance up. 'Ruby! Come and listen to this.'

Ruby ignored them. She was so tired after her long shift at RAF Leecliff's hospital that she could do no more than grunt a greeting. She flung herself upon her bed and closed her eyes. A ten-minute nap. That was all she asked. Then she would somehow summon up enough energy to ask what had happened.

Her mattress dipped with a creak of springs as someone sat by her feet. She groaned and opened her eyes to see Holly grinning down at her. She scowled. 'Leave me alone.'

Holly gave a sympathetic tilt of the head. 'Bad day?' But her blue eyes were dancing, and Ruby could see she was bursting to share her news.

'The worst.' Ruby dragged herself to a sitting position, resigning herself to the fact that Holly wouldn't let her rest. 'Half of the ground crew seems to have picked up a vomiting bug. I've been mopping floors and washing out basins nonstop.' She narrowed her eyes at her two friends. 'You two picked a good day to have off. What have you been up to?'

'Oh, just a trip into Bristol. But that's not important. You'll never guess what we've heard!' Holly bounced on the bed.

Ruby groaned. 'Will you let me sleep once you've told me?'

Holly beckoned Meg forward. 'You tell her, Meg. You're the one Squadron Officer Fleming collared after breakfast.'

Meg perched on the next bed. 'The RAF is starting up an Air Ambulance Service and they're asking for volunteer nursing orderlies.'

'Fleming said Meg would be perfect for them,' Holly added.

'Probably trying to get rid of me.' Meg gave a self-deprecating smile.

'Rubbish!' Ruby hated it when Meg talked herself down. 'You're the best nursing orderly we've got.' She glanced at Holly. 'It does sound exciting. Are you volunteering too?' She felt a twinge of dismay at the prospect of her two best friends leaving. They had been together ever since their training, and she'd been overjoyed when they had been posted to the same RAF station on the outskirts of Bristol.

'Of course!' Holly said. 'I put your name down too.'

Ruby sat bolt upright, all her weariness gone in an instant. 'Then you can cross it out! I'm not doing it.' Panic clawed at her innards.

But when she saw how upset Holly looked, she regretted her outburst. 'We have to volunteer together,' Holly protested. 'We're friends. We stick together.'

Coming from anyone else, Ruby wouldn't have taken it so seriously, but she knew how important their little circle of friends was to Holly. They had only been together a week when Holly had told Ruby and Meg that she was an orphan. She had been brought up by an aunt and uncle who had made no secret of their reluctance to bring up another child just when their two sons had left home. Although she hadn't gone into much detail, Ruby had got the impression that Holly's childhood had been very lonely and she had been only too happy to join the WAAF the moment she was old enough. Ruby bit her lip, hating to upset Holly, knowing how hard it would be on her to break up the group, but how could she explain that the very thought terrified her?

'I'm sorry,' she said finally, 'I don't think I can.'

'Why not?' Meg was regarding her with a furrowed brow. 'Are you scared of flying?'

'Something like that.' It was easier than admitting the truth.

Holly sprang to her feet. 'Okay. I'll tell Fleming that we're not volunteering after all. I'm really sorry I didn't ask you first. I just thought you'd be as excited as Meg and me.'

'Thanks.' Then Holly's words sank in. 'Wait. You're taking all our names off the list? But I thought this was something you really wanted to do.'

'Only if we're all together.'

This wasn't an attempt at manipulation, Ruby was certain. She knew her friend too well and knew Holly would never stoop so low. 'You should do it. I can see how much this means to you. Don't let me hold you back.'

'It does mean a lot, but my friends mean more,' Holly replied. 'I'd much rather us all stay together than go our separate ways.'

This was too much for Ruby to bear. 'What do you know about the job?' she asked. 'Where would we be based?'

Meg answered for her. 'We don't know an awful lot at the moment.' She glanced at Holly. 'Volunteering is no guarantee of getting the job, because we have to go through an interview first. Then there would be training at RAF Starsden.'

Ruby perked up. Starsden was on the northwestern outskirts of London and not far from her parents, who lived in High Wycombe. And really, she couldn't bear to disappoint her friends, who both looked eager to pursue this new opportunity. 'Maybe it wouldn't be too bad after all,' she said. She drew breath to ask about the interview but was enveloped in a cloud of violet scent as Holly pulled her into an enthusiastic hug.

'Thank you!' Holly pulled her to her feet and they were capering around the hut in an impromptu polka. 'You won't regret it, I promise. And we'll do all we can to help you get over your fear, won't we, Meg?'

Meg was pulled into the celebrations. 'It's really a very safe form of transport,' she said. 'And we won't be flying into action. I'm sure you'll get used to it.'

'Absolutely,' Holly told her. 'The important thing is, we'll be together.'

But Ruby wondered how they would react if she told them she wasn't scared of flying but of the responsibility. Working in a hospital was easy. It might be messy and unpleasant at times but at no point did she make any decisions to do with a patient's care. She just did what she was told. She had given up nursing because she was terrified of making a mistake that could end up killing a patient.

In the days running up to the interview, Ruby persuaded herself all would be well, even if she was selected. The RAF was recruiting WAAFs as nursing orderlies, which was the role she was already doing, and she had never been expected to do anything more demanding than take a temperature or change a dressing. For the most part, she acted as an assistant to the nursing staff and worked under their supervision. She was never in sole charge of a patient and surely it would be the same in the Air Ambulance Service – there had to be a trained nurse or doctor on the crew.

Therefore, she was feeling much more confident when Squadron Leader Norton arrived from RAF Starsden four days later to conduct the interviews.

Ruby joined Holly, Meg and the other candidates in the break room while they waited to be called into Squadron Officer Fleming's office for their turn. Holly was too agitated to sit and paced in front of her friends until Ruby felt dizzy watching her. 'I couldn't bear it if we got split up,' she said. 'I never thought to ask if we'd all be sent to the same base. Wouldn't it be awful if we were all accepted but still weren't posted together?'

Meg caught her arm and pulled her towards a seat. 'Sit down. You're giving me a crick in the neck. It'll be fine. This is just an interview, remember. We can pull out if we decide it's not for us.'

The sight of her friend's nerves made Ruby forget all her own misgivings as she did her best to soothe Holly's anxieties. 'I'm sure there will be a chance to ask questions, so we can find out if we're likely to be separated. Let's agree to do the best we can and compare notes afterwards. If you're not happy we can withdraw our applications.'

Some of the colour returned to Holly's cheeks, and she nodded. However, before she could reply the door opened and Fleming appeared in the doorway. 'Leading Aircraftwoman Fairweather,' she called.

Meg grimaced and rose, straightening her uniform. 'See you in the NAAFI,' she muttered, then followed Fleming from the room.

Ruby had to watch Holly and two other WAAFs be called into their interviews before her summons came. She rose, silently reciting her own advice to the others: *do your best and find out as much as you can about the Air Ambulance Service*. An unwelcome thought intruded: wouldn't it be awful if she was the only one to fail the interview? Their close-knit group would have to split up and it would be all her fault. She clasped her hands behind her back to disguise their trembling and followed the squadron officer into her office.

'Take a seat, Morris.' Fleming indicated a chair in front of the desk.

Ruby sat and found herself facing a man in RAF uniform who must be Squadron Leader Norton. He was a nondescript sandy-haired man who appeared to be in his late thirties or early forties. His most notable feature was a moustache that completely concealed his upper lip.

After Fleming had made the introductions, Norton gave Ruby a pleasant smile and began. 'You won't know much about the new service so let me explain a few things before I start the interview proper.' He leaned forward, regarding her with serious eyes. 'The first thing I need to make clear is that while all care will be taken, we cannot guarantee your safety. Although we will only be flying around the British Isles, there is always a chance of enemy attack. Are you prepared to accept the risks associated with this job?'

Having had her head full of her own and Holly's worries, this was something that hadn't occurred to her. How would her friends have reacted? She immediately knew that neither would have been put off. Meg had an adventurous streak and Holly had clearly been swept away by the thrill of doing something different. As for herself, she could honestly look Norton in the eye and say, 'I understand, sir. As far as I'm concerned, I've had to take care of patients during air raids and I know I can do my duty even when I'm in danger.'

Norton smiled. 'Good. Now, tell me about your background.' He glanced at the open file on the desk in front of him. 'I see you started nursing training but left despite excellent reports. Why was that?'

She settled on the excuse she had given at the time. 'My mother was taken ill partway through my second year and I left to take care of her. When she recovered I wanted to do something for the war effort straight away so I joined the WAAF.' This was true as far as it went. What she didn't say was that her mother had protested that she didn't need Ruby's help. It was Ruby who had grasped at the chance to leave a profession that, frankly, terrified her.

'Very commendable, I'm sure, and nursing's loss is our gain.'

She smiled and thanked him as she was expected, wondering what Norton would think if he knew the agonies she had suffered when the WAAF had made her a nursing orderly. She had hoped for a clerical role or something where lives didn't depend on her actions but as soon as they discovered her nursing experience, her fate had been sealed. It was only after she had discovered that she wasn't required to do things like draw up dosages that she had started to relax and enjoy her work. The prospect of being a nurse and responsible for administering potentially lethal drugs had filled her with dread. As an orderly she could take care of her patients without the overwhelming sense of responsibility.

Norton asked a few more questions about her work and skills which she had no problem answering. From his expression she could tell he was impressed and she relaxed, feeling that she wasn't letting Holly down. Finally, he asked if she had any questions.

'Will we get full training before we start?' she asked.

'Of course. You already have the skills we're looking for but we will make sure you are fully proficient with the challenges of working in an aircraft before you get sent out for real.'

'And where would we be based?'

'At RAF Starsden. That's where all the air ambulances are operating from, at least for now.'

So it looked as though the successful applicants would all be posted together. That would keep Holly happy. And herself, if she was honest. Her friends meant a great deal to her and she didn't like the idea of being split up either.

All in all she felt more positive about the job when she went to the NAAFI canteen to meet her friends.

'How did it go?' Holly asked before she had even sat down.

'All right, I think. How about you two?'

Holly and Meg both agreed that they also thought they had made a good impression. 'And we'd still be posted together,' Holly said happily. 'I do hope we all get in. It sounds marvellous.'

Three days later, Ruby sat with Meg in their sleeping hut, involved in a 'domestic evening' with all their off-duty hut mates. The floor had been swept, all surfaces dusted and polished and now the women were gathered around the stove, polishing their uniform buttons or darning.

Holly burst in like a whirlwind. 'It's up!' she cried. 'The list is up.'

'The air ambulance list?' Meg had turned a shade paler. When Holly nodded, she asked, 'Did we make it?'

'I don't know. I couldn't bear to look. The ward sister told me when I went off duty.'

All the girls who had applied immediately sprang up and pulled on jackets and scarves. All except Ruby. Suddenly she felt sick. Whether she was included or not, she was going to feel awful, either for letting down her friends, whom she was sure would be on the list, or from fear of the new job if she was accepted.

'Come on!' Holly pulled her to her feet, and she followed everyone outside on leaden feet. It was a mild evening for March, but Ruby shivered with nerves all the way to the hospital and the common room where they had been told the list of accepted candidates would be posted.

No sooner were they in the room than Holly made a dive for the board. Ruby lagged behind. Her vision tunnelled until all she could see was Holly, her head moving as she looked for the right list. Then she froze. A chill settled in the pit of Ruby's stomach. In that moment she knew that she feared letting down her friends more than she feared the job because she was sure Holly wouldn't be standing so still if all three had been accepted.

Then Holly spun round, her face ablaze with joy. She met Ruby's gaze. 'We got in!' she cried. 'All three of us!'

Chapter Two

Five days later, Ruby was part of a group of a dozen WAAFs gathered in a hut on the edge of RAF Starsden's airfield. There was one other girl from Bristol and the rest were from bases around the country. They had arrived at the station in northwest London two days before and had spent the previous day touring various departments, getting their arrival chitties signed as they were assigned kit and attended medical inspections.

Today, however, they were going to get their first training in the air ambulance side of their duties. Ruby's nerves, which had calmed upon learning that much of their work would be the same as before, were playing up again, and she felt as though her breakfast was having a party in her stomach. Seeing the other girls had got out their notebooks, she did likewise, only to drop it on the floor and then drop her pencil when she leaned down to pick up the notebook.

She had only managed to get herself organised when the door opened and Squadron Leader Norton strode to the front. There was a screech of chairs scraping against the polished concrete floor as all the women scrambled to their feet, but Norton waved them back into their seats.

'At ease, ladies, and welcome to the Air Ambulance Service.' He paused until he had complete silence and the gaze of each woman was riveted upon him. 'I'm going to start by telling you how we envisage the service will work.

As you know, the air force has men and women posted all over the British Isles, and sometimes they get injured or fall ill. If they can be treated at onsite facilities or at local hospitals, all well and good. However, if they need to be moved further afield, this can present a problem, especially if they are serving in a remote location or need to be taken to a distant specialist hospital such as the one in East Grinstead.' Norton paused again and glanced around at the WAAFs.

Ruby nodded to show her understanding. Only a few weeks before her transfer, she had helped care for a pilot who had been badly burned when his plane had caught fire on landing. It had been a difficult case, and she had hated knowing that any treatment must have caused him agonising pain. He had been transferred to the Queen Victoria Hospital in East Grinstead, which had become a pioneering centre for treating burns victims. She had worried about how the poor man would cope with the long ambulance ride to West Sussex, and now she thought about patients needing to take far longer journeys.

'That's where the Air Ambulance Service comes in,' Norton continued. 'Travelling by aeroplane, patients need only be on the move for an hour or two when going all the way by road or train might take a day or more. And you, the nursing orderlies, will accompany our patients to care for them while they are in the air.'

Some of Ruby's fears eased. So they wouldn't be dealing with critical patients. This wasn't the same as riding in an ambulance with a patient who had just been knocked down by a car. Her patients would already have received hospital treatment and would therefore be in a stable condition. While Norton went on to explain about the aircraft they would be flying – Airspeed Oxfords – and the crew – pilot, navigator and wireless operator – Ruby pictured herself at work with her friends, holding the hands of brave, handsome pilots while they sped through the air. Surely there would be less time for her to make a mistake with a patient than there would be in the hospital. For the first time she felt a thrill of excitement that she would be flying. She had never flown before and had always wondered what it must be like to swoop through the clouds. Now she would find out.

She forced herself to pay attention when Norton went on to explain their usual working routine. 'You will be rotating between air ambulance duty and shifts in the hospital. That's right,' he said when a few of the WAAFs made exclamations of surprise, 'you won't be flying every day, so you will continue with your usual ward duties for the most part. But, of course, none of that will start until after your training.

'Now, most of your training will be led by Sister Macintosh from the hospital. She will be working you hard over the next six weeks, teaching you all you need to know about caring for your patients in the air. At the end of six weeks, you will be required to sit exams. If you pass you will be fully qualified members of the Air Ambulance Service. Any questions?'

Holly's hand shot into the air, and Norton said to her, 'Name please?'

'LACW Hardwick, sir.'

'And what is your question, Hardwick?'

'What happens if we fail the exam?'

'You will return to hospital duties.'

'But will we be allowed to retake the exams?'

'That will be discussed on a case-by-case basis.'

When Norton took a question from another WAAF about extra pay, Meg muttered, 'In other words, this is all so new, they don't really know how many nursing orderlies they need. They don't want to promise allowing us another chance in case they don't need any more of us.'

'We'd better make sure we all pass first go, then,' Holly whispered. 'We have to stay together.'

Ruby returned her attention to the class in time to hear an elegant, blonde WAAF called Roberta Jones ask, 'When will we make our first flights?'

All the women, Ruby included, sat straighter and fixed Norton with intent stares. A zing of electric anticipation charged the hut's atmosphere.

'You will all be doing a flight today.'

'Today?' Ruby squeaked, forgetting herself. When Norton's gaze settled on her, she said, 'Sorry, sir.'

Norton's eyes twinkled. 'And your name is?'

'LACW Morris, sir,' Ruby replied, feeling her face burn.

'Well, Morris, in answer to your question, however inadvertently asked, yes, you will all be flying today. The reason for this is because before we spend time and money training you for service in an air ambulance, we need to know that you can all cope with flying. I'm sure you will all appreciate that when you are transporting a patient, your full attention must be upon him. If you suffer from airsickness or a debilitating fear of flying, you will be no good to us and, regretfully, we will require you to return to your former duties. I'm sure you will agree that it is better to find that out now rather than after you have undertaken training that could have been allocated to another WAAF.'

'Yes, sir, thank you, sir,' Ruby muttered, feeling deflated. Having got herself all excited about flying, it hadn't occurred to her that she might be unable to handle it. The other women all received the news with sombre expressions, and she knew that none of them wanted to be sent home now. Not for so humiliating a reason as panic or travel sickness.

Norton dismissed the class shortly after, instructing them to report back in an hour, dressed in their battledress.

Holly looked grim as they made their way back to their quarters to change. 'This is awful. I couldn't bear it if I was sent back to Bristol just because I was travel sick. I couldn't bear it if it happened to any of us. We have to stay together.'

A short while later the whole group was back in the classroom, dressed in their battledress uniforms, which they had been assigned upon arrival. Battledress consisted of trousers and a waist-length jacket that buttoned onto the waistband of the trousers. At least, they were supposed to be waist-length. Ruby was only five foot two, and her jacket was so long on her that when she fastened it to her waistband, the jacket ballooned out.

'Great,' she murmured to her friends. 'I'm going to be walking around the base looking like a blue marshmallow.'

They had also been allocated sheepskin lined jackets and boots, and Meg in particular seemed delighted with them. 'I feel like Amy Johnson, dressed like this,' she confessed.

Ruby didn't say anything but wished Meg had chosen someone who hadn't died flying. While the prospect of going up in an aeroplane had seemed so exciting back in the humdrum hospital life at Bristol, now she was facing an imminent flight, she was painfully aware of the dangers. And what if they ran into enemy aircraft? No one else seemed afraid, though, so she kept her thoughts to herself.

'Of course, having flown before, I know I'll be all right,' one girl said. Ruby remembered her name was Roberta.

'Really? What is it like?' a wide-eyed WAAF asked.

'Oh, yes. My older brother joined the RAF before the war, and he managed to wangle me on a flight. It was amazing, and I didn't feel at all ill. But then, I'm rarely ill.'

Holly murmured in Ruby's ear, 'Imagine the humiliation of being sick and sent away in front of Miss Perfect. I think I'd die of shame.'

Ruby didn't say anything but she had to agree. There was something grating about LACW Jones's voice, or was it simply that her accent spoke volumes and betrayed a lifetime of privilege that Ruby could only dream of?

'Serve her right if she did get sick,' Meg commented in a low voice.

Ruby had no time to reply for the door opened and Squadron Leader Norton strode in, accompanied by another man with sergeant's stripes on his sleeves. There was an immediate ripple of interest among the WAAFs, and Ruby was aware of more than one of them standing straighter and shooting the man flirtatious glances. She couldn't blame them. With his blond hair, piercing blue eyes and muscular build, he could have been a Viking in an earlier life.

Norton cleared his throat, and from his faint smile, Ruby guessed he knew the reason for the women's sudden attention. 'This is Flight Sergeant Foster,' he said with a gesture towards the Nordic god. 'He's another of our pilots. We have two aircraft – both Airspeed Oxfords – and we'll both be taking you up one at a time for twenty minutes or so.' He consulted a piece of paper. 'Arkwright, Barton, Beale, Grover, Fairweather and Hardwick, you'll be with me. The others will be with Foster. Arkwright, come with me now and Jones, with the flight sergeant. The rest of you wait here.'

The wide-eyed girl who had been speaking to Jones turned out to be Arkwright, and she followed Norton looking as though she was going to her execution. Jones smiled, with a confidence that Ruby could only envy.

'Good luck!' Ruby called, and the others joined her in wishing the first fliers the best.

Left to their own devices, the remaining women formed into two groups, depending on which pilot they were with. Ruby shot a longing glance at her friends' group but this would be a good opportunity to get to know some of the other WAAFs. She found herself standing beside a girl with a dark complexion and thick wavy black hair. Ruby had heard that some girls from the West Indies had joined the WAAF, although she hadn't met any yet. Perhaps this was one of them. 'Hello, I'm Ruby Morris,' she said to the girl. 'From Buckinghamshire.'

'Winnie Parry,' the girl responded with a smile. She spoke in the broadest Welsh accent Ruby had ever heard. 'From Cardiff.' Ruby's surprise must have shown for Winnie chuckled. 'My mam tells me my real father came from Jamaica but he was on the crew of a ship that docked in Cardiff for a few days and was back in Jamaica before my mam discovered she was expecting me.'

'That must have been hard on your mother.' Growing up, Ruby had been taught to look askance at unmarried mothers, but years of tending to injuries inflicted by war had taught her that there were far worse things in the world.

Winnie shrugged. 'Not really. She met my da soon after and they fell in love and got married in time for me to be born in wedlock.' She grinned. 'My brothers and sisters are all pale and fair-haired and I stick out like a sore thumb. But Da won't hear a word against me or Mam.'

'He sounds like a lovely man.'

'He really is. I miss him. He was so proud when I told him I was joining the Air Ambulance Service. I couldn't bear it if I failed to get in because I couldn't take the flight.'

'I'm sure you'll be fine.'

As she spoke, a roar split the air. As one, the girls rushed to the windows, from where the airfield could be seen.

Meg gave a little cry and pointed. 'Look!' she cried, unnecessarily, for the twin-engined aircraft that sped into view was clearly visible.

Ruby watched with her heart in her mouth as it raced down the runway gathering speed. When it rose into the air, all the girls cheered and clapped. For a heart-stopping moment it seemed to hover dangerously close to the rooftops, then it was climbing higher and higher. In her time in the WAAF, Ruby had seen many takeoffs and had become blasé at the sight. Now she watched as though it was her first time and wondered how it felt to those inside the aircraft. When the second Oxford tore across the runway, her stomach knotted. It would be her turn soon. What did it feel like to leave the ground? How would she react? She'd better not disgrace herself by throwing up.

Once both aircraft were out of sight, the women drifted back to their seats. It felt like an age passed before they heard the sound of returning aero engines, but a glance at her watch told Ruby that it had only been twenty minutes, as Norton had said.

A short while later, Jones walked in looking smug. 'It was a breeze, just as I thought.'

The others gathered around her to ask all about it, and Ruby had taken a reluctant step towards the huddle when Flight Sergeant Foster put his head around the door. 'LACW Morris, with me, please.'

On wobbly legs, Ruby left the room. Holly and Meg patted her back as she passed.

'Good luck!' Meg called. 'You'll be fine.'

If Ruby's mouth hadn't gone so dry she would have demanded to know why she needed luck if Meg was so sure she would be fine.

Flight Sergeant Foster was waiting for her outside. He took one look at her face and burst out laughing. 'Anyone would think you were going to the gallows,' he said.

'It feels like it.'

'I promise it won't be bad. All we're going to do is fly over London, see the sights from the air. You'll love it.'

'If you say so.' Then Ruby clapped her hand to her mouth, shocked that she had answered back to a man who outranked her. 'I'm so sorry, Sergeant. That was my nerves speaking.'

Thankfully, Foster saw the funny side. 'Don't worry about it. We don't stand on ceremony here.' He led the way to the dispersal point where the Airspeed Oxford stood. It was a squat aircraft compared with the elegant one-seater Spitfires and Hurricanes she had become accustomed to seeing. It had twin engines and a broader fuselage, obviously intended to hold more crew members.

'Welcome to the Ox-box,' Foster said with a grin. 'That's what we call the Oxfords. With affection, of course. They might not look as streamlined as a Spitfire, but they're true workhorses. The RAF wouldn't manage without them. You'll get a full guided tour later, assuming you don't throw up all over the controls, of course, but for now you simply need to know that the two Oxfords we've got at Starsden have been adapted for use as an air ambulance, so there's an extra flap cut into the fuselage to allow access for stretchers. As we're only flying around London, we won't need a navigator, so you can sit in the navigator's seat.'

So saying, he helped her climb through the cabin door. There was already another man on board, hunched over a wireless set.

'This is our wireless operator, Flight Sergeant Rhys Powell,' Foster told her.

Rhys, a cheerful-looking young man with dark hair and the bluest eyes she had ever seen, gave her a wave. 'Welcome on board,' he said in an accent that was as Welsh as his name might suggest.

Foster pointed to the front of the plane where two seats were placed in front of an array of controls. The navigator's seat was placed further back to accommodate a chart table. 'Strap in, and we'll be on our way.'

He showed her how to buckle herself into the harness and also demonstrated how to attach herself to the intercom. Then, as she got herself settled, she watched Foster as he strapped himself into his seat and started to flick switches on his control panel.

She felt a tap on her shoulder. Turning around, she saw Rhys Powell grinning at her. He handed her a paper bag. 'Just in case.'

She took it, sincerely hoping she wouldn't need it. But when the propellers roared into life and the Oxford vibrated as though it were straining at the bit, her stomach lurched.

At a signal from a man on the ground, Foster eased the throttle and the Oxford moved forward.

Ruby couldn't help it. One hand gripped the edge of her seat and the other crumpled the paper bag that she still clutched.

'You'll be fine,' Foster said, and the total lack of strain or fear in his voice helped her relax. 'We're going to taxi to the head of the runway and wait for the signal to take off. It might get a bit noisy and bumpy before we take off, but once we're in the air it will feel much smoother.'

Having Foster explain what he was doing as he went along helped ease her fears even more, and when they reached the head of the runway and paused, he called out, 'This is where it gets noisy. I need to rev up the engines against the brakes.'

There followed an ear-splitting din that she felt in her chest. Then a green light flashed at the far end of the runway, and the Oxford leaped forward. The vibration in the cabin increased as the plane gathered speed, and just when she thought she couldn't endure it any more, the vibration ceased.

'And we're away!' Foster called.

Looking out of the window, Ruby was stunned to see the ground falling away beneath them. It was as though her fears remained on the ground, while she was suddenly unmoored and floating free. She was pressed into the back of her seat as the Oxford climbed higher and, gazing out of the window, she was mesmerised by the sight of the land below. They were high enough now to see the network of streets and it was strange how different everything looked when viewed from above. It took her a moment, studying a cross-shaped building surrounded by green to work out that it was the church.

'Oh, that's the church,' she said, pointing down. 'It's funny how the tower doesn't look any higher than the rest of the building.'

'Look at the shadows,' Foster told her.

It took her a moment but then she found the church's shadow, a black smudge across the churchyard, and the tower's shadow stretching far beyond the rest. Now she knew what to look for, it helped her decode the rest of the view.

'Of course, the sun has to be out for it to work,' Foster said, 'and even then, if it's noon at high summer, the shadows won't be long enough, but it's a handy trick, especially if you have to make a forced landing and you need to check for telegraph poles in a field.'

He continued to speak, pointing out landmarks and explaining what he was doing, telling her when he was going to bank so she wouldn't be frightened when the ground seemed to tilt up to meet them. Ruby was thoroughly enjoying herself and she was glad that she had been assigned to Foster's group, because she felt able to ask questions that she would have hesitated to ask the squadron leader.

'We're at eight thousand feet now, so I'm going to pull out of our climb,' he said a short while later. 'You might think we're falling, but I promise you we're not.'

She was glad of the warning, for a moment later she clutched the edge of her seat when her stomach gave a swoop and she felt as though she would lift out of her seat.

'How are you feeling?' Foster asked. 'Do you feel like you might need the bag?'

She shook her head. 'I feel fine. This is fun. Where are we going?'

'Do you fancy seeing the River Thames and the Houses of Parliament? I thought I'd give you a tour of London.'

'Can you really recognise buildings from up here?'

'If you know what to look for.'

'How will you find your way?'

'Look out the window. It's like a giant map down there. See that long, straight road? That's the A5. It goes all the way into the centre of London.' As he spoke, he adjusted course until they were flying along the length of the road. 'We're well above the barrage balloons, so I think we can afford to lose a little height.' So saying, he pushed the control column forward, and Ruby's stomach gave another swoop.

She laughed. 'I went on a roller coaster once, but this is far more fun.'

He grinned back. 'You're still not feeling queasy at all?'

'Not in the slightest.' She had never felt such exhilaration in her life. 'If I'd known it would be so much fun I wouldn't have been nervous to begin with.' Then she shot him a sideways glance. 'Although I hope you'll warn me if you're going to do any loop-the-loops.'

'We can give the aerobatics a miss. This is going to be an air ambulance, after all. I won't be flying upside down when we've got a patient on board.'

Ruby would remember this first flight for the rest of her life. She stared, entranced, as the map of London appeared below her: the large green spaces that were the parks, the wide Thames that was more a silty brown than the blue it appeared on maps, spanned by tiny thread-like bridges.

Foster followed the river a short way then pointed at one of the banks. 'The Houses of Parliament.'

She would never have picked them out without his help – from above they looked nothing like the pictures she had seen. Close by was a large cross-shaped building. Wait. Cross-shaped? She gave an excited squeak. 'Is that Westminster Abbey?'

Foster chuckled. 'Top marks! You're getting the hang of this.'

'I've never been to London before. To think that the first time I've seen it is from the air.' It was a magical feeling, seeing the famous sights laid out beneath her as though she were a deity, looking down at the city from the clouds. It was hard to remember that the people living in the tiny model houses had endured the Blitz, and that the Palace of Westminster itself had been hit. From the ground she would be able to see the scaffolding.

'You'll soon get to know it. It's easy to get to by bus or Underground, so it's a popular place for a night out.'

On the return flight, Foster continued to bank and change height at intervals, probably still testing her for airsickness, but she didn't suffer at all. Her only nervous moment was when Foster sideslipped steeply on their approach to Starsden. When he calmly explained exactly what he was doing, she found that she could distract herself from the sensation of falling by picking out landmarks below. Then, almost before she knew it, the runway was rushing up to meet them and there was a slight jolt as the wheels hit the ground.

'That was amazing!' she said as Foster taxied back to their dispersal point. 'I can't wait to go up again.'

'Well, you survived your first flight, so as long as you pass your exams at the end of the course, you'll be taking plenty more flights and for longer.'

Ruby dashed back to the hut, feeling as though a whole new world had opened up for her.

Chapter Three

Much to Ruby's relief, Holly and Meg both returned from their flights saying how much they had enjoyed the experience. The same wasn't true for all the women, however, for three of them returned in tears having succumbed to airsickness, and one had been paralysed with fear at her first sight of the ground far below and had begged to be returned to the ground. If Roberta Jones could be believed, she had sailed through the flight and had practically flown and landed the Oxford herself. Ruby was much more pleased to find that Winnie Parry had also been fine and would be continuing to the training. In total, eight of the women who had arrived at Starsden were to take the course.

'I had hoped there would be more of you,' Squadron Leader Norton said at the end of the day, and only the women who had passed the flight test were present. 'I dare say we'll manage, but I expect you all to pass the end of course exam, or we will be very short-handed until we can recruit more.'

Their course kicked off the next day, and they gathered in the classroom the next morning eager to make a start. Ruby and her friends grabbed desks at the front of the class and had just arranged their pencils and exercise books in front of them when the door opened and a nursing sister strode in. She was carrying a large black bag that looked like a doctor's bag; she walked to the front and placed it on the table.

'Good morning, girls,' she said, a warm smile taking the edge off her brisk tone. 'I am Sister Macintosh, and I usually work up at the base hospital. But for the next six weeks I will be taking you through the training you will need to be air ambulance nursing orderlies. I know you have all already been working as nursing orderlies at various hospitals around the country, but while some aspects of the course will act as a refresher, there is plenty that will be new to you, as you will have to do some things differently in the air ambulance. And, of course, you need to be prepared to deal with any emergencies alone, as you will be taking sole responsibility for your patient while you are airborne.'

The words hit Ruby like a punch in the stomach. Surely she had misheard. She put up her hand.

Sister Macintosh paused and said, 'You have a question?'

Ruby nodded. 'Did I hear correctly? There will be only one nursing orderly per flight?'

'That's correct. Is there a problem?'

'Well, I mean...' Ruby struggled to arrange her thoughts. She swallowed and tried again. 'Wouldn't it make more sense to have two nursing orderlies on the flight in case of emergency?'

'It undoubtably would, LACW...?' The sister raised her eyebrows at Ruby.

'Morris.'

'I'm sure it would be easier, LACW Morris. However, if you've seen the interior of the Airspeed Oxford, then you will know that there will barely be room for one of you in the cabin, once there is a stretcher inside, let alone two.'

'Yes, of course. I should have realised.' Ruby had been so absorbed in the flight that she hadn't examined the interior of the aircraft in much detail but from what she could recall, Sister Macintosh had a point. Why hadn't it occurred to her before? If she had known she would be expected to take sole charge of a patient, she wouldn't have been so happy about passing her first flight.

The sister seemed to understand some of Ruby's worries, for her expression softened. 'Remember, the Air Ambulance Service is not an emergency service. You will be transporting patients whose conditions have already been stabilised at a hospital, and even your longest flights won't last more than two hours. Where necessary, patients will be sedated before travel. We don't anticipate you needing to do anything more critical than administer oxygen and pain-killing injections.'

'Yes, thank you, Sister,' Ruby said, then lowered her head to her exercise book and made a show of scribbling copious notes so no one could see her flaming face. Half of her wanted to stammer her excuses and say she'd made a terrible mistake and actually she was terrified of flying. She probably would have done had not two things stopped her. First was the squadron leader's statement that he had hoped to recruit more of them and the other, main reason was the knowledge that she would be letting her friends down. Holly had been desperate for them to stay together, and Ruby couldn't bear to upset her.

All she could do was cling to the hope that Sister Macintosh was right, and her patients wouldn't need any emergency interventions.

Making an effort to pay attention to the class, she looked up in time to see Sister Macintosh open the bag. 'Before we start work on the medical procedures you will need to be familiar with, I want to introduce you to your most important pieces of equipment. Each of you will be supplied with a medical bag like this, which you will bring to every flight.' She started to unpack it, producing syringes, a thermos flask, dressings and various other items. 'It will be your responsibility to keep your bags stocked. The air ambulances themselves do not contain any supplies.' Here she began to list the items they would need, ordering them to write it all down.

By the time the class finished, Ruby's head was spinning. They were sent to the canteen for a frugal meal and then the afternoon was spent taking a tour of the hospital and collecting their medical bags. By the time they were returning to their billets in a large house that had been requisitioned for the nursing orderlies, the day seemed to have both sped by and lasted for ever.

'Fancy a trip to the cinema?' Meg asked once they had dumped their bags and books in their room.

Holly was keen, and Ruby's heart sank. The knowledge that she would soon be solely responsible for her patients was a heavy weight on her mind and she wanted some time alone to get her thinking straight. The last thing she needed was to sit in a noisy, crowded cinema. 'You go,' she told them. 'I'll stay here. Maybe I'll go for a walk later. Get to know the area a bit.'

'Are you sure you're all right?' Holly asked. 'You've been quiet all day.'

'I'm fine. I just need some peace and quiet after everything we've had to take in today.'

But Holly didn't look happy. 'Please come with us! I don't like to think of you being alone all evening.'

Ruby had always found it impossible to say no to her friends, and tonight was no exception. She bid a silent goodbye to her longed-for solitude. 'Oh, all right. But I'll have to catch you up. I've rubbed a hole in the heel of my stockings and I need to change them.' She kicked off her shoes and displayed the offending heel.

'Fine. We'll see you there.'

It didn't take long to change stockings, rinse out and hang the worn ones so they would be dry for darning the next day. Then she set out after her friends, determined to make use of her brief walk alone to think things through. There was a small park on her route to the centre of Starsden, and she headed that way, longing for a few minutes away from the noise of the streets.

What should she do? She had given up her nursing training when she had been overcome by the fear of making a fatal or life-changing mistake. She had only resigned herself to her role in the WAAF once she had accepted that her work would always be closely supervised. After a while she had even started to enjoy it, glad to feel that she was finally helping people. Why hadn't she bothered to find out exactly what the air ambulance job entailed before being persuaded to apply? She would never have done it if she had known she would be alone with patients, and she could probably have persuaded her friends to remain in their current roles so that they could all have stayed together. Now if she requested a transfer she would be letting down not only her friends but also the Air Ambulance Service.

It was no good. No matter how much she dreaded her new duties, she couldn't bear to let anyone down. She would have to live with the fear and work as hard as she could so that she would never make a mistake.

By this time she was approaching the park gates. Or where they must have been, for now there were just two stone columns where the gates should have stood. She guessed they had been taken away for the iron, along with so many of the country's gates and railings.

Despite the fuel rationing, the road was still busy, with buses and military vehicles roaring past in addition to the few civilian vehicles that the owners could still afford to run. Ruby was about to go inside the park when a shiny green Bentley approached. It was an old model with headlights that stuck out. Ruby had always liked to see old cars like that, thinking they looked like they had faces with a surprised expression. She paused to watch it go by.

From the corner of her eye she caught a flash of brown, and then there was a screech of brakes and a yelp. A moment later and the Bentley sped off, leaving a dog, shivering and whimpering in the road. It had all happened so fast that it took her a moment to realise that the flash of brown she had seen had been the dog running into the road where it had been hit by the car.

'Oh, the poor thing!' Ruby flung herself down beside the injured animal and ran gentle hands over it, searching for injuries. The dog, a light brown mongrel that looked as though it had a fair amount of terrier in its ancestry, looked up at her, its eyes mournful brown pools.

'What's the matter, boy? Where are you hurt?'

The dog whined and licked his flank.

'Is that where the nasty car hit you?' she crooned, probing the spot with gentle fingers.

She didn't notice she had company until she heard footsteps, and a pair of shiny black shoes and the blue-grey serge of RAF uniform trousers appeared in her line of sight.

'Can I help?' asked a man's voice.

'Oh, yes please. I—' She glanced up only to meet the concerned gaze of Flight Sergeant Foster. All coherent thought fled. He really was *very* good looking.

'It's Morris, isn't it. What's happened?'

He remembered her! *Stop it! Focus on the dog. That's the important thing right now.* She stammered through an explanation of the accident, concluding with, 'I suppose he needs to be seen by a vet, although I've no idea where to find one.' Or how she would afford the bill, come to that. But she wasn't prepared to leave the injured dog in the street.

He crouched beside her. 'Is it bad?'

'I don't think so. I can't feel any broken bones, but of course he could still have internal injuries.'

'I suppose we ought to try and find the owners.' He looked around as though expecting someone to materialise out of thin air, carrying a lead.

'He doesn't have a collar.'

Foster examined the dog. 'He doesn't look thin enough to be a stray.'

At that moment a woman came hurrying out of the nearest house. 'Is he all right? Oh, I feel so guilty.'

'Is this your dog?' Ruby asked.

'No. It's a stray that appeared in the area a week or so ago. I've no idea where he came from. I can only think that his family had to move away suddenly and couldn't take him with them. He looks like he's been well cared for until now. If it had been a year ago I would've supposed he came from a home that had been bombed out, but it's been quieter recently. When he came to my door a few days ago I wanted to take him in but our rations are little enough for me and my children. I couldn't afford to feed him properly. I felt sorry for him, though, so I fed him a few scraps. But when I saw him hit by that car... if I'd taken him in, he would never have been in the street to be hit.'

'You can't think like that,' Ruby said. 'You were kind to feed him when I'm sure plenty of others must have turned him away.' She turned to Foster. 'I've got an idea. Why don't we keep him as a mascot? He could live in our crew room.'

Foster looked doubtful. 'We don't even know how badly he's hurt and you want the Air Ambulance Service to adopt him?'

'What's the alternative? You heard that lady. It's the same for everyone. No one is going to want to take in a pet when they're struggling to feed their families on their rations. Who in their right mind would want to keep a strange dog?'

'I suppose there's always the Battersea Dogs Home. Or maybe there's somewhere closer. The RSPCA might be able to help.'

'But he's so sweet. Wouldn't you rather keep him?' Ruby could hardly believe that she was pleading like a child begging a parent for a puppy. She would never normally dare to speak to a superior like this but faced with his obvious kindness and care for a stray dog she had let down her guard. Somehow, she didn't feel like a subordinate with him but like an equal.

Foster stroked the dog's head. It whined and licked his hand. He sighed, took off his coat and wrapped it around the animal before picking it up, cradling it to his chest. 'Come on, then.' He strode down the street.

Ruby hurried after him, painfully aware that her friends would be waiting for her. 'Where are we going?'

'I know someone who might be able to check the dog over without it costing us an arm and a leg.'

'How far is it?' She was having to jog to keep up with his long strides, and she couldn't maintain this pace for long.

He shot her a glance. 'Sorry.' He shortened his stride to match Ruby's. 'It's not far. About a ten-minute walk.'

'Oh. Hang on. I'm supposed to be meeting my friends at the cinema.'

At this moment, Winnie appeared around the corner like an angel of mercy, heading in the direction of the shops and cinema. Ruby called to her, and she crossed the road, her face creasing in sympathy when Ruby explained what had happened. 'The poor thing,' Winnie crooned, tickling the dog between its ears. 'Can I help?'

'I don't suppose you could find Holly and Meg at the cinema? They'll be waiting for me,' Ruby said.

'No problem. I was heading there anyway. I'll let them know what's happened.'

'That's a relief. Thank you.' She watched Winnie stride away then stroked the dog's ears. The dog gazed back at her with melting brown eyes, and she knew she had already lost her heart to the creature. 'I hope your friend can help him.'

'Not my friend. My brother. This way. We're going to my parents' house.'

He turned into another road and led them through a residential area until he eventually stopped outside a semi-detached house that could have been the twin to the house Ruby had grown up in. 'Do you mind opening the gate?' He nodded at the bundle in his arms. 'My hands are full.'

She did so then stood aside to let him reach the front door first. It was opened by a woman of about fifty years of age with silvery blonde hair and twinkling blue eyes.

'Laurie!' She opened the door wide and stepped back to let them in. 'This is a lovely surprise.'

'Hello, Mum,' he said, kissing her on the cheek. 'Is Adam in?'

Her mouth turned down. 'When isn't he in?' She looked at the dog and then Ruby. 'Are you going to introduce me to your friends?'

'This is Leading Aircraftwoman Morris. She's a nursing orderly at RAF Starsden.'

Ruby stepped forward. 'Hello, Mrs Foster. You can call me Ruby.'

'That's a lovely name. Call me Lettie. And is this your dog?'

Ruby shook her head. 'He was hit by a car. Flight Sergeant Foster hoped his brother would be able to help.'

'I see. Poor thing.' She looked at Foster. 'Adam is in the back room. I hope your friend can persuade him to help. Maybe taking care of a dog is what he needs to bring him out of himself.'

'We can only hope.'

'Come in. I'll make tea.'

Foster turned to Ruby. 'This way. And call me Laurie. You can save the Flight Sergeant Foster stuff for when we're on duty.'

He led the way down the narrow quarry-tiled passage and opened a door at the end. It led into a small room with three armchairs around an unlit fireplace and a four-person dining table beneath a rattling sash window. There was a wireless playing a musical programme and in one of the armchairs sat a young man who bore a close resemblance to Foster – Laurie, Ruby corrected herself. This must be Adam. He had a tartan blanket draped around his knees and he stared blankly into the dark fireplace. He jumped when Laurie placed the dog, still wrapped in his jacket, upon his lap. Until that moment, Ruby would have sworn he hadn't noticed his visitors.

'Hello, Adam,' Laurie said. 'We were hoping you could help us with this chap.'

As he explained about the accident, a spark of interest seemed to shine in Adam's eyes and he had already started to lightly probe the animal's flanks and ribs before Laurie had finished speaking. 'Let's get him on the table,' he said. 'Can one of you carry him? And we ought to cover the table with newspaper or Mum will go spare.'

Seeing a basket of newspapers beside the fireplace, Ruby took some from there and spread them across the tabletop. Once the table was covered, Laurie picked up the dog and placed him upon it. Although she had her attention firmly upon the animal, she couldn't help but notice the way Adam struggled to stand and needed to lever himself up using the arms of his chair. Was he ill? Laurie was certainly worried about him, for he cast several surreptitious glances in his direction while soothing the dog.

He seemed to walk easily enough, although he was a shade paler by the time he reached the table. 'Right. Let's have a look at you.' He glanced at Laurie. 'What's his name?'

Laurie shrugged. 'No idea. He's a stray.'

'We can't have that, can we, boy?' Adam addressed the dog, still probing for injuries. 'He's got to have a name.'

'How about Bentley?' Ruby suggested.

Laurie pulled a face. 'You want to name him after the car that hit him?'

Ruby chuckled. 'Put it like that, it doesn't sound good. But I remember thinking how the Bentley looked like it had a happy face, and this dog has the same expression.'

'I think Bentley's a good name,' Adam said. He fondled the dog's ears. 'What do you think, boy – are you a Bentley?'

The dog tilted his head and both of his ears stood up.

Ruby laughed. 'See – he recognises his name.'

'Bentley it is, then,' Laurie conceded. 'Is he badly hurt, Adam? I was hoping you could fix him up without us having to find a vet.'

'Oh, aren't you a vet?' Ruby blurted in surprise. From the assured way Adam had examined Bentley, she had thought he must be. It would have explained why he wasn't in uniform, for vet was a reserved occupation.

'I started my training but didn't get as far as taking my final exams.' Adam was busy inspecting Bentley's left foreleg and so had his face turned away from her. Ruby had the impression he didn't want to explain himself.

He took his time examining the dog, taking particular care over the places where his touch caused Bentley to whine. Finally, he straightened. 'I don't think there are any broken bones or internal injuries.'

'Thank goodness!' Ruby exclaimed.

'I'd better keep him for a day or two to keep an eye on him just in case,' Adam went on. 'What are you going to do with him after that, though? Mum will never let him stay permanently and I don't want to throw him out onto the streets, either.'

Ruby caught Laurie's eye and silently begged him to let the dog stay at Starsden.

Laurie's lips twitched. 'Oh, very well. I don't know how I'm going to explain it to the squadron leader, but it looks like the Air Ambulance Service has a new mascot.'

Chapter Four

Quite how Laurie persuaded the CO to take Bentley on, Ruby never knew, but two days later, Bentley the dog was installed at RAF Starsden and spent his days in the crew room and his nights in Laurie's quarters in the Sergeants' Mess. He was popular with the whole air ambulance team and soon everyone was saying they couldn't imagine the place without him. Adam had confirmed her opinion that although he was a mongrel, he looked like he had a lot of terrier in him. Ruby adored him, whatever his breeding, and often managed to sneak him scraps from the canteen. She also found him an excellent listener. When she was alone with him, she could pour out her fears and he would regard her with his solemn eyes, tilting his head this way and that. She always felt better afterwards.

It never lasted, though.

By this time her six-week course was well under way, and she and the rest of the nursing orderlies were working with Sister Mackintosh on all aspects of being a nursing orderly in the Air Ambulance Service. Some of the things they covered were refreshers on what she already knew, but others were procedures not normally expected of an orderly working in a hospital. For example, although she had trained in giving injections, she had never been required to administer one in reality, for the trained nurses had always done that. Now, Ruby was in possession of a medical bag containing morphine. It didn't matter that Sister Macintosh assured them it was unlikely to be needed; the fact that the training covered it meant there was a real possibility. Even though they were issued with syrettes, each containing a pre-measured dose, she still feared that she would somehow administer a fatal amount. Bentley was the recipient of all her fears over this, because she couldn't bring herself to confess them to her friends.

Holly and Meg had taken to the course with enthusiasm. Both had loved their flights as much as Ruby but, unlike her, they were eagerly awaiting the end of the course when they could start their duties and take to the air once again.

'Won't it be marvellous when we get to work properly?' Holly enthused on their first Saturday in Starsden. The course only took place Mondays to Fridays, so the friends had declared they would make the most of their weekends together, knowing they would be back on shift work once they had qualified. 'To think we'll be doing something as exciting as flying.'

Meg nodded, stirring her tea. They had voted to explore Starsden High Street that morning but had only got as far as an inviting cafe when the heavens had opened and they had dashed inside for shelter. Now they could only view the street through the rivulets pouring down the outside of the diamond-taped windowpanes. 'I can't wait. It will be good to have something exciting to write home about at last. My mother has always been going on about my older sisters and their children, or the important work my younger sister is doing in the Wrens. She never seems to think what I do is good enough.'

'That's unfair!' Ruby exclaimed. 'You were one of the best orderlies back in Bristol. There are plenty of patients who thought what you did was very important.'

Meg shot her a grateful smile. 'That's what I keep telling myself, but it's hard when I'm treated as just average.'

Ruby would have been quite happy doing something humdrum and average. Anything that didn't mean having sole responsibility for a patient's wellbeing. However, she didn't say so and joined Holly in telling Meg that if she ever met Meg's family, she would explain exactly how important her work was.

In fact, the only thing that worried her more than the responsibility was the exams she would sit at the end of the six-week course. She was constantly torn between hoping she failed so she could return to her safe and undemanding job in Bristol and wanting to stay with her friends here in Starsden, for Holly and Meg were both handling the course with ease and Ruby was sure they would pass with flying colours.

Usually she didn't like to share her worries, but this time she felt she had no choice. Holly in particular viewed the possible breaking of their group with horror, and Ruby wanted to prepare her for the possibility that she might not pass. 'I'm not looking forward to the exams,' she confessed. 'I'm terrified I'm going to fail.'

'You'll be fine,' Meg said. 'You didn't have any trouble with the last lot of exams.' She was referring to the exams they had taken at the end of their initial training.

'I know but we're only a week in and there is so much more to learn. What if I mess it up?'

'You can't!' Holly's eyes were wide, her distress plain, and Ruby's heart squeezed. 'Anyway, you're doing well in class. Sister Macintosh even said you did a good job when she picked you to explain how to control a haemorrhage.'

'Yes, but that was because nothing was riding on it. I'm worried I'll fall apart in the exam.'

'Then we'll help you.' Holly was firm. 'You're an excellent nursing orderly. To be honest, I don't know why you didn't train to be a proper nurse. We can't afford to lose you.'

'We can help each other,' Meg said. 'I know what we can do. Every night, we'll test each other on what we've covered that day. By the time we get to the exams, it will all be second nature, and you'll sail through, just you wait and see.'

'That's an excellent idea.' Holly's expression eased. 'In fact' – she glanced out of the window with a grimace – 'we might as well go back to our digs and start now because this rain doesn't look like it's going to stop any time soon. Starsden High Street can wait.'

With her friends' help, Ruby's fears about the exams gradually faded. When the other girls on their course went out in the evenings to dances or the cinema, Ruby, Meg and Holly stayed in with their books, drilling each other on procedures until they seeped into Ruby's dreams.

'You know, I dreamed I was taking Flight Sergeant Foster's blood pressure last night,' she said one evening after correctly stating the normal blood pressure for a twenty-year-old man.

'Oh yes?' Holly exchanged a grin with Meg. 'I bet it was elevated. He fancies you, you know.'

'Don't be ridiculous.' Although Ruby felt an inexplicable rush of pleasure at Holly's statement.

'He does,' Meg insisted. 'Anyone can see it. He tries to be all calm and professional around us but he always smiles more when you're around.'

Ruby tried to bite back her own smile. 'Why, what's he like when I'm not around?'

'He's perfectly nice but distant, if you know what I mean.'

'I don't find him distant. He always strikes me as being friendly and approachable.'

'My point exactly!'

'Yes,' Holly put in, 'you should have seen him the other day when an Admin WAAF invited him to that dance in London. She was fawning all over him.'

'Really?' An unpleasant spike jabbed her gut.

Meg pulled a face. 'Oh yes, I remember. Not that I blame her because he's really good looking, but it made me feel queasy to watch her. She was pretty, though. Lovely wavy blonde hair, a bit like yours, Ruby, and tall and thin enough to look good in her uniform.' She glanced at herself in the mirror with a sad sigh.

'Don't you dare say that you're not as pretty as her,' Holly said, looking fierce.

'But I'm not. I've got ordinary brown hair and I'm fat.'

'You're not fat! You've got curves that beanpole of a WAAF would die for.'

Much as Ruby agreed with Holly, she thought they were straying from the point. 'You look amazing, Meg. I'd love to have a figure like yours. But did Laurie go to the dance?'

'Course not. He can see right through her. He told her he was busy. But I bet if *you* had asked, he'd have gone like a shot.'

'I'm sure he wouldn't. Anyway, I'd never have asked. Even if he wasn't a flight sergeant, I'd never dare to ask out a man.'

'Why not?' Holly asked. 'We're not living in Victorian times now, you know. There's nothing wrong with asking out a man.'

'What if he said no? I'd never live down the shame. Not that I'd ever want to ask,' Ruby added hurriedly.

Holly grinned. 'I don't think you need ever worry about him turning you down.'

An inexplicable warmth lingered with Ruby for the rest of the day. Yet it was accompanied by a twinge of unease. She had been made to look foolish once before, and she couldn't bear for it to happen again.

The six weeks of the course passed all too quickly for Ruby. She got through each day by telling herself she wasn't alone in the air with a patient *yet* and tried to simply enjoy the training and the time with her friends. But nothing could stop or even slow down time, and she couldn't escape the fact that the exams were rapidly approaching. The comfortable five weeks to go became four then three. April segued into May, but Ruby was too buried in her studies to pay much heed to the spring flowers and blossoming trees. Although the work she, Meg and Holly did every evening helped her face the exams with more confidence, she couldn't avoid the consequences of the results. Either she would fail and let down her friends and the Air Ambulance Service or she would pass and have to do a job that terrified her. She still couldn't decide which was the greater evil.

One thing tipped the balance in favour of passing. While the nursing orderlies were in class, the air ambulance crews underwent training flights. At times, Ruby would gaze out of the window at an Airspeed Oxford circling overhead and remember the thrill of being in the air. If she failed, she would be sent back to work full-time in hospital and might never fly again. As the exams drew closer, she knew she would always regret it if she failed.

Finally the morning of the exams arrived, and she woke with a cold lump of dread in her stomach. The WAAFs dressed and went to breakfast in a more subdued fashion than usual. Instead of the animated chatter that echoed around the cookhouse rafters, a bubble of silence surrounded the tables occupied by the nursing orderlies. All had exercise books open beside their plates and their heads were down, studying as they ate.

'The radial artery is found on the thumb side of the wrist,' Ruby muttered as she took a bite from her toast. She chewed it several times before the dryness filtered through to her consciousness and she realised she had forgotten to spread it with margarine or jam. Not that it mattered. She felt too sick for more than a couple of mouthfuls. She pushed away her plate with a grimace.

'I keep forgetting,' Meg said. 'To relieve a patient's pain, can you inject a second dose of morphine after a twenty-minute wait or is it thirty?'

Ruby stared at her friend. 'Only if you want to kill your patient. It's two hours.'

Meg grinned and patted Ruby's arm. 'Just checking. See – you'll be fine. Now, stop worrying and eat your breakfast. You'll pass out if you try getting through the day on what you've eaten so far.'

Meg's attempt to reassure her, feeble though it had been, helped unknot Ruby's stomach, and she managed to finish her toast. However, nothing could completely dispel her nerves, and it was almost a relief when it was time to troop out to their classroom for the first exam. In no time at all, Ruby found herself at a desk near the back of the room with paper, pencils and a question paper face-down in front of her.

Sister Macintosh stood at the front of the room, and when everyone was seated, she said, 'You have an hour and a half. You may now turn over your papers and start.'

Ruby stared at the first question. *Describe the type of respirations associated with severe internal haemorrhage.* She knew the answer. She could do this. Drawing a deep breath, she picked up her pencil and began to write.

'How do you think you did?' Holly asked.

It was the end of the gruelling day, and the girls were walking back to their house. Although there had been breaks between the two written papers and the practical, they had been too busy swotting for the next exam to analyse the papers they had already sat.

'I honestly don't know,' Ruby replied. She was so drained it was an effort to speak. 'I didn't do badly on the first paper but I'm not so sure about the second. As for the practical…' She winced. 'Let's say it wasn't my finest hour and leave it at that.'

But Holly wasn't going to let it go that easily. 'Why – what happened?'

Ruby groaned. 'It was awful. Sister Macintosh asked me to take a patient's pulse, and it was only then that I realised I hadn't wound my watch that morning, and it had stopped.'

'That's not so bad. You must have noticed straight away.'

'Yes, but I was all fingers and thumbs. Even after I'd managed to wind it up, it took me ages to find the patient's pulse.'

'You mustn't worry about it. Sister Macintosh will take exam nerves into account, I'm sure. You got there in the end, didn't you?'

'Well, yes, but only after I'd got in a complete muddle. I timed the pulse for a full minute just as Sister Macintosh taught us, but then I got confused with that trick some of the nurses at Leecliff used and multiplied the number by four.'

Meg burst into a fit of giggles. 'But you only do that if you count the number of beats in fifteen seconds.'

'I know. Sister Macintosh looked most alarmed when I announced the patient's heart rate was 280.'

'I'm sorry,' Meg said, wiping her eyes. 'I'm not laughing at you. Well, maybe I am a bit but more about Sister Macintosh's reaction to hearing the patient's heart was about to explode.'

'Even she was trying not to laugh,' Ruby said glumly. 'At least I gave her some entertainment, I suppose. I realised what I'd done straight away and corrected it, but I cringe every time I think of it. There's no way I'm going to pass now.'

'But you didn't have any trouble with anything else, did you?' Holly looked anxious.

'No. The pulse debacle was the first thing I did. After that I was so sure I'd failed I relaxed. Everything else was fine. What about you two?' Ruby was desperate to turn the focus of the conversation away from her.

'I think I did all right,' Meg said. 'I nearly made a mistake with that dosage question, but I noticed just in time and corrected it. Sister Macintosh looked pleased with me after the practical, so I'm fairly confident I passed that. What about you, Holly?'

Holly crossed the fingers on both of her hands. 'I struggled a bit with question five on the second paper but everything else was fine. I hope. I just don't know how I'm going to survive the weekend waiting to hear if we all passed.'

'What we need,' Meg said, 'is a distraction. We've been working so hard, we haven't really been out since we arrived. But it's Friday night. There must be a dance on somewhere.'

At that, Winnie, who had been walking ahead with her friend Claire Parker, turned and said, 'I hope you don't mind me butting in, but I couldn't help overhearing. There's a dance on at the Red Lion Hotel tonight. We should all go!'

'Perfect!' Meg turned to her friends with shining eyes. 'Tonight we paint the town red!'

Chapter Five

The Red Lion turned out to be a large red brick Georgian building on the outskirts of Starsden. Although it was within walking distance, the friends took a bus, not wanting to be too tired to dance by the time they got there. The strains of 'Pennsylvania 6-5000' reached their ears as soon as they climbed off the bus and guided them to the doors of the hotel ballroom.

Inside, through a haze of smoke, they were met with a heaving dance floor, packed with couples dancing with varying levels of expertise. Around the edges of the room were several tables, and Ruby immediately spied Winnie and Claire occupying one not far from the band. Winnie saw her at the same time and waved enthusiastically, beckoning them.

'We saved seats for you,' she said when they had negotiated the crowd and made their way across the room.

'Anyone else here we know?' Ruby asked, taking the vacant chair beside Winnie.

Winnie pulled a face. 'Only Bobby.' This was Roberta Jones, who had informed the class at the start of training that she preferred to be called Bobby. 'She's with some of the girls from Admin. Oh, and Flight Sergeant Foster.' She jerked her head towards the bar where Bobby's blonde head stood out.

Ruby found it hard not to compare herself unfavourably with Bobby. Although her own hair was also blonde, something about the cheap soap she was forced to use had turned it dull, whereas Bobby's gleamed like summer sunshine. In fact, it wasn't just her hair that made her stand out but her whole appearance. Even in uniform, she could have walked out of the pages of *Vogue* magazine. Ruby had a sneaking suspicion that she had taken her uniform to a tailor, for she was the only WAAF in the room whose uniform fitted her perfectly, accentuating and enhancing her willowy figure. Ruby was strongly conscious of the way her own uniform swamped her short, slender figure, making her appear dumpy. Not the look she would choose for a dance.

Then her gaze slid from Bobby and over the equally well-groomed WAAFs she was with to the tall, handsome young man standing beside them. It was Laurie. Her heart sank. 'Did Bobby and Flight Sergeant Foster come here together?' she asked, striving to keep the dismay from her voice.

'I don't think so,' Winnie replied. 'But the girls she's with seem to know him, and one of them is the WAAF who asked him to the dance in London. She's been glued to his side ever since he arrived. Do you know who the man is that he's with? He's not in uniform.'

It was only then that Ruby noticed Adam standing at Laurie's other side. Some of the dismay she'd felt at seeing Laurie with Bobby drained away. 'Oh, that's his brother, Adam. He's a vet, I think, or training to be one.' She tried to remember what Adam had said.

Winnie tapped her arm. 'I could use a drink,' she said with an arch smile. 'Why don't we go to the bar and get one? Coming, you two?'

Before she knew it, Ruby was in the middle of the group, being steered towards the section of the bar where Laurie stood. When they got closer, she saw a pretty brunette WAAF had her hand on Laurie's sleeve. It looked horribly possessive, and Ruby tried to pull away from her friends. 'I think we should come back later.'

'What, and leave poor Flight Sergeant Foster to a fate worse than death? Come on' – Holly pulled her arm – 'he needs saving.'

Ruby could only watch, half in embarrassment, half in admiration as Winnie squeezed herself into the minute gap between the WAAF and Laurie and only appeared to notice either after she had ordered her drink. She gave a dramatic double take that Ruby was sure fooled nobody. 'Oh, hello, Bobby. And Flight Sergeant Foster, how lovely to see you. I was only saying to Ruby here that I wondered if we would see anyone else from the base.'

'Yes, it's strange how the only dance within walking distance of RAF Starsden should have attracted so many of us,' Laurie replied with a twitch of the lips. He went on to introduce Adam, saying that he was working at their father's ironmongery in Starsden.

Ruby happened to be looking at Bobby when he said that, and saw her sneer. No doubt she thought an ironmonger's son was beneath her interest. However, when prompted by Winnie, she introduced her friends from Admin.

She had just announced the name of the brunette who'd had her eye on Laurie – Fiona – when the band launched into 'The Waltz You Saved for Me'.

'Oh, that's funny,' Winnie said. 'Ruby here was just saying how much she looked forward to dancing a waltz, weren't you, Ruby?'

Ruby could only stand and stare at Winnie, wishing the floor would open up beneath her. Or beneath Winnie. She wasn't fussy. Was her crush on Laurie so obvious that even Winnie had sensed it? She'd thought it was only Holly and Meg who had noticed.

Laurie, however, turned a smile on her that reduced her knees to jelly. 'It would be a pleasure to dance with you.' He offered her his arm.

Feeling light-headed, Ruby took it, thankful that she didn't seem to be required to speak at the moment, because she didn't think she would have been able. As she stepped towards the dance floor, she couldn't help glancing at Bobby's Admin friend, Fiona. Her face was screwed up so tightly she looked as though she had just drunk a pint of vinegar.

When Laurie took her in his arms and guided her across the floor, she finally found her voice. 'I'm sorry for barging in on you like that,' she said. 'I hope you didn't feel pressured into asking me to dance. I don't know what got into Winnie's head.' She was babbling. Drawing a deep breath, she tried to get herself under control. She struggled to think of something else to say but her mind had gone blank.

Thankfully Laurie chuckled. 'She did me a favour. I wanted to ask you to dance anyway.'

'You did?' Ruby's voice was barely more than a squeak.

'Yes, I wanted to thank you for the help you gave to Adam.'

'Adam?' It took her a moment to work out who he meant until she remembered his brother. 'Oh. I didn't realise I'd helped him.'

'You did. Very much.' He paused as though ordering his thoughts then said, 'I don't know if you noticed that he's not altogether in the best health?'

'Well, I thought he struggled to move around. I wondered if he'd been injured.'

'He was. At Dunkirk.'

'Oh. So he was in the army?' But the Dunkirk evacuations had been two years ago. His injuries must have been extensive for Adam still to be suffering.

Laurie nodded. 'Those first few weeks after he was brought back were... terrible. We thought he was going to die. He'd received a bullet wound that had damaged his spine and made a mess of his stomach. Then, when it became clear he would survive, there was the worry that he would be paralysed. And all the times I visited him in hospital I kept wondering if I could have prevented it. He's my little brother. I should have tried harder to persuade him to stick with his training. Then he'd have ended up in a reserved occupation and wouldn't have gone anywhere near Dunkirk. Only that would have been hypocritical of me, considering I joined the RAF as soon as war was declared.'

Ruby wanted to ask what he had done before the war, but this was hardly the time. Not when he was pouring out his heart about his brother. She had the sense that he had kept all these feelings bottled up and now he had found someone willing to listen he needed to unburden himself. 'I'm sure it must have been hard seeing him put himself in danger but if he was old enough to volunteer then he would have been old enough to know his own mind. It wasn't up to you to stop him.'

'I know.' He gave a sad smile, and Ruby guessed he must have told himself this many times. 'And when he started to recover and the doctors told us he would walk again, we thought all would be well. Adam was keen to build up his strength and return to the army, so I suppose that proves he had no regrets about joining in the first place. But anyway, it doesn't really matter because it turned out that the bullet had caused some permanent damage. He was on sick leave for a long time, refusing to give up hope, but a few months ago, the doctors told him he would never be strong enough to return so he was discharged on medical grounds.'

'Oh. Poor Adam.' The words felt wholly inadequate, but Ruby felt she had to say something. Then she remembered what Laurie had said at the start of the dance. 'I don't see how I've helped him, though.'

'Well, you and Bentley between you, to be precise. He's had a few unpleasant encounters recently, with strangers demanding to know why he wasn't in uniform.'

'But that's awful!' Ruby exclaimed. 'There could be any number of reasons, and it's none of their business.'

'That's exactly what I told him, but I'm not the one who has to face up to the questions. Anyway, you treated him with kindness and respect and it showed him that any nice person would act the same way as you.'

'I should hope so.' She was horrified to hear that complete strangers might think they had a right to pass judgement on Adam. 'I'm glad I could help, even if it was only by behaving like any civilised person should.'

'Between you and Bentley, you've really helped. He's improved a lot since he had the dog to take care of. He's even been going out and about a bit more and he's working more regular hours at our dad's shop.'

She recalled that Adam had mentioned something about not finishing his veterinary training. 'Do you think he might go back to college?'

Laurie pulled a face. 'That's the problem. He could but he's lost a lot of confidence. Even treating Bentley doesn't seem to have helped him regain it completely.' There was a pause while he steered them around a corner, avoiding another couple who were approaching from the other direction.

Ruby relished the feel of his hand upon her back and the hard ridges of muscle that she could feel through his sleeve. It had been a long time since she had enjoyed a man's company this much. She tried not to think too hard about the last time she had had the kind of feelings that Laurie elicited. Last time had not ended well.

Finding a quieter spot on the dance floor, Laurie continued. 'I can understand why Adam feels as he does. If I were to be invalided out of the RAF, I would feel as though I'd lost my purpose in life.' He tore his gaze from her then, looking down, and he muttered, 'Not that I'm serving much purpose at the moment.'

'What do you mean?' Ruby seethed. 'The Air Ambulance Service is incredibly important. I wouldn't have volunteered if I didn't think that. Imagine what it must be like for those who are badly injured or terribly ill, who at the moment have to endure hours in a bumpy ambulance. We'll be able to make it so much easier for them. Never think helping people is of lesser importance to fighting or dropping bombs.'

'I' – his startled gaze met her own – 'you're right. I'm sorry. I didn't mean to imply your work is less important than those who are fighting. But I can understand how Adam feels. The news is full of the fighting on various fronts. His friends are out there. Even though he's no longer in the army, I think he's finding it hard to admit that his fighting days are over.'

The song ended at that point, and they broke apart to applaud the band. When they returned to the bar to join the others, Ruby thought about what Laurie had said. Not so much about his brother, although her heart went out to him, but about his muttered comment about not serving much purpose. What had he meant? She couldn't ask now, because they were back with their friends. And Bobby, Fiona and the other Admin WAAFs.

The band struck up a lively number, and Fiona, with a sly glance at Laurie, announced, 'I love this song. I can never hear it without wanting to dance.'

With a hint like that, Laurie had no option but to ask her to dance. Fiona shot Ruby a triumphant look as she took his arm.

Something twisted deep in her chest. She could no longer deny the truth: she was developing feelings for Laurie and felt nothing but stinging jealousy at the sight of Fiona in his arms, gazing into his eyes.

Someone tapped her arm, and she dragged her gaze from the couple on the dance floor to see Meg giving her a sympathetic smile. 'I'm sure Flight Sergeant Foster has got enough sense to see that Fiona's a shallow flirt.'

Ruby would have been happier if she hadn't observed how much men seemed to like shallow flirts. Especially if said flirts were in possession of a pretty face and an attractive figure.

She bought a lemonade and took it to their table. Holly made to follow then but paused and glanced at Adam. 'You're welcome to join us.'

Adam's face lit up with a smile. He collected his beer and followed them. When he sat down, Holly said to him, 'You're lucky to have your brother posted so close.'

Adam pulled at his collar. 'Actually, it didn't happen by chance. He was flying with Coastal Command for some time but when I was... injured, he requested a transfer so he could be closer to home. He was moved to a posting in Essex for a while – much closer than Devon where he was before. But then when the Air Ambulance Service was set up so close to home and they were looking for pilots, it was on record that he had requested a posting close to home so I suppose he was selected for that reason.'

Ruby, whose attention was half on the dancing couple, couldn't resist listening in, drinking in every scrap of information she could glean about Laurie. She still couldn't shake off the feeling that Laurie wasn't entirely happy with his job and wondered if he resented flying with the Air Ambulance Service instead of his work at Coastal Command. Still, he was obviously concerned about his brother and it must set his mind at rest to be near to him. But when he had spoken about Adam being faced with returning to civilian life when the men in the armed forces were getting all the praise and attention, she wondered if he hadn't been speaking about himself. When people spoke of the RAF, they generally spoke of the men flying Spitfires and Hurricanes in Fighter Command or pilots flying long, gruelling missions in Bomber Command. But what of the men flying patrols in Coastal Command or those in the soon-to-start Air Ambulance Service? They were both vitally important, but was it possible that Laurie didn't feel he was making as valuable a contribution to the war effort as other pilots?

The song ended, and Ruby's heart sped up. Would Laurie choose to stay with Fiona or would he join Ruby and Adam at their table?

Fiona tugged his arm, clearly intending to lead him to the table where her friends were sitting. At that moment, however, he looked in Ruby's direction and his gaze fell on Adam. He gave a wave and then said something to Fiona. He left her and came to join them.

Ruby's victory was short-lived, however, for Adam gave an enormous yawn only five or so minutes after Laurie had sat down.

Laurie instantly shot him an anxious look. 'I'd better see you home, or Mum will have my guts for garters for wearing you out.'

Chapter Six

Ruby spent the rest of the weekend endlessly reliving her dance with Laurie. Although they had stayed long after Laurie and his brother had left, and she danced with several other men, the dance that stood out was her waltz with Laurie. She couldn't forget the warmth that had suffused her whole body when she'd been in his arms, not to mention the thrill she'd felt when he had confided in her about Adam. Of course she had been sorry to hear of his brother's suffering but never before had she been with a man who had wanted to share something so personal. The other men she had danced with had been more typical of her experience; they had either been silent, only speaking to apologise when they had stumbled or trodden on her toes, or they had spoken of themselves and spent the whole dance boasting of how they were practically winning the war all on their own. While her conversation with Laurie couldn't be described as romantic, they had at least spoken from the heart.

With all that to think about, Ruby almost forgot to be nervous about the exam results. Until they returned from Church Parade on Sunday morning and were told their results had been posted in the common room at Poplar Court. Poplar Court was the large house where the nursing orderlies had been billeted. It had been a private residence but had been requisitioned soon after the start of the war and was now home to many of the WAAFs who worked at the hospital. Being only a ten-minute walk from the hospital, the women found it very convenient, not to mention that it was easier for them to sneak in and out unobserved than if they had been living on base. To Ruby and her friends, who had slept in freezing cold Nissen huts at their previous posting, it was the height of luxury. Instead of sharing a hut with a dozen other girls, they now slept five to a room, and even though they had less space, it was warmer and they didn't have to traipse outside to visit the ablutions block. The only disadvantage was having Bobby for a roommate.

'I feel sick,' Holly muttered as they trooped into the common room, too anxious to learn their fate to put away their coats and hats.

However, their anxiety was short-lived. Winnie was already gazing at a list pinned to the noticeboard when they walked in, and she looked up with a beaming smile. 'We've all passed. Isn't that wonderful!'

Holly gave a whoop and performed a jig on the spot. 'That's wonderful. Congratulations to all of us!'

A wave of relief washed over Ruby. She hadn't let down her friends.

'Shame Bobby passed, though,' muttered Meg. 'Now we've got to put up with her telling us all about how she single-handedly performed an appendectomy on a patient while simultaneously fighting off a load of enemy fighters.'

Ruby snorted and opened her mouth to add to the story when Winnie called out, 'They've posted the duty roster too. Ruby, you're flying tomorrow, lucky thing.'

'What?' Ruby felt as though someone had tipped a bucket of icy water over her head. She went to stand beside Winnie. Then she remembered what they had been told during their training. 'But that doesn't necessarily mean I'm actually flying, does it? I'm just to be on call in the crew room in case I'm needed.'

'It says here you're to report to the crew room at 0700.' Winnie tapped the typed orders. 'Sounds like they've got a patient already lined up. Probably someone who's been waiting for transport for a while.'

With a sinking heart Ruby realised that was all too likely.

'Lucky thing,' Holly said, reading the orders over Ruby's shoulder. 'I'm not on ambulance duty until Friday.'

Her only shred of comfort was that it was probably better to get her first flight out of the way than spend days agonising about it.

She gave her friends a shaky smile. 'Help me go over my notes again?' she asked. 'I need to be sure I'm ready for tomorrow.'

Ruby was a bag of nerves by the time she reported to the crew room the following morning, carrying her medical bag and feeling very self-conscious in her flight boots. She was surprised but pleased to find her pilot was Laurie, having expected Squadron Leader Norton would want to pilot the first mission. She was also pleased to see Flight Sergeant Rhys Powell would be their wireless operator again. Laurie introduced her to an officer she hadn't met before – Flying Officer Neil Maitland, their navigator.

The crew room was a Nissen hut with a pipe stove in the centre, around which was gathered a set of mismatched chairs. There was a board at the back with lists of duty rosters, and lockers lined the walls. There was also, she was pleased to see, a kettle small enough to fit on the stove and a selection of mugs, tins of powdered milk, cocoa and tea on a shelf. She already knew from her training that if they weren't flying they would be required to wait in the crew room on days they were rostered for air ambulance duty in case they were needed.

Laurie wasted no time in outlining the day's mission, his words accompanied by the sound of Bentley noisily lapping from his water bowl that had been placed in a corner. 'We're going to Kirkwall in Orkney to transport a pilot with lung cancer to London. He wants to be closer to his family.'

Lung cancer! Ruby's heart twisted in sympathy. She had been prepared for patients with terrible injuries but hadn't expected to see patients with cancer. From Laurie's tone of voice, she gathered the pilot wasn't expected to live long.

'Get kitted up, everyone,' Laurie instructed. 'We're taking off in thirty minutes.'

Ruby's nerves were such that she had to nip to the nearby latrine. When she returned, Laurie handed her a life jacket. 'You'll need a Mae West in case we have to ditch in the sea.' He showed her how to fasten it. She could immediately see why it was called a Mae West, because it made her chest twice the size. It was hardly the most flattering gear, and she wished Laurie didn't have to see her like that.

All the same, she couldn't help being excited about flying all the way to Orkney. She had only the vaguest notion of where it was and had to consult the chart pinned to the wall to see their destination was in a group of islands some miles from the northeastern tip of Scotland. Quite an adventure for her first outing! The thrill helped mitigate her nerves about having a patient to care for on the return flight, as well as the fact that the patient was not critically injured meant that she wasn't so worried about being the only medic on the flight. Therefore, when the time came to board the Airspeed Oxford, she wasn't as nervous as she had been earlier and listened with interest from her seat in the cabin while Laurie went through the preflight checks. Then, when they were racing down the runway, she felt the same rollercoaster rush of exhilaration she'd had on her first flight.

The navigator looked up from his chart and, catching her eye, gave her a smile. 'The thrill never gets old,' he said. Then he turned to give Laurie his bearing.

'How long will it take us to get there?' she asked when he turned back to his charts.

'About two hours, assuming the forecast wind speeds are correct. The most direct route would have us flying over the North Sea for some way past Tyneside, but that would put us in greater danger of running into enemy aircraft, so I'm plotting a course further west that will keep us over land for longer.'

Enemy aircraft! Ruby gazed out of the window, half expecting to see a swarm of Messerschmitts swooping out of the clouds. 'Are we likely to run into trouble? I thought we had red cross markings so the Germans wouldn't shoot at us.'

'I still don't want to risk it. The Germans do honour the red cross markings on the whole, but who knows what might happen if an enemy pilot was dazzled by the sun and didn't see the markings until it was too late?'

Laurie must have been listening in, for he called back, 'No alarming the nurse, navigator.' Ruby had noticed that many people tended to refer to the nursing orderlies as nurses even though they didn't have the same qualifications.

'Sorry, Skipper,' Maitland called.

'Ignore him, Ruby,' Laurie said. 'I'm keeping my eyes open even if my navigator isn't, and I won't take us anywhere near trouble.'

Even though she knew they wouldn't be able to outrun a fighter aircraft, she still felt reassured. She was in safe hands with Laurie.

As the Oxford sped north, Ruby divided her time between gazing at the scenery below and mentally rehearsing everything she had learned. She checked the oxygen, in case her patient might need any, and went through her medical bag. Would he be in pain? She checked her pain relief medication. She shoved dressings out of the way, knowing that those wouldn't be needed. She also had a flask of water to hand in case he became thirsty.

Her common sense told her that she was as prepared as she could be, yet she couldn't shake off her fear that something would go wrong.

Maybe Laurie could sense her fear or maybe he was simply remembering her excitement of seeing London from the air, for after she had rummaged through her bag for the third time he called, 'We're about to fly over Loch Ness. Want to look out for Nessie?'

She gazed out of the window and gave a cry of wonder when she saw glittering water and then fields and moorland. Remembering Laurie's advice, she picked out the higher hills by the deep shadows they cast upon the lower land. 'It's beautiful. I've never been to Scotland but I've always wanted to go.'

She remained transfixed by the view as they followed the east coast further north, picking out the settlements, a rare sight against the empty moors and forests. Then the land came to an end and she spied a cluster of islands, emerald green against the grey-blue sea. They began to lose height, and she found herself gazing in wonder at a huge, sheltered bay, surrounded by islands on all sides. As they descended, the outlines of many ships became visible. This had to be Scapa Flow – the anchorage for Britain's Home Fleet.

There was no time to look around and drink in the sight for they were losing height rapidly now, and Laurie was talking over the radio to someone at RAF Grimsetter.

The harbour disappeared and they were flying over land. The plane banked, and the sky disappeared, replaced by a fast-approaching cluster of buildings. As they got closer, Ruby could see it was more than a small group of houses but a sizeable town. Another harbour appeared, this one on the other side of the island. They continued to lose height, banking all the time. When they levelled out, they were above an aerodrome. The ground rushed up to meet them then, and just as they were about to touch down, they lurched violently to the side. Ruby let out a yelp as she was flung against the fuselage. A split second later, they levelled out again and there was a jolt as the Oxford's wheels struck the ground. Ruby released a shaky breath.

'Sorry about that,' Laurie called. 'We got hit by a freak crosswind. No harm done.'

Except to Ruby's ribs where she was sure her heart had hammered a hole through them. Someone on the ground was signalling to them, and Laurie taxied in the direction indicated.

Once the Oxford came to a halt and the propellors swished to a stop, ground crew dashed up to place chocks against the wheels.

'Here we are,' Laurie announced somewhat unnecessarily. 'We're a little ahead of schedule, and the ambulance hasn't left the hospital yet. They should be here in twenty minutes. Gives us a chance to stretch our legs.'

Ruby was grateful for the opportunity to leave the cramped cabin. She also felt that she couldn't claim to have been in Orkney if she didn't set foot upon the land. As soon as she stepped outside, she discovered the reason for the rocky landing when a gust of wind tore off her cap. She dashed after it but Laurie, who had been speaking to one of the ground crew, must have seen what happened for he broke into a sprint and managed to catch it. He handed it back with a grin.

'Can't have you getting in trouble for losing your kit on your very first trip.'

'Thanks.' Another violent gust ruffled her hair, and she decided against attempting to put her hat back on, convinced it would only fly off again. She tucked it under her arm instead.

The chase had put several yards between them and the group huddling in the lee of the Oxford, and Ruby became conscious that this was their first time alone since they had danced together on Friday night. She racked her brains for something to say. 'I hope your brother enjoyed the dance,' she said eventually.

'He did. Taking care of Bentley has done him the world of good. It seems to have taken him out of himself, if you know what I mean.'

She didn't really but she smiled and nodded. 'I'm glad. And I'm really pleased he could help because I can't imagine the place without Bentley now.'

'No, it would feel empty without him.'

His piercing blue eyes bored into hers, and she felt quite breathless. *Don't be an idiot. He doesn't fancy me. He's just being friendly. He would have never asked me to dance if Winnie hadn't backed him into a corner.* She'd had several stern words with herself on the subject over the weekend because she knew how damaging a crush could be. She didn't want to fall into that trap again.

'Ruby, I—'

But the roar of an engine made him break off. Ruby looked across the aerodrome and saw an ambulance approaching. 'That's my cue,' she said and hurried back to the Oxford, part relieved that their patient's arrival had provided a distraction and part wishing the ambulance could have waited until Laurie had finished what he had been about to say.

Chapter Seven

Ruby waited with a thundering heart as the ambulance pulled up as close as possible to the Oxford. In a matter of minutes she would be taking sole charge of her first patient. First the excitement of seeing Scotland from the air and then her flustered emotions at being with Laurie had pushed it from her mind but now the worries came crowding back. Would she be good enough? Would she make a mistake that would make the patient worse?

The ambulance doors opened and a nurse emerged first. She made straight for Ruby. 'You must be the nursing orderly.' At Ruby's answering nod, she carried on, 'This is Flying Officer Mark Peterson. He has lung cancer and is being transferred to Harefield to be closer to his family. He's been sedated for the journey so there shouldn't be much for you to do apart from put him on oxygen. If he wakes, he might need pain relief.' She went on to explain the dosages while Ruby made hasty notes.

Together they supervised Peterson's loading onto the aircraft, using the wide door flap that had been specially fitted. Then the ambulance crew departed. 'Take good care of him,' was the nurse's parting remark. 'We shouldn't have favourite patients, but he's mine, all the same.' She handed Ruby Peterson's small bundle of possessions, explaining that the rest of his things were being sent by boat and train.

By this time the Oxford had been refuelled, and they were ready to leave. Ruby stowed his bag under the stretcher and took her place beside Peterson, looking at him properly for the first time, taking in his condition. Her heart twisted. He was gaunt with deep hollows around his eyes, and his skin had a yellowish tint. He was clearly dying, and her heart went out to him, having been forced to go through his illness so far from his family. Was he married? she wondered. Even accounting for the ageing effect of illness, he looked older than most of the pilots she knew, perhaps in his late thirties or early forties. More than old enough to be married with a family of his own.

In her concern, her anxiety left her. All she could think was that he needed her care and she was determined not to let him down. She no longer worried that she would make a mistake with the valves while administering oxygen. Now it felt like second nature as she fitted the mask and set the oxygen flow to the desired amount.

He didn't stir even when Laurie opened up the engines on full throttle for takeoff and battled the cross-currents once more to take to the air. Assured her patient was as comfortable as could be, she gazed out of the window at the shining lochs and harbour, bidding a silent farewell to Orkney. She could hardly believe that she had flown all that way in a single day! She couldn't wait to tell her friends.

Peterson didn't wake until they were almost over England. Seeing him stir and push at the oxygen mask, she leaned over him. 'Hello. I'm LACW Morris. Are you in any pain?'

He shook his head and pulled the mask away.

'You should leave it on,' she told him.

But he shook his head again and batted away her hand when she tried to replace it. 'I hate those things,' he said, and his voice was strong enough that she allowed him to remove it. She turned off the oxygen.

'Do you need anything? I've got some water here if you need it.'

'You don't have any whisky, do you?' There was a faint twinkle in his dull eyes.

'Afraid not. The pilot would throw me out without a parachute if we had a party back here.'

'It'll have to be water, then.'

She poured a little water into the flask cup and raised his head to help him drink. He had taken three sips when the plane jolted, spilling water over Peterson's face.

'Sorry!' Laurie called, having to shout to be heard over the engines' roar. 'Hit a bit of turbulence.'

Peterson chuckled. 'Good thing it wasn't whisky. Would have been a terrible waste.' He twisted his head in an attempt to see the front of the plane but gave up with a grimace. 'How good's the pilot? I don't like being flown by chaps I don't know.'

'He's the best,' Ruby said. It didn't matter that she had only flown with him once before; she had felt completely safe with Laurie at the controls and she was sure he must be one of the best.

'That's good.' Peterson coughed, and when the fit was over, Ruby insisted he go on oxygen for a while. He soon pushed aside the mask, though, and said, 'It feels good to be in the air again. Flying's the best job in the world.'

'What aircraft have you flown?'

'I started off on Hurricanes. Everyone goes on about Spitfires, and they're beautiful to look at, but Hurricanes were the unsung heroes of the Battle of Britain. We'd never have got through without them.'

'You flew in the Battle of Britain?'

Peterson nodded but broke into another coughing fit before he could reply.

Ruby insisted he use the oxygen again and while she helped him on with the mask, said, 'I remember reading everything I could about our fighter pilots during the Battle of Britain. You were all so brave, doing what you did. It's a real privilege to meet one.'

After a while, Peterson had recovered enough to dispense with the mask again and speak. 'I never felt brave at the time,' he said. 'I don't think I am a particularly courageous person. It's just that I didn't feel I had a choice. I have a wife and two children. I did it for them. To give them a future. I was scared all the time, but I got through by not allowing myself to think of the things that could go wrong. I took every day, every hour and every minute as it came and didn't look too far ahead. There's nothing brave about that.'

He needed oxygen again, and this time he didn't object but closed his eyes and fell asleep. He didn't wake again during the flight, and Ruby spent the remaining time mulling over what he had said about bravery. He was right, she realised. She knew she wasn't brave and she had dreaded the responsibility but as soon as she had seen him she had forgotten her fear and got on with her job. Because Peterson had needed her.

As Peterson was being admitted to a London hospital, they landed at Starsden. This wouldn't always be the case. If a patient was being admitted to a hospital elsewhere, they would land at the nearest aerodrome and then make a third flight back to Starsden afterwards. Ruby was glad that after what was probably the longest flight she would have, they were returning directly to base.

Thanks to the accurate arrival time that Rhys had signalled ahead, there was an ambulance already waiting when they landed. She bid a fond but sad farewell to Peterson, knowing she would never see him again.

Once the ambulance had driven off, she returned to the Oxford to clean everything in the cabin and leave it in good order for the next flight. Finally she collected her medical bag. While she had been doing that, Laurie had been speaking with a member of the ground crew, and he finished his conversation at the same time as she left the aircraft. The two other crew members were already walking back to the crew room so with a flutter of spirits Ruby realised they would be walking alone. She had been sure he had been about to say something serious in Kirkwall, before he had been interrupted by the ambulance's arrival. Was he about to pick up that conversation now? For a wild moment it had flashed into her mind that he was going to ask her out.

'Ruby?'

She spun round to gaze at him, moving so fast she stumbled and had to grab his arm to stop herself from falling. 'Yes?' She was too breathless to say more.

'Don't forget to fill in your log-book,' Laurie told her. 'You won't be needed again today, so you can leave as soon as you've done that.'

'Oh. Thank you.' She waited for him to say more, but he walked the rest of the way in silence.

Feeling as though the wind had been knocked out of her, she stowed her gear in her locker and sat at one of the tables to complete her log-book entries. As she recorded the details of her two flights she shot several sidelong glances at Laurie. He frowned in concentration as he wrote in his own book but gave no sign of wanting to speak to her or even of noticing she was still there. Thoroughly deflated, she finished by noting the times of both flights and then petted

Bentley while she waited for the ink to dry. It seemed to take an age. 'At least you're happy,' she murmured to Bentley, whose eyes were half closed in ecstasy.

'Did you say something?' Laurie asked without looking up.

'Only to Bentley.' She closed the log-book and put away her pen. 'Well, goodbye.' She hesitated. 'If you're sure it's all right for me to leave?'

Laurie finally glanced at her. 'Yes, I'm sure. Enjoy the rest of your afternoon.' And that was all.

Idiot! Fancy letting her imagination get the better of her like that. Of course Laurie wasn't interested in her. She had been foolish to think so.

She couldn't leave fast enough.

—

Laurie resisted the temptation to call Ruby back. It was a good thing the ambulance had arrived at RAF Grimsetter in time to stop him asking her out. On their return flight, although the engine noise had prevented him from hearing most of her conversation with Flying Officer Peterson, he had heard her saying how much she admired the brave fighter pilots of the Battle of Britain. He hadn't done anything brave. While the likes of Peterson had been saving Britain from a Nazi invasion, he had been in Coastal Command, flying routine patrols. He had volunteered to retrain as a fighter pilot but had been told that his role in protecting the fleet was vital. Hearing Ruby praising fighter pilots had touched a nerve. Would she really be interested in him? She would certainly never have a reason to gaze at him admiringly and tell him how brave he was.

As soon as he was officially off duty he called Bentley to his side and clipped on his lead. 'Shall we go and see Adam?'

The little dog immediately tore towards the door, tail wagging, forcing Laurie to run after him if he didn't want to dislocate his shoulder. 'I'll take that as a yes, shall I?' Not that he was complaining. Being posted so close to his family was, after all, the main reason he had not protested when he had been transferred to the newly formed Air Ambulance Service. It had been agony being far from home when Adam had been injured, so while he wasn't performing the daring feats he felt were his duty, he did appreciate being able to spend much of his off-duty time with his little brother.

His father was already home when he arrived, having closed up his shop for the day. He clapped Laurie on the shoulder. 'Good to see you. Flown anywhere exciting?'

'Actually, yes.' Laurie was pleased to be able to report his first mission. 'I went to Orkney and back. Transferred a patient to London.'

'Ah, well. I suppose you can't expect to be in action all the time. I remember a time in France...' And he was off, relating more of his experiences as a pilot in the Royal Flying Corps during the Great War. If even half the stories his father told were true, he had been responsible for shooting down most of the aircraft in the German air force. Laurie had drunk in every story as a boy; they had inspired him to join the RAF as soon as war broke out. They still inspired him, although he now understood they were his father's way of coping with the deadly danger he had faced and the terrible sights he had seen.

He followed his father into the back room where he was greeted by his mother and brother.

'Will you be eating with us?' Lettie asked.

Laurie, catching the flicker of anxiety in her eyes, hastened to reassure her. 'No, I can't stay that long. I'll eat in the Sergeants' Mess.' It was enough of a struggle for the family to make their rations stretch as it was, without him adding to the burden. 'I just thought I'd pop in to see how you all are.'

'We're doing well. Adam managed a couple of hours' work at the shop, didn't you, Adam?'

Adam grinned at him, and Laurie could tell he was fighting the urge to roll his eyes at being treated like a five-year-old. 'Yes, Mum, I did.'

'Go on with you. But it's good to see you out and about more.' Lettie turned to Laurie. 'You'll at least have a cup of tea? And there's still a slice of fruitcake left over from last week.'

'Sounds lovely, Mum.'

She bustled out, and his father left the room at the same time, saying he needed to fix the henhouse.

Laurie dropped onto the sofa next to Adam. 'It's really good news that you're feeling well enough to go out more. Any chance you might think about going back to veterinary college?'

Adam reached down to pet Bentley. 'Maybe. I'm thinking about it.' But there were shadows in his eyes.

Laurie could guess why Adam sounded less than enthusiastic. Being a vet was all his brother had wanted to be, and the whole family had worked hard to send him to college. Laurie hadn't resented it at all and had willingly worked long hours at the shop to help them make enough money. The joy in Adam's eyes when he had started was all the thanks he needed. Yet, probably for similar reasons to Laurie, he had joined the army at the outbreak of war. Even now, when he had been formally discharged on medical grounds, he couldn't completely let go of his desire to serve his country as their father had done in the Great War. Returning to college would be finally acknowledging to himself that there was no returning to action.

'I had a letter from Sam today.' Sam was his friend in the army.

'Oh? How's he doing?'

'He's doing well, I think. I know he can't say much, but he's in North Africa now. He and the lads seem to be having fun.'

There was a pause, punctuated only by the clock ticking on the mantelpiece.

'I just wish I was still out there. I feel useless here.'

'You're not useless. You've done your bit. You nearly died, for God's sake.'

Adam gazed into the fire. 'I know. It doesn't stop me feeling I should be doing more, though. I hate going out in civvies, seeing girls staring at me, wanting to know why I'm not in uniform.'

Laurie's heart sank. 'I'm sure they're not thinking that. They're probably wondering who the good-looking young man is and if he'll introduce them to his even better-looking brother.'

He'd expected to raise a reluctant smile. Instead, Adam rubbed his temples, squeezing his eyes tightly shut. He seemed to be holding an inner debate. Finally he pulled a crumpled envelope from his pocket. 'I got this today.'

Laurie looked at the envelope. There was no address on it, just Adam's name, written in block capitals. He glanced at Adam, in a silent request for permission. When his brother nodded, he pulled out a sheet of paper and read what was written on it, also in block letters.

YOU'RE NOTHING BUT A YELLOW-BELLIED COWARD. YOU SHOULD BE

ASHAMED OF YOURSELF. BRAVE MEN ARE DYING WHILE YOU SIT AT HOME.

Laurie gazed at it, feeling sick. Making a supreme effort, he gave a grin and said lightly, 'Short and sweet.'

Adam wasn't smiling, though. His eyes were fixed upon his brother, his misery plain in every taut muscle.

Laurie laid a hand on Adam's shoulder, feeling him quivering. While they weren't a demonstrative family, touch seemed the only way to get through to him. 'You know it's not true, don't you? You fought and nearly died. You're only home now because you were willing to give your all for your country.' He waved the letter in front of Adam's face. 'Whoever wrote this is a sick individual and knows nothing about you. There's only one thing this letter deserves.' He crumpled the paper in his fist and flung it in the fire. The flames flared briefly then dwindled as the paper shrivelled to ash.

Adam still said nothing, so Laurie squeezed his shoulder. 'Tell me you know it's a lie.'

His brother swallowed. 'I do. Of course I do. But it feels so personal. It was addressed to me. It's not like someone just approached me in the street and handed me a white feather.'

That was true. Laurie still had the envelope. He looked at it, searching for anything that might identify the sender, but there was nothing apart from the name. He peered inside, looking for what, he didn't know. It wasn't as though the sender would have handily dropped a calling card inside. It was empty, as he had known it would be. One thing did catch his attention, however.

'This is good quality paper. Pre-war stock, I would say. Why would anyone waste something so good on something so hateful?' He frowned, remembering how the weight and thickness of the letter itself had felt between his fingers. 'The same with the notepaper. It should be a crime to waste a whole sheet of paper on three sentences.' He snorted. 'Mum would have my guts for garters if she knew I'd burned it instead of putting it in the salvage basket.'

Some of the colour returned to Adam's face and he gave the ghost of a smile. 'I promise not to tell.'

'It wasn't addressed so how did you get it? Was it pushed through the door?'

'It didn't come here. I found it at the shop. I thought it was for Dad at first until I read the name properly.'

'Good thing you noticed in time.' Laurie dreaded to think how their father would have reacted had he read the note. With his name being Alan, there had been occasions when he had accidentally opened mail meant for his son. 'Any idea what time it arrived?'

Adam's brow furrowed. 'Not really, but I found it under the other letters, so whoever it's from must have delivered it before the post arrived this morning.'

'That doesn't really help,' Laurie said glumly. 'It gives us a time anywhere between when Dad closed on Saturday and the arrival of the post on Monday morning.' He glanced at the envelope, hesitated, then threw it in the fire. It was briefly consumed in bright flames before withering into ash beside the remains of the letter. 'Hopefully that's the last you'll see of that,' he told Adam with more conviction than he felt. As his brother had said, the attack felt personal. 'Promise you'll tell me if you get any more.'

'I promise.'

Laurie wanted to say more, make Adam see how brave he was for the battles he had fought, both literally, when he had been in the army, and figuratively when he had been forced to come to terms with his injuries. However, Lettie returned to the room at that moment, bearing a tray with tea and the promised cake. Adam caught his eye, sending a silent plea not to say anything in front of her, and Laurie gave a barely perceptible nod. He saw no need to alarm his parents.

But the cake, that he had been looking forward to, seemed tasteless and he struggled to choke it down. While he made light conversation, joking and pretending that nothing was wrong, he trembled with anger. He made a silent vow that he would find whoever had done this to his little brother and make them pay.

Chapter Eight

'We should do something tonight,' Meg said, flinging herself onto her bed with a sigh. She had just returned from a flight to Lancashire, transferring a badly burned pilot to East Grinstead hospital. 'It's the first time in ages we've all had time off together, and I want to forget the poor patient we had today.'

Ruby sat beside her and gave her a sympathetic hug. 'Burns patients are always distressing.' She'd had one only last week, and it had taken every ounce of her strength to smile at the man whose right side was a raw, ugly mass of burns and speak to him calmly to put him at ease. It was one thing to know you shouldn't let the patient see your horror but putting it into practice was quite another. Although she had seen burns patients during her time at Bristol, she had always been following the instructions of a nurse or doctor and had found it easier to follow their example.

A whole month had gone by since her flight to Orkney, and she had made three more trips since then; her logbook was filling up nicely. While she was still nervous about the responsibility, she hadn't had problems with any of her patients. As Sister Macintosh had told them right at the start of their training, with flights being no more than two hours, and many of them much shorter than that, patients who had been sedated or given pain relief before the flight would be unlikely to need any further intervention before they reached their destination. By putting her patients' needs first, she was able to repress her doubts and fears. For the most part.

Holly walked in at that moment, returned from a shift at the hospital. 'Urgh! Corporal Lewis can't get those casts off his arms soon enough. If I have to scratch his nose one more time...' She shuddered and dropped onto the bed beside her friends. The springs creaked ominously.

'We were just saying we should do something this evening,' Ruby told her. 'Any suggestions?'

Holly brightened. 'Let's go to the pictures. *The Man Who Came to Dinner* is on at the Majestic, and I've been wanting to see that for ages.' She tugged off her shoes and massaged her feet with a groan. 'Plus I don't think I could do anything that involves standing.'

'Good idea,' Meg said, but then a look of alarm crossed her face. 'Unless there's going to be an air raid. I'd hate to be trapped in a cinema.'

'We'll be fine,' Holly said. 'The Germans are targeting other cities at the moment.' Cities like York and Exeter had borne the brunt of recent attacks, and London was experiencing a lull.

Meg appeared reassured, and so they agreed to go to the cinema. Ruby would have preferred a walk or even a visit to the pub – somewhere they could talk – but as the others were keen to see the film, she didn't argue. Therefore at seven o'clock they were sitting on the creaky fold-down seats at the Majestic, laughing at the cartoon reel.

Ruby was chuckling at a joke when Meg nudged her arm. 'Look who's in front. Want to move forward?'

Ruby tore her gaze from the screen and peered at the silhouetted heads of the row in front. It was Laurie and Adam. Her heart gave a little flutter. She hadn't seen him much recently, having been flown by other pilots since Orkney, but there was no mistaking his strong profile.

'Well?' Meg whispered. 'There's an empty seat next to him. You know you want to.'

'Idiot,' she whispered back. 'You know I'm not interested.' This was the story she had told following his cold dismissal after that first flight. Not wanting to worry her friends, she had hidden her hurt and declared that she didn't feel anything beyond friendship for the handsome pilot. She hadn't breathed a word about that moment on the airfield when he had appeared to be on the brink of asking her out, nor had she mentioned that she would have said yes had he asked.

The trouble was, it was one thing to sternly tell herself she wasn't interested, but it was quite another to get the message across to her heart, which skipped in a most disconcerting manner whenever she happened to catch a glimpse of him. It meant that her gaze continually slid from the action onscreen to the back of his head. When the main feature started, she was so transfixed by a lock of hair that didn't lie quite flat that she could hardly follow the action at all.

'Richard Travis is so good looking,' Holly said when they trooped outside much later. The sun was setting over the rooftops, casting pink and gold streaks into the sky. 'He reminds me a bit of Simon.' She went on to extol the virtues of the sweetheart she had met before joining the WAAF.

Ruby, who had heard it all before, didn't pay much attention. 'I suppose he was all right,' she said absently, scanning the departing cinema goers for a sight of Laurie.

'Oh, and the bit when Jimmy Durante hit his head had me in stitches,' Meg remarked.

'Oh, me too.' Ruby's heart gave a jolt when a tall man in RAF uniform crossed her eye line and then subsided when she realised it wasn't Laurie.

'I don't remember that,' Holly said.

'Don't worry,' Meg said with a sly smile. 'There's nothing wrong with your memory. It never happened. I was just testing Ruby.' She turned to Ruby with an arch smile. 'Did you watch any of the film, or were you drooling over Laurie the entire time?'

'I'm not going to dignify that with a response.'

The others laughed and much to Ruby's relief Holly changed the subject. 'I don't feel like going back to Poplar Court yet. Come on, we've got late passes. Why don't we go to the Three Horseshoes?' This was the pub on the outskirts of Starsden that, being only a five-minute walk from the base, had been adopted by RAF Starsden's personnel. It was an old, half-timbered former coaching inn with a snug that made a cosy retreat for anyone who didn't want to face the rowdier elements in the public bar.

'Sounds good to me,' Meg replied. 'I'm not tired. What about you, Ruby?'

'I'm game.'

It was typical that the first person Ruby should see when they entered the snug was Laurie, sitting in a quiet corner with his brother. Neither Holly nor Meg appeared to notice them as they trooped to the bar. With any luck they would continue not to spot the men, and she could enjoy her drink without their constant teasing.

Sadly, this wasn't to be. Meg was the first to leave the bar and made a beeline for Laurie's table. Ruby was forced to follow.

'Mind if we join you?' Meg asked Laurie.

'Be my guest.' Laurie shifted to make room, and whether by accident or design, Ruby found herself sitting in the middle of a bench seat, squashed between Laurie and Holly.

Laurie looked at her with an expression that was somewhat warmer than the one he had turned on her when he had dismissed her after their last flight together. 'I see we're on ambulance duties together on Tuesday,' he said. 'How have you found the experience so far?'

'It's gone well, I think. I mean, I would say I've enjoyed it, only it doesn't seem right somehow, considering the condition of the patients, but it's good to know I'm doing useful work.'

'I'm glad to hear it. I've heard nothing but good things about you from the other crewmen.'

She felt her cheeks burn from a blush and hoped that in the dim light he wouldn't notice. He had spoken of her with the other men! Did that mean he was interested in her after all?

'I've heard good things about all of you,' he went on, turning to Meg and Ruby. 'You should be proud of yourselves for what you've accomplished.'

Meg and Holly thanked him but Ruby felt deflated. So he hadn't been thinking of her in particular but had been keeping an eye on all the nursing orderlies. She supposed it was his job as skipper to know the strengths and weaknesses of all his crew. He wasn't interested in her. She needed to get over this crush before it started affecting her work.

She was trying to think of something sensible to ask Adam about Bentley's care when the wail of air raid sirens cut through the hum of conversation. She leaped to her feet, her mouth dry. This was the first time there had been an air raid since she had arrived in Starsden and although she knew the locations of all the shelters at the base, she had no idea where to find the ones in Starsden.

Thankfully the landlord took control with quiet authority. 'Down into the cellar. There's plenty of room for everyone.' He lifted the counter and showed them the door that led to the cellar steps.

In the crush, Ruby got separated from the others. Seeing Meg just ahead of her, she grabbed her arm. 'Let's try and stay together,' she said.

The smell of damp and dust hit her as she shuffled down the stone steps. Once she reached the cellar, she saw that there was, indeed, plenty of room. It was illuminated by a single light bulb which cast deep shadows among the stacked barrels and bottles standing upon the flagstones.

'There are empty barrels in the far corner.' The landlord went to where he was pointing and turned some of the barrels that were there onto their sides. 'Sit on them if you like but if I catch any of you stealing any drink, you'll be banned for life.'

This was a dire threat, and Ruby was sure no one from the base would risk being banned from their nearest pub. People began to arrange themselves around the cellar, pulling on coats and jackets against the damp chill, and settled in for a long wait. She still couldn't see Holly or Laurie so she went to claim a barrel.

Meg turned one on its side and rolled it against the wall. Then she half perched, half leaned against it. 'This is even less comfortable than the seats at the Majestic,' she said, and patted the space beside her. 'There's just about room for you.'

Ruby joined her, only belatedly noticing Adam propped against the wall beside them. 'Have you seen the others?' she asked.

He nodded. 'Holly tripped and twisted her ankle.' He held out his hands in a soothing gesture at the women's exclamations of dismay. 'It's nothing to worry about, but Laurie's waiting for the crush around the steps to lessen before he helps her down. He sent me to tell you and also say that he's sure this is a false alarm so not to worry.'

'I hope he's right,' Meg muttered. Only then did Ruby notice how she was twisting her hands together and shivering.

'Are you cold?'

Meg shook her head. 'Sorry. I can't help it.' And it dawned on Ruby that her friend was terrified.

She put an arm around her shoulders. 'We've been through air raids before and you always seemed so calm.'

'I know, but that was when we were in RAF Leecliff. If I was on duty then I had patients to look after, and I was so busy helping them I didn't have time to be frightened. If I was off duty, I would take my knitting into the shelter. I wish I'd brought it with me tonight. It helps me stay calm.'

Ruby couldn't bite back a grin. 'I don't think people would have appreciated the click of knitting needles through the film.'

Her words had the intended effect – Meg giggled.

'Anyway,' Ruby went on, 'I think Laurie's right, and this has to be a false alarm.'

Her words would have had more authority if they hadn't been immediately followed by a loud crash overhead. The room shook, and the light bulb swung wildly upon its cable. Shadows danced on the whitewashed walls, making Ruby feel like she was sitting inside a zoetrope.

Meg gave a squeak of fright and hugged her arms to her chest. The cellar echoed with people crying out.

'Have we been hit?' one man cried.

'No, we'd know if we had,' said another.

'Or, rather, we wouldn't,' a third man said with grim humour. 'I reckon it was a good hundred yards away.'

A woman who hadn't sat down but had been pacing around the room, muttering to herself, now launched herself at the man she was with. 'It's my house, I know it is. You promised I'd be safe here.'

Without waiting for a response, she swung around and marched up to a man standing nearby who wore RAF uniform. 'And what are you doing down here? You're a pilot! You should be up there, protecting us. And you' – she pointed a trembling finger at Adam, who started as though wakened from a dream – 'you're not even in uniform. You should be ashamed of yourself!'

—

Laurie had helped the limping Holly down the steps and had just found her a place to sit when the crash set everyone panicking. He looked round frantically for Adam and saw him just when the terrified woman launched her tirade. He felt a surge of anger towards her, which deepened when his brother seemed to shrink into himself.

He swiftly spoke to Holly. 'Will you be all right alone for a moment?'

'Of course. I—'

He didn't wait for her to finish but pushed his way towards his brother.

Before he could get there, Ruby placed a gentle hand upon Adam's shoulder and left it there for a few seconds. Then she rose and faced the woman. There was no anger in her face, and when she spoke her voice was gentle. 'I'm sorry you're frightened but please leave my friend alone. It's none of your concern why he can't be in uniform but believe me when I say that he's more than played his part.'

The woman didn't speak but stood staring at Ruby, her trembling lips pressed tightly together. Then another woman approached and put an arm around her waist. 'Come over here, Jean, and sit with me. I don't hear any more aircraft, so I think we'll be all right.' Jean allowed herself to be drawn away, and Laurie saw Ruby's tense shoulders relax.

A second later, he was at his brother's side. 'Are you all right?'

'I'm fine.' Then, appearing to recover from his frozen attitude, Adam added, 'Really, I don't need you to come charging to my rescue.' He seemed to realise how ungracious that must appear to Ruby for he reddened and said to her, 'But I appreciate what you said. Thank you.'

The man who had been with Jean hesitated then approached. 'I apologise for my sister. She was living in Hackney during the Blitz and she lost everything.' He addressed Adam. 'She doesn't know what she's saying when she gets like this, and I just wanted you to know that no one else thinks that way. I'm friends with your father, and he's told me all about you. I know what you've done for us.'

Adam gave the man a shaky smile. 'I understand. It's all right.'

Laurie was torn between thanking Ruby and comforting Adam but decided his brother's need was greatest. Besides, Ruby was speaking to Meg in a low tone so he decided not to interrupt in case she didn't want to be overheard. 'I'm sorry I wasn't here,' he said to Adam. 'Are you sure you're all right?'

'I'm fine, really. She shook me up but it was good of her brother to explain. I don't mind so much now.'

Laurie gave him a doubtful look and would have said more but he remembered he had left Holly to her own devices, so he went to help her walk over and join her friends. They started a game of riddles which made them laugh and helped take their mind off what might be happening overhead. Laurie tried to join in but his thoughts were full of Ruby standing up for his brother and they wrecked his concentration. She had been magnificent. When he had considered asking her out before, he had been put off by hearing her speak of the bravery of fighter pilots. It had made him doubt his worth in her eyes. But now he knew he would always regret it if he didn't ask, because there was no woman he would rather be with. As soon as he got a chance, he would ask her.

The all-clear sounded soon after, and the group climbed up the cellar steps muttering heartfelt thanks that they had survived unscathed.

'Must have been a bomber gone astray,' said a pilot Laurie vaguely recognised from one of the other squadrons on the base. 'I only heard one aircraft.' Laurie was inclined to agree.

When he stepped outside he was met by the sight of a red glow coming from the next street. Someone ran off to investigate and returned to breathlessly report that St Winifred's school had been hit but there were no casualties as it had been empty. 'They're asking for volunteers to help put out the fire,' he finished.

Laurie hesitated. He wanted to help but he didn't want Adam to feel obliged to do so as well when he wasn't fit enough for firefighting. Then he saw Holly standing awkwardly with her friends, favouring her twisted ankle, and had a brainwave.

'I should go and help with the fire,' he said to Adam, 'but Holly needs help getting back to Poplar Court. Could you give her a hand?'

Laurie was on the point of dashing off to the school then he paused. There was no time like the present, and if Ruby liked brave men, then it was time he acted like one. 'Can I have a word, Ruby?' he called.

Chapter Nine

Ruby couldn't imagine what Laurie wanted to say. He hadn't shown any interest in her since Orkney and so it was clear he wasn't interested in her.

'I'll catch you up,' she said to Holly and Meg and waited until they had started the walk – or hobble, in Holly's case – back to Poplar Court. 'Is anything wrong?' she asked Laurie once they were alone.

'No. Well, I hope not anyway.' Laurie took off his cap, twisted it in his hands before seeming to notice what he was doing. He shook it out and jammed it back on his head.

Ruby regarded him in surprise. She had never known him to be lost for words before. 'What's this about?' A horrible thought occurred. 'Have you heard a bad report of me? Did I make a mistake on my last flight?'

'What? No! Why do you say that? I've only heard good things about you.'

'Oh.' Ruby's face burned. 'What do you want to say, then?'

Laurie grinned. 'Isn't it possible that I might have something complimentary to say?'

'I don't know.' Ruby was wary. Flirting was unfamiliar territory and she was starting to suspect that Laurie was skirting the edge of it. From what she had seen in films, she was supposed to say something funny and clever at this point but all she could do was blurt, 'Do you?'

'Yes! Look, I don't have long – I have to help with the fire – but I wondered if you might like to come to the cinema with me one evening. Are you free on Saturday night?'

His words came out in a rush and Ruby got the impression he had about as much experience of asking out girls as she had of being asked. She felt her face stretch into a huge grin. He was asking her out! 'I'd like that. Yes, I'm free on Saturday.'

His smile matched her own. 'Wonderful! I'll meet you outside Poplar Court at half past six.' And then he was gone, sprinting after the other firefighters.

Ruby watched him, pressing her hands to her burning cheeks. Had that really happened? She had thought about it for so long but now it didn't seem real. Or, rather, it didn't feel as she'd expected, she reflected as she jogged to catch up with the others. Her experience of romance was limited to just one relationship until now, not that you could call it a relationship as it had been entirely one-sided, she now understood. She quickly shut down that train of thought before she was overwhelmed by humiliation. Her experience with Dr Flint had not been happy.

Yet that was all she had, apart from what she had picked up from books and films, and compared to those, Laurie's approach had been so... normal. Where were the violins and heavenly choirs?

'What did he want?' Holly demanded the moment she reached the others.

'He asked me out!' The words escaped before Adam's presence registered. Oops! Laurie had better not mind his brother knowing.

'I knew he liked you!' Meg exclaimed. She glanced at Adam. 'How would you feel about having Ruby as your sister-in-law?'

'Meg!' Ruby was scandalised. 'We're just going to the cinema, not eloping to Gretna Green.'

Thankfully Adam chuckled, so he didn't seem bothered at the prospect of her seeing his brother. 'It's good to hear he's finally decided to get a social life. I won't tell him that I know, though. I'll wait to see how long it takes him to confess.'

'What film is showing?' Holly asked, saving Ruby from the embarrassment of having to discuss Laurie with Adam.

'I don't know.' She hadn't thought to ask, and she couldn't remember the list of upcoming films from the cinema.

Holly snorted. 'So you're going to be with him, not to see the film.'

Ruby couldn't deny it and bore her friends' ribbing with all the good grace she could muster for the remainder of the walk.

It was only when they had bid Adam goodbye and Holly had to ask for a hand to help her upstairs that Ruby properly remembered her twisted ankle.

'I'm sorry,' she said, taking Holly's arm. 'I never asked how you were.'

'It's not too bad. I turned it in the rush to get to the cellar but I don't think it's a serious sprain.'

'Good thing you're off duty tomorrow so you can rest it up. I'm really sorry I didn't check up on you before, though. What kind of a friend does that make me?'

'One who was distracted by a handsome man?'

She couldn't deny it but made a promise to herself that however her relationship with Laurie turned out, she would never neglect her friends.

Holly turned out to be correct in her assessment and she was up and about a day later and able to go about her duties unhindered by her ankle. It enabled Ruby to look forward to her date free from worry on her friend's behalf, and by the time she was back on air ambulance duty on Friday, she was jittery with anticipation.

That day they were flying to Newcastle to collect a WAAF with TB. Corporal Linda West required transportation to a sanatorium in Devon to be closer to her family. It was a good thing that Squadron Leader Norton was her pilot that day as she doubted her patient would get her full attention had it been Laurie at the controls. It was also a relief to have a patient who was in no immediate danger and needed nothing more than a sympathetic ear.

'I can't believe this has happened,' Linda said when they had taken off from RAF Blakelaw. 'I thought I was coughing because I was used to the clean air of Dartmoor. It was a terrible shock when the MO told me I had TB.'

'I'm sure it was.' Ruby patted her hand.

'And now I'm going to be right at the other end of the country from my fiancé.' Linda had to break off to cough.

Ruby handed her a clean handkerchief and helped her into a sitting position.

When the fit had eased, Linda took a sip of water then said, 'Well, it can't be helped and there are so many people worse off than me. What about you? Have you got a nice fellow?' Ruby nodded, blushing, and Linda smiled. 'Tell me all about him. I could do with something to take my mind off the state of my lungs.'

'Well, it's early days yet,' Ruby hedged, painfully aware that the crew could probably hear what they were saying.

'How many times have you been out?'

'We haven't,' Ruby confessed. 'First time tomorrow.'

'How exciting! You must be looking forward to it.'

'I really am.' It felt good to be able to honestly admit it. Meg and Holly had teased her unmercifully and although she hadn't minded, knowing she would have done the same had it been one of her friends who had been so obviously smitten with a good-looking man, she had held back from admitting her true feelings to them. Maybe it was because she simply wasn't used to speaking of her deepest feelings. It wasn't something encouraged by her family. She also held back because she knew she was falling for Laurie and didn't know how deep his feelings ran. For all she knew, he just saw her as a friend and she didn't want her friends to worry about her if that turned out to be the case. It was simpler to pretend she wasn't counting down the hours and minutes until she could be alone with him.

There was also another fear lurking in the back of her mind. What if she was wrong about Laurie? What if he was just like the doctor from her student nurse days?

That thought was so terrifying that she pushed it from her mind and gave Linda a bright smile. 'I am looking forward to it,' she said. 'I've got a good feeling about him. I really like him.' And in that moment, she allowed herself to acknowledge her thrill that Laurie had singled her out. A man as kind and good looking as him could have any girl he wanted yet he had asked her. She smiled at Linda until she thought her chest might burst with happiness, and the spectre of Dr Flint faded.

Linda smiled back. 'Tell me about him. What's his name?'

Ruby faltered, her eyes drifting to the men in the crowded cabin. Linda intercepted her look and raised her eyebrows. 'Ah. I understand. My fiancé works at the same station as me, too, and I know what it's like. Especially when it's early days. But if you want my advice, don't let love slip you by. You never know what's around the corner. I'm so glad I took a chance on David – that's my fiancé – even though we knew things would get difficult if he was injured or posted elsewhere. Of course, we never dreamed *I* would be the one to end up in hospital, but at least I've got the comfort of knowing our relationship is solid enough to see us through.'

'Why don't you tell me about your fiancé?' Ruby suggested. 'If you feel up to it.'

And so, for the remainder of the flight, she listened while Linda described the kind man with the loving nature, wicked sense of humour and twinkling eyes who had captured her heart. Ruby couldn't help wondering if she would ever look back on her first date with Laurie with the same fondness as Linda recounted the details of hers. She went on to speak eagerly of regaining her full health and anticipated the day when she would finally be able to marry the love of her life. Would Ruby have a similar story, although minus the illness, she fervently hoped, or would she part ways with Laurie after just a few dates? She dared to admit to herself that she hoped it would be the former.

Saturday finally arrived, and after a panic over which lipstick to wear (she opted for a dusky rose that went well with the blue-grey of her uniform) and how to do her hair (Meg kindly arranged it in a sophisticated roll at the nape of her neck) she dashed outside only five minutes late and found Laurie already there.

'I'm sorry I'm late,' she said, patting her hair to check it wasn't coming down. 'I had a bit of an emergency with my hair but' – she drew a breath, aware she was in danger of starting to gabble – 'well, I'm here now.'

'You're worth waiting for,' Laurie said, gazing at her in a way that sent delicious tingles down her spine. 'And anyway, you weren't late.'

He offered her his arm, and Ruby found herself strolling towards the High Street feeling as though she would float into the air if Laurie didn't hold onto her. The strange thing was, though, that while she had never had a problem talking to him before, now she could hardly think of a thing to say. Maybe Laurie had a similar affliction, for after his greeting, which had left her flustered and breathless, he also seemed to struggle to find words.

'How is Holly's ankle?' he asked after an uncomfortable silence.

'It's much better, thank you.'

More silence.

'Have you seen—?' she began at exactly the same moment as he started speaking.

They both laughed.

'You first,' she said.

'No, after you.'

'I was just going to ask if you knew what film is showing.'

'Oh.' Laurie stopped dead, bringing Ruby to a halt beside him. He slapped his forehead. 'Do you know, I completely forgot to look.' He looked mortified. 'What an idiot! What kind of chap asks a girl to the cinema without checking what's on?'

Ruby giggled, and all the tension left her. 'I don't mind. Let's make a deal. Whatever is showing, however bad, we have to see it.'

'Done!'

All the awkwardness between them disappeared, and they carried on walking, making ever more outrageous suggestions of what they might be forced to watch.

When they reached the Majestic and saw the board outside, Ruby collapsed into giggles.

'*Hoppity Goes to Town*,' Laurie read. 'What on earth is that about?'

Ruby recovered herself enough to point at the number of children in the queue. 'Whatever it is, it seems to be family friendly.'

'Well, we made a pact.' Laurie pointed to the end of the queue. 'Shall we?'

'Absolutely. Anyway, if we did something else, I would spend the whole evening wondering who or what Hoppity is.'

Hoppity turned out to be a cartoon grasshopper, fighting to save his insect town when humans moved in to build a skyscraper. Ruby enjoyed the film more than she thought she would although she found the story more difficult to follow after Laurie put his hand over hers. And when he laced their fingers together she could hardly have recalled where she was, let alone explained the plot of the film. His hand was warm and strong and felt totally right around hers. They stayed like that for the remainder of the performance and gradually her worries fell away. She felt as though she and Laurie were encased in their own tiny bubble, shielded from all the cares of the outside world.

When they left the cinema neither was in a hurry to return to their billets. Still holding hands, they strolled through the town admiring the golden glow cast by the low midsummer sun. As the sun sank lower, Ruby grew increasingly jittery. Would he kiss her? It was something she yearned for and dreaded in equal measure. Perhaps it was to do with her only other attempt at romance, and that had left her with a horror of ever again making a fool of herself over a man. Kissing seemed such a complicated business. What if Laurie went to kiss her on the cheek when she thought he was aiming for her lips? Or even if he did kiss her on the mouth, how did she know when to finish? The longer the walk continued, the more these worries consumed her.

'I had a lovely time tonight,' Laurie said when they finally turned towards Poplar Court.

'Me too.'

'When's your next day off?'

Was he asking her out again already? Ruby felt so light she could swear her feet floated off the pavement. A brief conversation revealed that they were both available the following Saturday and she happily agreed to spend the day with him.

'How about a day in London? I remember you saying you'd never been.'

'I'd love that. I've been longing to go.' She and her friends had been too busy studying at first and now they were working they either didn't have the time off together or they were too tired to go so far when they did.

At the door to Poplar Court she said, a little breathlessly, 'Well, goodnight. I've really enjoyed tonight.'

She turned to go inside but Laurie caught her hand and tugged her towards him. 'Do you know what would make the evening totally perfect?'

'What?' she squeaked, although she had a pretty good idea from the way he was stooping over her, bringing his face close to hers.

'A kiss.'

She swallowed. This was it. For a horrible moment she was tempted to bolt inside. But then she remembered Corporal Linda West, her TB patient, and the love she clearly had for her fiancé. *Don't let love slip you by. You never know what's around the corner.* Linda was right. She mustn't let one bad experience cause her to throw away this chance with Laurie.

Ruby summoned her courage, put her hands on his shoulders, raised herself on tiptoes and pressed her mouth to his. He returned the kiss, placing his hands lightly on her waist. It was only a brief kiss, gentle and full of promise, yet it made her head spin. When it ended, she was so befuddled she hardly knew what she said before she fumbled with the door, pulling when she should have pushed. She finally got it open and then she was leaning with her back against the door, waiting for her heartbeat to subside. She retained enough wits to sign in and then she was floating up the stairs to her room.

Everyone else was there, already in their pyjamas; all bar Bobby turned expectant faces towards her.

'Well?' Meg demanded.

'Well what?'

'Come on, tell us all about your evening. How did it go?'

Ruby gave up all pretence of nonchalance. 'It was wonderful.' Even if she had tried to play it cool, the huge grin making her face ache would have given her away. 'We went to the cinema and then had a walk afterwards. I know it doesn't sound all that amazing when you put it like that, but he was lovely.'

'It sounds very romantic.' Meg's eyes had gone misty. 'I'm so pleased the two of you have got together. I wish I could meet someone who looked at me the same way as Laurie looks at you.'

'Why – how does he look at me?'

An inelegant snort came from Bobby's corner of the room. 'The same way you look at him. The way Bentley looks at anyone when he wants a treat.'

Ruby cringed. Bentley had a good line in melting, pleading looks. 'I don't, do I?'

'No!' Holly replied, shooting Bobby a glare. 'I think it's lovely. Don't mind Bobby. She's just jealous because Laurie didn't ask her out.'

Bobby looked up from her writing case, which was open on her knees and returned Holly's look with a haughty stare. 'Oh, please! Why would I want to go out with an ironmonger's son when I'm engaged to the son of an earl?'

'What's wrong with being an ironmonger's son?' Holly flared up. 'Laurie's a lovely man. That's all that should matter to Ruby, not whether he can trace his family tree all the way back to William the Conqueror. Who was a thug if you ask me, so being descended from him is nothing to be proud of.'

Ruby felt the crushing dread that always consumed her when others were bickering. Desperate to put an end to the discord before it turned into a full-on argument, she said, 'I didn't know you were engaged, Bobby. Why haven't you told us before?'

Looking slightly mollified, Bobby replied, 'He got his commission in the army when it became clear there was going to be a war. So he was posted early on. I haven't seen him for a long time.' In a quavering voice she added, 'I miss him.'

'Oh, I'm sorry. I hope you see him soon.'

Not long after, Bobby put away the letter she had been writing and climbed into bed, turning on her side with her back to the others.

Holly pulled a face. 'I hope we didn't spoil your evening.'

'You didn't.' Ruby hung up her tunic then unpinned her hair and started to brush it out. While she did so, Holly, Meg and Winnie gathered on the other side of the room from Bobby, sitting on Winnie's bed, so they could continue the conversation with the minimum of disturbance.

'Come on, then, spill the beans,' Winnie urged in a low voice. 'You haven't even told us if he kissed you.'

'Yes, tell us everything,' Holly said. 'Was it the perfect evening, like my date with Simon?'

Ruby and Meg both groaned while Winnie looked curiously at Holly. 'Who's Simon?'

'My boyfriend.'

Meg rolled her eyes. 'Who you've been out with once.'

'Yes, because he was joining the RAF the next day. But we've been writing to each other ever since.'

'They met at a dance,' Meg began in a sing-song voice, indicating that she was reciting a story she had heard countless times, 'and it was love at first sight. They had one perfect evening together when they danced every dance together and told each other all about their lives. Now they're just waiting for the war to end so they can live happily ever after.' She grinned at Holly. 'Did I miss anything?'

Holly scowled. 'You forgot the bit where he sent me *Anne of Green Gables* for my birthday.' She pointed at the much-creased book that took pride of place on her shelf. 'It's always been my favourite book, but I never told him.'

Bobby gave a dramatic sigh, flung back her covers and sat up. 'You're a red-haired orphan. How hard was it to guess?' She turned to Ruby. 'Now are you going to finish telling everyone about your date so I can get some sleep?'

Ruby spoke quickly before Holly could get angry again. 'Well, I don't know if my evening was as perfect as Holly's but it was lovely. And to answer your question, Winnie, we did kiss. Although it would be more correct to say I kissed him.' She felt a warm glow at the memory.

Meg gave a soft cheer. 'So the two of you are definitely an item?'

'I think so. He asked me out again. We're going to have a day in London next Saturday.' As she said it, she spared a thought for Bobby, hoping this news wouldn't turn her even more against Ruby. It must be hard for her, not having seen her fiancé in all this time. She hoped he came home soon. Maybe it would put Bobby in a better mood.

Chapter Ten

Ruby's thrill at the date, the kiss and the upcoming London trip remained with her in the days that followed. However, not even that could quell her nerves over her air ambulance duties. Even though she had now made four flights without anything terrible happening, it could only be a matter of time before she made an awful mistake. When she was on air ambulance duty again – two days before their planned trip to London – her stomach was a mass of knots. She made her way to the crew room feeling as though she was on her way to the gallows.

She was flying with Squadron Leader Norton that day. He greeted the crew with a cheerful 'good morning' before announcing, 'We're off to Anglesey today. We've got a patient with severe burns who needs transferring to hospital in East Grinstead.'

Burns! Ruby shuddered. She had already helped transport one burns patient and, despite him remaining asleep for the entire journey, she'd hoped never to repeat the experience. She couldn't forget the sight of raw, blistered skin, the odours of the wounds and the dread of being unable to relieve his suffering should he wake. And now she would once again be in charge of a poor man with burns just like those. For an hour or more.

In other circumstances she would have enjoyed the flight to Anglesey. It was a clear day, and the land below them grew ever wilder as rich, pastoral fields and hillsides gave way to rugged moorland and mountains. However, as much as she tried to look at the view instead of feverishly checking the contents of her medical bag, she couldn't appreciate the sights unrolling below. Only when the Oxford's nose dipped and an island came into view did Ruby tuck away her bag and pay more attention. Anglesey was separated from the mainland only by a narrow strip of water, yet its green and gold patchwork of fields were a striking contrast with the parched, rocky landscape they had just crossed.

All too soon, they were circling the aerodrome at RAF Angle. Ruby hugged her arms to her stomach as they came in to land. *You can do this; you can do this.* If she repeated it enough times, she might start believing it.

The plane touched down with barely a jolt, and then they were taxiing towards a dispersal point. When they rounded a bend it gave Ruby a clear view of the perimeter road. And the approaching ambulance.

Once they had come to a stop and climbed out of the Oxford, the only thing that gave Ruby the strength to walk to the ambulance was the knowledge that however anxious she was, that was nothing compared to what her poor patient must be enduring. It was time to put aside her fears and give him her full attention.

Squadron Leader Frank Riches was, thankfully, asleep and the nurse who had accompanied him in the ambulance assured her that he was likely to remain so for the duration of the flight. He had burns to the head, arms and torso which were covered in gauze dressings.

'We've had to be cautious with pain relief because of his head injury,' the nurse said.

'Head injury?' Ruby's heart sank. This didn't sound good.

'Yes, he also suffered a fractured skull when he crash-landed. Because of that, the doctor opted not to sedate him for the journey but gave him morphine instead. Give him another dose in half an hour if he needs it.' The nurse flashed her a smile. 'He'll be fine, though. I'm sure you'll have a quiet flight.'

Easy for you to say. Ruby bit back the retort and instead thanked her and helped carry the stretcher into the Oxford.

For the first part of the journey it looked as though the nurse was right and Ruby would have an uneventful trip. However, twenty minutes into the flight Squadron Leader Riches stirred and moaned. She leaned over the stretcher and spoke in soothing tones.

'Not far to go. I think we're over England now.' She glanced across the cabin and gave Neil Maitland a questioning look.

He nodded. 'Another forty minutes.'

She turned back to her patient. 'Did you hear that?' She repeated what the navigator had said. Normally she would soothe a patient by taking his hand but as Riches' hands were both badly burned and covered in dressings this wasn't possible.

The right side of Riches' face, including his eye, was also obscured by dressings but his left eye blinked open and focused on her face. 'Forty minutes,' he repeated. His voice rasped.

'Don't talk if it hurts, Squadron Leader,' Ruby cautioned him.

' 'S not too bad. And call me Frank.'

'All right, Frank.'

'What's your name?'

'Ruby.'

'Pretty name for a pretty WAAF. Didn't expect to see a looker like you up in an aeroplane.'

It must be the drugs making him ramble. Ruby happened to catch Rhys's eye and she scowled at him, promising dire retribution should he report Frank's words to Laurie. 'How bad is the pain? Is there anything you need?'

'No. It's fine.' But the deep lines scoring the good side of his face said otherwise.

What should she do? There were still – she glanced at her watch – five minutes before she could give him another dose of morphine. Did those five minutes really matter? Yes. She'd been given those instructions by someone more qualified than her, and she had to trust them. Yet she couldn't let Frank suffer longer than necessary, so she pulled one of the morphine syrettes from her medical bag, ready for when it was needed. She spoke to him, talking nonsense about the weather, the film she and Laurie had watched together... anything that popped into her mind. All the while she kept half an eye on her watch, counting down the minutes. Three more minutes... two... one...

Heaven help her, but she'd never had to inject morphine into a real patient before. Sister Macintosh had covered it thoroughly, but nothing could prepare you for the reality. If only she could have the nurse here now, to make sure Ruby did it correctly.

Her instructor's face floated into her mind's eye and she could hear her speaking as clearly as though she stood right at Ruby's shoulder: *Never give a second dose of morphine if the patient's respirations are twelve breaths per minute or fewer.*

Now she came to think about it, Frank did seem to be breathing slowly. She replaced the syrette in her bag and counted his breathing for a full minute. Eleven breaths. So even though he was in a lot of pain, she couldn't give him anything for it. What else could she do? It would be heartless to let him suffer without doing anything for him at all. Even though his eye had drifted closed, he radiated pain, and he was clearly awake and in distress. Why was his breathing suppressed? Was it something to do with the head injury? It was possible that it was more serious than the staff at RAF Angle had suspected, but if so, what should she do?

Oxygen! Idiot! What was she thinking? With trembling fingers, she placed the mask over his face, doing her best not to rub the burns. Then she adjusted the valves to control the flow. As she did so she continued to speak, urging him to stay awake. That's what you were supposed to do with head injuries, wasn't it? Maybe between that and the oxygen, his breathing would improve enough for more morphine. She felt so helpless watching him suffer.

No matter what she tried, his breathing didn't improve beyond twelve breaths a minute, still too low for a second dose. The minutes crawled by. At times Frank seemed more alert, and she coaxed him to speak, but he could never manage more than a couple of words before breaking off with a moan. When at last the Oxford's nose tilted into a descent, Frank was barely conscious. She was so focused on keeping him awake that she didn't even notice they were making their final approach until the Oxford's wheels struck the runway.

She called to Norton. 'Is the ambulance here? Take us as close as possible.'

She could have wept with relief when she opened the door and found a nurse waiting just outside. Finally – someone with more qualifications than her! She poured out her report, her words tumbling over each other in her haste to let the nurse take charge. Then she stepped aside so the nurse could examine her new patient and waited with bated breath for her verdict.

Finally, the nurse glanced up. 'I think you're right about the head injury. Don't worry. We'll take good care of him. He'll be fine.'

'Did I— is there anything else I could have done?'

'You did well. It's a jolly good thing you didn't give him morphine. Don't worry – you did all the right things.'

There was so much more Ruby wanted to ask. She wanted to go through every minute of the flight and question her every decision, but the patient's needs had to come first. He mustn't be kept waiting. All she could do was watch helplessly while the ambulance drivers loaded Frank into the ambulance and then drive away.

It didn't matter that the nurse had said Ruby had made the right decisions. She felt like she had let her patient down. Was she really cut out for air ambulance duty?

—

'How was your evening with that nice young lady?' Laurie's mother asked as she picked up the tea strainer and poured the tea. He had hoped to catch Ruby that evening, maybe take her to the pub, but she was on air ambulance duty and was late returning. As it was a while since he had seen his family, he'd popped round for a visit.

Laurie shot a glare at his brother. 'Honestly, is there anyone you didn't tell?'

Adam grinned, although Laurie thought his smile looked strained. Please don't say Adam fancied Ruby as well. It would make things horribly complicated. That was the downside to having a posting so close to home. 'If you must ask her out in front of all her friends and me, what do you expect?'

'Not for you to blab it to our parents,' Laurie muttered. 'Just you wait until you start seeing someone. I bet you won't want me carrying tales to Mum.'

'No danger of that. I'll have the sense not to carry out a courtship in front of you.'

Laurie scowled but he couldn't feel too annoyed. Not when he had enjoyed the evening so much. If anyone had told him that the best evening of his life so far would be spent watching a cartoon about a grasshopper, he'd have thought they were off their rocker, but now he was convinced he'd enjoy watching paint dry as long as he had Ruby at his side. The more he saw of her, the more he liked her. The evening had shown him that in addition to her caring side and the courage that had caused her to leap to Adam's defence, she also had a keen sense of humour. Not many girls would have been impressed by his mistake at taking them to see a cartoon but Ruby had taken it in her stride and had seen the funny side. He couldn't wait until tomorrow and spending a whole day in her company.

'Laurie? Laurie?'

Only belatedly did he realise his mother was speaking to him. 'Sorry, what?'

'Honestly, you were miles away. Your date must have been a success if it's turned you into a daydream.'

'We had a good time,' Laurie said, determined not to be drawn into giving details.

'Are you seeing her again?'

'Yes.'

Lettie looked satisfied. 'That's all I needed to know.'

Soon after, she disappeared upstairs to fetch some darning. Their father was in the front room, working on his accounts, so Laurie and Adam had the back room to themselves.

'Sorry I dropped you in it with Mum,' Adam said. 'She was fretting over the air raid so I mentioned it to take her mind off her scare. But I should have left it up to you to decide when you were ready to tell her.'

Laurie felt bad for not considering how the air raid might have affected them. Having already come through the Blitz, they must be dreading a return to those dark days. 'That's all right. You know what she's like. She'd have probably wormed it out of me anyway.'

'So you really like Ruby, then?'

'I do.'

'I'm glad. I think she's good for you. And I'll never forget the way she stood up to that woman in the pub.'

It didn't sound like Adam had feelings for Ruby, yet he was clearly bothered about something.

Feeling his way carefully, he said, 'I'm sorry I haven't been round since then. I should have made sure you were all right. That Jean woman had no right to say what she did.'

'Maybe not, but she's not the only one.'

'Why? Has anyone else said anything?' Laurie went cold. 'Don't tell me you've had another of those letters?'

Adam didn't say anything but picked up his teacup and made a show of studying a crack in the glaze.

'Adam, you promised to tell me if you got any more.'

'I know but I didn't want to worry you, all right? It's bad enough that you're having to send so much of your pay to help out because I can't pay my own way without burdening you with my troubles as well.'

'They're not a burden. It's more of a burden when you try and hide things from me. So,' he went on when he had paused to draw a calming breath, 'have you had any more letters?'

Adam nodded. 'One came yesterday.'

'What did it say?'

'Pretty much the same as the last one. I can't remember exactly. I burned it like you told me.'

Laurie was having second thoughts about that. 'Look, I know I told you to burn them but we might be destroying vital evidence. I didn't seriously expect you to get any others. I thought it was some unbalanced person who was sending similar stuff to others in the neighbourhood. But now you've had another one, it looks like someone is targeting you.'

'I can't keep them. What if Mum or Dad found them? They'd go spare.'

'Give them to me. If they contain any clue about the sender, I'll find it. I promise.'

'I shouldn't have told you,' Adam said. 'Now you're going to make a huge fuss.'

'Don't be an idiot. I don't want to worry Mum and Dad any more than you do. But I do want to make these letters stop. Perhaps we should go to the police.'

'Oh yes, because having the police stomping all over the place, questioning the neighbours, wouldn't bother Mum or Dad at all.'

Laurie had to admit Adam had a point. 'All right then. But I never know exactly when I can get here because I work irregular hours, and I don't want you hanging onto the letters here for any length of time.' Quite aside from the risk of one of his parents finding them, he didn't like the thought of Adam having a constant reminder of the poison the letters were spewing. 'I think the best thing to do is post them on to me and include a note telling me where you found it, at what time and if you can narrow down the times it was delivered, all the better.' What the censor would think of the poison pen letters, he hated to think but he didn't have a better suggestion.

Adam gave a grudging nod. 'I suppose I can do that. It's not like I've got anything better to do with my time.'

Laurie gazed at him in dismay. 'I thought you were working more hours at the shop. And what about returning to college?'

'I am working more hours. It just doesn't seem so important when my brother and friends are fighting the Nazis and I'm selling boot polish to housewives.'

'I'm not exactly taking the fight to the Nazis myself.'

'No, but you're doing something important. Imagine how much easier it would have been for me if I could have been flown straight back to Britain when I got wounded instead of having to wait around for days getting worse, and then having to cross the Channel in someone's fishing boat.'

Laurie winced, hating to think about what his brother had endured. 'But you were there and you got wounded in action. I don't know how many times I have to say this, but you've already played your part and I bet you've done far more than whoever wrote those vile letters. Don't let it worm its way into your head. That's what the writer wants.' He gave a chuckle he didn't feel, trying to lighten the mood. 'Besides, some of those housewives can be very intimidating when they can't find exactly the right shade of boot polish. Dad must be grateful for your help.'

Adam laughed and the conversation turned to another subject. It was only after he had left that Laurie realised he hadn't answered his question about veterinary college.

After completing his final flight the following day, Laurie returned to the Sergeants' Mess on light feet, eagerly anticipating his day with Ruby.

He found a letter waiting for him. It was hand delivered, addressed in Adam's handwriting and he opened it with a heavy heart. Inside was a second envelope with Adam's name written upon it in the same block capitals as before. Adam had written a note to accompany it, and he read it, scowling.

> *Dear Laurie,*
>
> *Dad found this on the mat when he arrived at the shop at seven this morning. He didn't open it, thank goodness, but now he's teasing me for having a girlfriend who sends me love letters. I suppose that's better than him knowing the truth. I was the last to leave at 7.30 last night, and it definitely wasn't on the mat then. Don't come dashing round because I know you're busy. I only sent this because you made me promise.*
>
> *Adam*

With a sick feeling in the pit of his stomach, Laurie removed the poison pen letter from its envelope and looked at it.

COWARDS LIKE YOU SHOULD BE HANGED.

He crumpled it in his fist then jumped a mile when someone slapped him on the shoulder. 'What in blazes— oh, it's you, Rhys.'

Rhys cocked his head on one side, looking a lot like Bentley in that moment. 'Caught you at a bad moment?'

'You could say that.'

'How about a trip to the pub? That should sort you out.'

'Not this time. Something's come up at home.'

Rhys's eyes clouded. 'Is your brother ill again?' He knew about Adam's injury, Laurie having confided in him not long after his transfer from Coastal Command.

'Something like that.' Laurie didn't want to say anything about the poison pen letters. 'Look, I'd better dash. See you later.'

Although Adam had told him not to come, there was no way Laurie was going to leave Adam alone a moment longer than necessary after getting a message like that. He grabbed a quick bite to eat in the mess and then headed out.

He reached the place where he could either turn right to reach the High Street or left to go home, when he realised that Adam might still be in the shop. On reflection, it made sense to go to the shop, considering that was where the letters were being delivered. Walking at a brisk pace, he reached the High Street in ten minutes and then turned into George Street, where the ironmongery was situated.

By this time the shop was closed but peering inside he could see his father placing stock on the shelves. He tapped on the glass and his dad called, 'We're closed,' without looking up.

'It's me,' Laurie called.

His dad looked up, his frown turning to a beaming smile. He unlocked the door and ushered him inside. 'Hurry up. Don't let anyone see me. I've had Mrs Evans pestering me for curtain hooks for days. She doesn't seem to understand that these things aren't easy to come by at the moment and I've run out of ways to tell her the new stock hasn't arrived.'

Laurie laughed. 'I think you're safe. No one's lurking outside.' He glanced around and when he didn't immediately see Adam, asked, 'Is Adam here?'

His dad pointed to the next room. 'He's in the electrical section.'

Laurie had loved visiting the shop as a child. It was like an Aladdin's cave, with several rooms, crammed with everything from buckets to picture hooks. The bit he liked best was behind the counter in the next room. The wall behind was lined with tiny wooden drawers, all painstakingly labelled. Within each drawer was a specific item – a tap washer of a certain size, nuts, bolts, fuses and much more. He found Adam replenishing the five-amp fuse drawer.

'Need a hand?' he asked.

Adam glanced up. 'What are you doing here?'

Laurie glanced into the open box on the counter. 'Restocking your thirteen-amp fuses if you'll let me.'

'Oh, go on, then. But you know what I mean.' Adam shot a glance into the other room, where their dad was still working. He lowered his voice. 'I said you didn't have to come.'

'I know, but I wanted to.' Laurie set to work unpacking the fuses and placing them in the correct drawer. 'That last letter was vicious. I wanted to make sure you were all right.'

'I'm fine. I don't need a nursemaid.'

'I know. But you can't expect me to see something like that and not want to check up on you. You're my brother. You'd do the same for me.'

'I suppose. I just—' Adam slammed a drawer shut with unnecessary force. 'I feel so useless sometimes. I know, I know, I've played my part. You keep telling me that, and I know it's true. I mean, I wouldn't last five minutes on active service. But if you were in my position, tell me you wouldn't feel like you needed to do more if you got a letter like that, or even if you got a letter from one of your friends who was fighting for his country.'

'I understand. I really do,' Laurie told him. He wondered if he should encourage Adam to contact the veterinary college again but decided that he wasn't in the right frame of mind. 'Look. I asked you to send me the letters for a reason. The Poison Pen has sent you three now and—' He broke off when he noticed Adam wouldn't meet his eyes. 'There have been others, haven't there.' It wasn't a question.

Adam nodded.

'Tell me about it.'

'I had one a couple of days before the one I told you about. I burned it.'

'Same paper? Same handwriting?'

'Yes and yes. Definitely the same person.'

'Why didn't you tell me?'

'Because it said much the same as the others: it called me a coward and said I should be ashamed of myself. I didn't see the point of showing you. I thought if that's all they were going to say, I could forget about it as long as Mum or Dad didn't see. But when I saw the latest one… well, I couldn't ignore it.'

'No,' Laurie said grimly. 'It shook me up when I saw it, so I can only imagine how you felt. Are you sure you won't let me take it to the police?'

'No!' Even a Shakespearean actor would have struggled to inject the same amount of vehemence into that one short word. 'I know I complained about you acting like a nursemaid but I didn't really mean it. Anyway, you're not here most of the time so I don't have to put up with your mollycoddling for long.'

'Thanks,' Laurie said dryly.

'But Mum and Dad have been hovering over me, acting like I'm an unexploded bomb ever since I came home.'

'Can you blame them? They were terrified.' Laurie had been posted in Devon when he had heard that Adam had returned from Dunkirk seriously injured. His CO had managed to get him compassionate leave ten days later when Adam was already on the road to recovery. Even so, he had been shocked by the sight of his brother looking so frail. His parents had been able to visit him in hospital as soon as he was allowed visitors so had seen him in a much worse state.

'I do understand, but that was ages ago and they still act like I'll die of pneumonia if I go outside without a coat. It's getting annoying. Can you imagine how they'd react if they saw those letters? But if we showed them to the police, there would be no way of keeping it from them.'

'Very well. I'll keep quiet about it for now, but I don't like it. In return you have to promise me you'll send all future ones to me straight away.'

'Don't worry. I will.' Laurie got the impression that Adam had been more shaken by the mention of hanging than he'd like to admit.

'Make sure you do. Now, I've got the day off tomorrow, so why don't we take advantage of Dad's mollycoddling and ask him to give you the day off too? We could do something together.'

Adam brightened. 'Really? I miss the bike rides we used to have when we were kids.'

'Then that's settled. We'll cycle out of London, enjoy the sunshine and find a nice pub. Forget all about the war and poison pen letters for the day.'

'Hang on, weren't you supposed to be seeing Ruby?'

'I was but there was a mix-up with schedules. You know how it is.' Laurie felt bad at lying to his brother, almost as bad as he felt about cancelling his date, but Adam needed him and he wasn't going to let his brother down.

Chapter Eleven

Ruby stood at the mirror, trying to decide how to arrange her hair for the much-anticipated day out with Laurie. Should she roll it around a ribbon as she usually did or attempt something more stylish?

Winnie came flying into the room. 'Laurie's waiting for you outside.'

'Already?' Ruby wailed. He wasn't supposed to arrive for another half an hour. 'I haven't got my things together yet and I can't find my hair grips.' After her horrendous flight with the burns patient, she needed this day to be perfect.

'Tell him to wait. I'm sure he'll understand.'

Ruby wasn't convinced. Last night she had mentally rehearsed all that she needed to do to be ready for Laurie on time, wanting to impress him with her effortless organisation, and now his early arrival had thrown everything out of kilter. Still, she didn't have much choice so she left her hair loose around her shoulders and dashed down the stairs to the main door.

'Can you give me ten minutes?' she asked the moment she saw Laurie leaning against the wall outside. 'I must have got the time wrong and I—'

'I'm sorry, Ruby,' Laurie interrupted, 'something's come up and I can't make it today.'

'Oh.' The lightness of heart, the bubbling excitement that had been her constant companion since their cinema trip vanished in an instant, replaced by crushing disappointment. 'That's a shame,' she said, trying not to show how upset she really was. 'It was kind of you to tell me in person, though.'

Laurie frowned. 'You know I wouldn't cancel if I had any choice? But it's a family matter.'

'I understand.' And she really did. She was sure Laurie wouldn't cancel on her unless he had no choice so she tried to put him at ease by hiding her disappointment. 'I hope it's nothing too serious.'

'Nothing that can't be sorted out,' he said with a tight smile. 'Well, I'd better be off. Thanks for understanding.'

She watched him until he had turned the corner and then she took herself back to her room on dragging feet.

Winnie greeted her with an eager smile. 'I've found your hair grips. Do you need a hand arranging your hair?'

Ruby sank onto her bed with a world-weary sigh. 'No thanks. He only came round to say he couldn't make it.'

'Oh no! Why?'

'A family emergency apparently. Maybe his brother's ill, although he didn't say.'

'That's a shame, but you'll be able to go to London another day.'

Winnie had to leave for her shift at the hospital after that, and Ruby was left all alone. Holly was on air ambulance duty so would be out all day, and Meg was working in the hospital. Bobby would be coming off duty soon, and the prospect of facing her pitying sneer was enough to send her scurrying out for a walk, even though she had no idea where to go.

For some time she walked aimlessly, turning her brief conversation with Laurie over and over in her mind. One moment she was cross with him for being so vague when cancelling an arrangement they had made ages ago – had the situation been reversed, she would have given a full explanation on why she had to go back on her word – the next moment, she felt bad with herself for thinking that way. While it felt like she had known Laurie for ages, it wasn't all that long in reality and she certainly didn't know his family well enough to be informed of a matter that concerned them. This reminder satisfied her until she recalled that Laurie hadn't made any definite arrangement to see her again. Was this his way of breaking up with her?

It was like the Dr Flint fiasco all over again.

She scarcely knew where her feet were taking her until she found herself outside the church hall. A notice was pinned on the board outside and she read it for want of anything else to do in the way she would always read the back of a cereal packet when eating breakfast.

MEETING SATURDAY 27 JUNE, 11 A.M.

St Winifred's School Supplies

There will be a meeting in the church hall to discuss raising funds for St Winifred's school. After the bomb that destroyed the Infants' wing, the younger children are having to take lessons in the school hall. They are in desperate need of funds to replace lost equipment. If you can help, please come to the meeting.

Halfway through reading, Ruby's interest sharpened. This was happening today. While she wasn't sure what help she could offer, there was no reason she couldn't attend. If nothing else, she could offer to raise funds at RAF Starsden. Several of the men from the base, Laurie included, had helped tackle the fire, so the damage to the local school was well known among the personnel.

With a fresh sense of purpose, she filled the intervening time with a visit to the shops to restock her depleted supplies of soap and toothpaste and purchase some darning yarn then made her way back to the church hall in time for the meeting.

The woman organising the meeting greeted her graciously. 'Good morning. It's lovely to see someone from the RAF station here. I'm Mrs Copeland. My two daughters attend St Winifred's, and I've volunteered to chair the fundraising committee.'

Ruby introduced herself before admitting, 'I'm not really sure if I can help but I thought I'd see if there was anything I can do.'

'Anything, however small, would be wonderful. We know how busy everyone is on the base so we're very grateful to see one of you here.'

Ruby took a chair near the back and let her thoughts drift while more women filed in. Inevitably her mind turned to Laurie and the reason why he had let her down. Had Adam been taken ill? She sincerely hoped not – she would feel rotten if that was so. Yet Laurie had already told her that Adam had been badly injured so surely he would have told her if he'd had a relapse? It would have been far easier to accept than his vague 'family matters' excuse.

She was so deep in thought that she barely noticed Mrs Copeland had mounted the stage until she addressed the room.

'Thank you all for coming. I appreciate you making time in your busy days. I will keep it brief, as this is only an initial meeting to make you all aware of what the school needs and to invite ideas.'

Initial meeting? Ruby's heart sank. What had she let herself in for? Still, when Mrs Copeland launched into a detailed description of the damage that had been done and the supplies the school would need as a matter of urgency, her heart kindled with determination to help. She had fond remembrances of her own school days and wanted to do all in her power to help the children of Starsden have the best possible schooling.

'Now,' Mrs Copeland concluded once she had gone through the list of everything that needed to be replaced, 'one thing we can do is put out an appeal to anyone with older children who may have books, toys, slates and so forth that they would be willing to donate. I hope we can collect enough to at least tide us over to the summer holidays. But in the longer term the school needs money to replace textbooks, teaching and sports equipment, meaning the other thing we need to organise is fundraisers. Does anyone have any ideas for activities?'

Hands shot up all around the room, and jumble sales, a fundraising concert and knocking on doors to ask for donations were all suggested. These were quickly approved and volunteers offered to organise them.

'Anything else?' Mrs Copeland asked.

Ruby hesitantly put up her hand. She couldn't sit there and hear of all the school needed without offering to do something. 'It would be difficult for us to organise an event at RAF Starsden because many of us work such irregular hours, but I can put up notices around the base asking for donations and drum up support for your concert and jumble sales. We have a few choirs so maybe they could be persuaded to perform.'

'That's very kind of you,' Mrs Copeland said. 'We'd appreciate any support you can provide.'

And so it was that Ruby found herself appointed the Air Force Liaison, a grand title which would mostly involve putting up posters around the base provided by the fundraising committee.

The meeting broke up and everyone drifted to the refreshment table where tea and light refreshments had been laid out. Ruby hesitated to join them, aware that she was probably better fed in the WAAF than most of these women, who were likely struggling to stretch out their rations. She had just decided to leave when someone tapped her on the shoulder. She turned to see a middle-aged woman with wavy blonde hair smiling at her. She looked familiar although Ruby couldn't immediately place where she had seen her.

'How lovely to see you,' the woman exclaimed. 'I was only asking Laurie the other day when we might see you again, but I never imagined you'd be here.'

It was Lettie Foster, Laurie's mother.

'Lovely to see you too,' she said. Then ventured, 'I hope the family is all well?'

'Right as rain, thank you. Now Adam's so much better I can get out and about more. Of course, my boys haven't been in school for years but I did so want to help out when I heard what had happened. Quite dreadful. Thank goodness no one was hurt, though.'

'Yes, of course,' Ruby said, her mind racing. Surely Laurie's family matter couldn't be all that urgent if his mother was able to take time out to come to the meeting. 'Isn't Laurie with you today? I thought he said something about it.'

'Oh no. He and Adam have gone for a bicycle ride. Laurie persuaded his father to give Adam the day off.'

'Well, they've got nice weather for it,' Ruby commented, unsure how long she could hold up her smile.

'Are you staying for refreshments?'

'I'm afraid not. I'm needed back at the base.'

Ruby made a hasty exit, blinking back tears. So Laurie had stood her up to go gallivanting off with Adam? Well, at least she knew where she stood.

Having told Mrs Foster that she was expected back at base, she couldn't risk being seen around town, so she wandered back to Poplar Court on heavy feet.

'A bike ride!' Ruby paced in front of the sofa that Holly and Meg were sitting upon, having flung down her darning, unable to concentrate. The other occupants of the common room were gathered around the wireless set on the other side of the room, listening to a musical broadcast. It meant that Ruby could let off steam without fear of being overheard. 'He stood me up to go on a bike ride!'

Evening had fallen, bringing Holly and Meg back from their respective duties. The first thing they had done when they saw Ruby was express their surprise at seeing her back so soon and asked about her day. Ruby, who had bottled up her emotions all day, had promptly burst into tears. Holly had instantly raced down to the shared kitchenette to make her a large mug of Horlicks, and it had taken not only the comforting drink but also the last of the fruitcake sent by Meg's mother to calm her down. Then Bobby had turned up, and they had made a hasty exit for the common room, with a diversion to the bathroom for Ruby to rinse the tears from her face.

'Are you sure that's what it was?' Meg asked. 'It doesn't sound like Laurie to mess you around like that.'

'What else could it be? When he told me there was a family matter that needed his attention, I believed him. Didn't have any reason not to. I thought maybe Adam was ill again or something.'

'Adam's been ill?' Holly's concern was written plain across her face.

'No. I mean, not since we've known him.' She had already told them that he had been invalided out from the army, as that was no secret, although she hadn't told them of Laurie's worries about his state of mind. If she hadn't been so desperate to talk through Laurie's behaviour, she would have asked Holly why she was so concerned about Adam. As it was, she filed Holly's reaction away for another time. 'Anyway, there can't be anything wrong with him if he can go gallivanting off on his bicycle at the drop of a hat.'

'That's a relief,' Holly said. 'It does seem strange, though. I could have sworn that Laurie's really keen on you and isn't the type to mess you around. But cancelling on you just so he can go on a bike ride seems totally out of character.'

Meg nodded. 'There's something else going on. You mark my words.'

'I hope so. I mean, I don't hope there's any major family problem, but I do hope he wouldn't change our plans unless there was a very good reason.' Ruby dropped back into her chair with a sigh. 'This is Dr Flint all over again.'

Holly leaned forward. 'Who's Dr Flint?'

'Oh.' Ruby hadn't meant to let slip about her one and only earlier romance. Not that it had ever been a proper romance because it had turned out to be completely one-sided. She'd never mentioned it to her friends because it was all too embarrassing. 'He was a doctor at the hospital in Oxford where I did my training.'

'And?' Holly leaned forward with a glint in her eye. 'You can't leave it there. What happened?'

Ruby groaned and shook her head. 'It was all so stupid. You're going to think I was a complete berk.'

'No we're not. How old would you have been – seventeen?'

Holly nodded.

'Well then, whatever happened, we're going to think you were very young.'

'It was only three years ago.'

'There's a big difference between seventeen and twenty.'

Ruby didn't feel any different but she let it pass. Maybe it was time she admitted what had happened. She only wished that she didn't come out of it looking so foolish. 'There was this doctor.'

Holly gave an impatient wave. 'Yes, we know. Dr Flint. Tell us something new.'

'Well, he was recently qualified and—'

'Don't tell me,' Holly cut in. 'I know the type. Full of self-importance. Loved having the nursing staff running around after him. Probably made his own mother call him "Doctor".'

Ruby felt her cheeks burn. On reflection, he had been every bit as bad as Holly described, but she hadn't seen it at the time. 'He was really good looking,' she said, feeling obliged to put forward a defence.

'As handsome as Laurie?' Meg asked.

Ruby thought about it. 'Maybe, but in a different way. He looked like Cary Grant.' Rather than a Norse god. She could now see that Dr Flint had known he was good looking whereas Laurie seemed oblivious to the admiring looks he received.

'So what happened?' Meg prompted.

'I remember the first time I really noticed him. The ward sister was giving me a dressing-down for failing to make a bed properly. I couldn't see what I'd done wrong but apparently I'd made a complete mess of the corners. Anyway, the worst part was that she'd done it in front of everyone on the ward, including Dr Flint. I was humiliated.

But Dr Flint came and sat with me in the canteen later and asked if I was all right.' She would never forget the thrill of being noticed by the best-looking doctor in the hospital.

'And then what?' Meg asked. 'He vowed always to protect you from ravening ward sisters and completely swept you off your feet?'

'No. But he was very kind and before he left he said we should meet up after a shift sometime.'

'And did you?'

Ruby sighed again. It sounded like nothing when she came to relate the details to someone else but it was impossible to put into words the elation of thinking that the handsome doctor had noticed her and wanted to see more of her. 'Not really. He would sit with me in the canteen sometimes and then he would arrange for us to do something together like go to the pictures or he would mention a dance but when the time came there was always a reason why he couldn't go.' And now she came to think of it, he hadn't explicitly asked her to the dance. He had said it was on and said it would be fun. She had agreed, breathlessly picturing the pair of them whirling around the dance floor, but he had never actually asked her.

Holly scowled. 'So he strung you along. He saw you liked him and it flattered his vanity to keep you interested even though he had no intention of going out with you.'

Ruby could only nod. She had never looked at it like that before. She had only seen it from her angle, blaming herself for falling for a man who didn't keep his word. But from another perspective, she understood that Dr Flint was far more to blame. He had seen her infatuation and encouraged it because it suited him to know that the student nurse on Ward Six worshipped the ground he walked on.

'I didn't know at the time, but he was going out with a theatre nurse. One of the students who was on a surgery rotation tried to tell me but I didn't believe her because I was so sure he liked me.' She gave a wry smile. 'But after I left, I saw his engagement to some society heiress announced in the paper. So he was stringing along the theatre nurse as well.'

'Lucky escape for her, if you ask me,' Holly muttered.

Possibly Meg could see that Ruby was still raw from the experience for she said, 'You do know that his behaviour was nothing to do with you, don't you? He was just feeding off your admiration.'

Ruby snorted. 'Infatuation, more like. I can see it now but at the time I was so hurt and bewildered. I didn't know what I'd done to make him behave like that. Maybe you're right and there really is a big difference between seventeen and twenty, because it seems so obvious now, but at the time I was completely taken in.'

Holly was frowning. 'But Laurie's nothing like that so what's the problem?'

Ruby shrugged. 'When he told me that something had come up, I was disappointed but didn't question it. Then when his mother said he'd been out for the day with his brother it all came flooding back. Dr Flint was forever making vague arrangements and then backing out at the last minute. Now I look back, I can see he would make the arrangements when he thought I was losing interest. I—' She bit her tongue, her cheeks burning when memory of one particular incident hit her.

'Go on,' Holly prompted.

'This is going to make you think I'm an utter halfwit. But there was a physical therapist who I'd got friendly with, and he asked me to the pictures. A definite date, not like Dr Flint's vague promises. Only Dr Flint must have got wind of it, because he came to find me at lunch and asked me to the same film. On the same night.' Ruby buried her face in her hands and groaned. 'Of course, I was overjoyed to be finally asked out on a proper date by the gorgeous Dr Flint so I turned the physical therapist down.'

Holly snorted. 'Let me guess. The lovely Dr Flint gave you the brush-off straight after.'

Ruby nodded. 'I can't believe I was so naive. I've kept this bottled up all that time but I wish I'd told you before. Just describing it out loud has made me see what a piece of work Dr Flint really was, yet I thought he was wonderful.' She sighed. 'Anyway, when Laurie's mum told me he'd gone for a bike ride, it all came flooding back. Now I'm worried Laurie's doing the same thing that Dr Flint did, making me fall for him just to feed his ego.'

'He's not. I'm sure of it,' Meg said, and Holly nodded.

'But how can I be sure? I mean, I know it seems obvious that Dr Flint was a... a...'

'A slimy toad?' Holly suggested.

'A git?' Meg offered.

Ruby thought about it. 'A gitty toad,' she said. 'But at the time I was completely taken in. What if the same thing is happening now?'

'It's not. First of all' – Holly counted on her fingers – 'neither Meg nor I think Laurie's anything like this Dr Flint, so if you can't trust yourself, have faith in *our* judgement.'

'I suppose I can try.' Ruby relaxed a little. 'What else?'

'Secondly, you *can* trust yourself. I don't think you'd fall for another Dr Flint precisely because you've already been through it and recognise the signs. And thirdly, and most importantly, Laurie already asked you out to the pictures and that date happened. You even kissed. So it's totally different from Dr Flint.'

It was the last point that convinced Ruby. 'You're right. I'm being silly. Just because Laurie went on a bike ride, it doesn't mean there wasn't an important issue that stopped him going out with me.'

'Exactly!' Meg said. 'Maybe he didn't want his mother to know what was wrong so just told her they were going on a bike ride.'

'I didn't think of that.'

All in all, Ruby felt much happier.

'Where did you meet Mrs Foster, anyway?' Holly asked.

'Oh, I nearly forgot.' And she told her friends all about the fundraising meeting for the school. 'I offered to spread the word on the base,' she concluded. 'Any chance you could help?'

'Why not?' Holly said. 'Sounds like a good cause. How were you planning on going about it?'

'Probably put some notices up around the place with information on where to send donations. I also said I'd tell people in the choir in case they felt able to sing in the concert. Oh, and I could put a notice in the newsletter.'

'That's a good idea,' Meg said. 'I'm seeing Sister Macintosh tomorrow, and she's in the choir. I'll mention it to her and ask her to spread the word.'

'Why don't we put on an event at the base?' Holly suggested. 'A dance or something.'

'I like the idea of organising something ourselves. We'd probably get more donations that way.' Ruby tried to sound enthusiastic but inside she was quaking. What had she let herself in for? A dance would take a huge amount of organisation, and she was still finding her feet with the air ambulance, not to mention trying to work out where she stood with Laurie. She didn't think she could take on something so demanding on top of everything else, but nor did she want to let down the children of St Winifred's school.

'It would take a lot of organisation,' Meg pointed out. 'And anyway, there are regular dances at the Red Lion.

There might not be enough interest in another dance here.' Ruby wanted to hug her.

'I suppose you're right.' Holly, thankfully, didn't look too downcast. 'How about a concert? A group of us could get together and sing songs from the musicals.'

Meg's eyes were shining. 'I like the sound of that, but instead of singing in one place, we could tour around the base and collect money. Like carol singing only it's summer.'

'I love that idea.' And this time Ruby was genuinely enthusiastic. This felt like something she could handle. 'We could sing for the patients too so they won't have to miss out. I'll ask Sister Macintosh tomorrow.'

The others agreed this was a good idea and Ruby picked up her darning in a better frame of mind than when she had flung it down.

Chapter Twelve

Three days after the cancelled London trip, Laurie entered the crew room with his stomach knotted in anticipation. He had flown every day since then and hadn't seen Ruby at all after telling her he couldn't make it. He couldn't regret going out with Adam, for the day spent cycling around the quiet lanes had done much to rid their minds of the shock from the latest poison pen letter. They had gone as far as Elstree and enjoyed a simple but hearty lunch at a cafe and returned home with their peace of mind restored. Adam, who had started the day with a pale, pinched face and shoulders a mass of tension, looked relaxed and his cheeks had a healthy bloom.

It was only when his mother had described her day that Laurie's worries returned although for quite another reason. When she told him that she had seen Ruby at the fundraising meeting and that she had mentioned the bike trip, he bitterly regretted not being more open with Ruby. What must she think, hearing that he had gone on a bicycle ride with his brother?

And now there was no avoiding her, for she was the nursing orderly on his crew that day.

She was already in the crew room when he walked in. The other crew on duty were also there, making the hut crowded.

Flying Officer Maitland, his navigator, occupied a table at the back of the room and had his charts spread around him. Laurie shot Ruby a smile, hoping it would convey his apologies and intention to speak to her as soon as possible. The smile she gave in return was tight and there was a wariness to her expression that made his heart sink. She immediately turned away, bending over Bentley and making a fuss of him.

Laurie wished he could go straight up to her and explain but they were due to leave soon and he needed to brief the crew. He approached Maitland. 'Have you got the course plotted?'

Maitland nodded, folding his charts. 'I'm ready to leave when you are.'

Laurie beckoned to Powell and Ruby to join them. 'Morning, everyone,' he said when the little group was gathered. 'We're flying to RAF Ballyhalbert in Northern Ireland where we're collecting a patient who was injured when he crash-landed yesterday. He has broken both his legs and also has extensive burns. The medics are most concerned about the burns, which is why we are transferring him to East Grinstead.'

He saw Ruby wince when he mentioned the injuries and wasn't surprised. He'd once had to drag a pilot from a blazing plane and would never forget the sight or the man's agony. No doubt Ruby had treated patients with burns and was remembering similar experiences.

He went on. 'You know the drill because we've done this before. We've got three flights ahead of us: first to Ballyhalbert, then to East Grinstead and finally the flight home. It's going to be a long day so get kitted up and be ready to leave in fifteen minutes.'

There was a general rush for the latrines and then to the lockers to collect their gear. Although this included parachutes, they were under orders not to use them if they had a patient on board as the patient would not be able to operate a parachute. He sincerely hoped they would never be faced with that stark choice.

He had intended to catch Ruby before takeoff but she had headed straight for the latrine when he had finished speaking and then chatted to Rhys upon her return while she pulled on her flying boots and jacket. Then there was no time for any more talking for they had to board the Oxford.

The flight to Northern Ireland was thankfully uneventful. As always he kept a sharp lookout for enemy aircraft, painfully aware that the Oxford had no defence should they come under attack. Even so, he was constantly aware of Ruby the whole time, jealous of Powell, who chattered easily to her. He couldn't help but wonder if she had been deliberately avoiding him back at the crew hut or if he was letting his imagination get the better of him. Maybe there would be a chance to speak when they reached RAF Ballyhalbert.

His hopes were dashed, however, for when he landed, he could already see an ambulance driving to meet them. Now there was no opportunity for speaking to Ruby alone for she needed to give her entire attention to her patient. He accompanied her to the ambulance. It had become his habit to speak to the patient while the nursing orderly took details of the injuries and any medication that had been administered. However, Flight Sergeant Emery had been heavily sedated and appeared to be asleep. For the patient's sake, he was glad that he seemed to be comfortable and could only hope that would last for the duration of the flight.

Once Ruby had been given her instructions, they lifted Emery on his stretcher into the Oxford. Then Laurie had to leave Ruby to get him comfortable in the cabin while he prepared to take off.

His opportunity finally came at Gatwick, where they were transferring Emery. The patient had been carried out to the waiting ambulance when Laurie spied a photograph lying on the floor, beneath where Emery's stretcher had been. It was a wedding photograph, he saw with a knot of pity, showing a bride and groom standing outside a church. The groom was dressed in RAF uniform and could only be Flight Sergeant Emery. Laurie recognised him from the half of his face that wasn't a mass of burns. The bride gazed at her new husband with adoring eyes. On the back were written the words:

> *I will never stop loving you. Alice x*

He dashed for the ambulance, thankfully getting there before the driver closed the doors. 'This belongs to the patient,' he told the WAAF driver. 'Please make sure he gets it.'

Ruby, seeing what it was, exclaimed, 'My gosh, how awful if he lost it. He woke up towards the end of the flight and asked me to hold it for him so he could look at it.'

'I'm surprised he could speak.'

'He couldn't. He kept tapping his chest with his good hand until I worked out there was something in his pocket that he wanted me to get for him. He grew much calmer when he could see it.' She paused while the ambulance drove away. Then she said wistfully, 'It must be wonderful to love someone so much that the mere sight of them makes you feel better.'

He nodded. While he couldn't claim to know Ruby as well as Flight Sergeant Emery knew his wife, seeing Ruby always made his day. He wondered if she would still like him if a terrible injury changed his appearance.

'Ruby, I really am sorry I cancelled our date.'

'That's all right. You already explained.' But her expression said otherwise.

'I saw my mother when I got back, and she said she'd seen you and told you I'd gone out with Adam.'

She nodded but said nothing. Still, she didn't walk away, which he took as encouragement.

'I know it must have been hurtful to hear I didn't take a promised trip with you just so I could go cycling with Adam, and I'm sorry you had to hear about it like that.'

'You don't have to explain yourself to me.'

'But I want to! I wish I could tell you everything, but it's not my story to tell. All I can say is that something really did happen with Adam and he needed to get away from the shop and Starsden for a while. Saturday was the only day I could go. I would much rather have spent the day with you. I want you to know that.'

The smile she gave in response looked more genuine than the others she had sent his way that day. 'Thank you for explaining. I hope everything is all right with Adam now.'

He frowned. 'I don't know, to be honest. I hope so.' As far as he knew, Adam hadn't received another letter and he was fairly sure that his brother wouldn't try hiding any more from him.

Another thought struck. 'By the way, my parents don't know anything about this either because Adam made me promise not to tell them. If you see my mother again, please don't mention it.'

'I won't.'

He cleared his throat. 'I know it's been a long day but if you feel up to it, would you like to go out with me tonight?'

This time her smile lit her whole face. 'I'd like that. What shall we do?' Her face fell. 'Oh, I don't have a late pass, so I can't stay out long.'

'Do you dare risking the cinema again? That will finish in plenty of time to save you from jankers.'

—

They didn't make it to the cinema in the end, because the film was one they had both seen before. Instead, Laurie suggested that they have a drink at the King's Head. This was a cosy pub on the High Street that was frequented more by locals than RAF personnel and was consequently quieter. The King's Head was so small that it didn't have a separate snug, but as the public bar was only occupied by elderly men who nursed their pints while quietly talking to their friends, it was just as peaceful, if not more so, than the snug at the Three Horseshoes. The only sound was the hum of conversation, the quiet click of dominoes from a game being played in the far corner and the occasional hum of a motor engine as vehicles drove down the High Street.

'This is my dad's favourite pub,' Laurie told her as he carried their drinks to a table, beer for him and a port and lemon for Ruby, as she was feeling daring. 'I think he comes here to avoid the risk of me running into him, so I hope he's not planning on coming this evening. He always says his presence lowers the average age to about seventy. I hope you don't mind not being somewhere more lively.'

'I don't mind.' Ruby sipped her drink and discovered she rather liked it. 'It's been... a difficult day, in many ways. I could use some peace and quiet.' Although her patient had been calm and as free from pain as possible throughout the flight, she had been on edge the whole time. Emery's injuries were so similar to those of her previous patient it had seemed inevitable that he would deteriorate and require treatment she was unqualified to provide. Even though it hadn't happened, she still quivered with tension. She took another sip, willing it to soothe her frayed nerves. Maybe it would work faster if she didn't also have worries about Laurie. She had wanted to believe him before when he had said he would have far rather been with her than Adam, but a part of her was still the confused teenaged girl who hadn't seen through Dr Flint's insincere smile. Since joining the WAAF and burying herself in her duties and new friendships, she had forgotten the intense hurt and longing of those days, but Laurie's cancellation had brought it all back. She couldn't bear to go through it all again. It didn't matter that this was now the second time she had been out with him and reason, as well as her friends, told her that Laurie was nothing like Dr Flint. It was hard to shake off old insecurities when they ran so deep. She was therefore glad of the chance to simply chat and get to know him better, hoping that time spent in his company would help allay her fears.

Laurie put down his beer mug with a grimace. 'We've transported a lot of burns patients since we started operating. It must be hard to nurse someone with such extensive injuries.'

Ruby nodded, moved that Laurie would consider the toll such work would take on her peace of mind. 'I try and tell myself that although it can't be easy on them to be moved, they've got the best chance of recovery at East Grinstead. Apparently the reconstructive surgery that goes on there is a marvel.'

It felt good to sit and talk. Laurie was different from Dr Flint in that respect. With the doctor she had always sensed him looking over her shoulder and he never quite seemed to have his full attention on her. Whereas Laurie was fully focused on her. He seemed genuinely interested in what she had to say and from what he said he had clearly listened to both what she said and what she left unsaid. Nothing like Dr Flint, who only seemed to wait for a gap in the conversation to speak of himself. She could see that now and was disappointed in her younger self for not seeing that before.

He smiled at her now. 'That's what I've heard too. And you do marvels with your patients, keeping them calm during the flight.'

'You really think so?'

'I know so. The rest of the crew always say how well you cope.'

'I can't tell you how good it is to hear that.' The tension that had been tying knots in her stomach ever since last week's awful flight dissipated. No doubt it would strike again before her next flight, but at least she could put the experience behind her until then.

Laurie, however, looked as though he could also use some reassurance. He studied his beer mug, tracing its handle with his fingers, seemingly lost in his own thoughts. Finally he said, 'I sometimes wonder if Adam would have made a better recovery if they had been able to fly him back from France, if he could have got proper medical attention sooner.'

'You can't think like that,' Ruby told him. 'The important thing is that he's alive and doing well.'

Laurie didn't look convinced so she made an effort to change the subject. 'Anyway, there's something I wanted to ask you. You know I went to that fundraising meeting?'

'The one my mum was at?'

She nodded. 'Well, I want to help in whatever way I can. I talked it over with Holly and Meg, and we thought of a fun singing event.' She explained their idea of a summertime carolling event around the base. 'But we won't be singing carols, of course,' she concluded, 'just popular songs.'

'As long as you can all sing well enough to be sure it's not torture for your patients.'

She swatted his arm in mock reproach. 'We'll practise first. Anyway, if we're that bad, people might pay us to stop. How's your voice? We could use some men in the choir.'

'Not bad. A bit rusty maybe.'

'But you'll help?'

'Of course.'

All in all, Ruby felt much better about Laurie backing out of their day out by the end of the evening. Before they left the pub they rearranged their day out for the next time they had a day off together, which was still three weeks away. But Laurie had also told her of another dance at the Red Lion on Saturday evening and, as they were both free that evening, he had asked her to go with him. She had eagerly agreed and was walking on air as he escorted her back to Poplar Court. This time their goodnight kiss was less hesitant and no less wonderful than their first kiss.

Her happiness lasted all the way upstairs to where Meg and Holly were polishing their uniform buttons, and they listened to her recounting how wonderful the evening had been.

'I told you there would be a reasonable explanation,' Meg said when Ruby had explained what Laurie had said about missing their date.

'It's still very vague if you ask me.'

Ruby jumped. She had been so full of her news, she hadn't noticed Bobby huddled on her bed. She wouldn't have repeated what Laurie had told her if she had known she was there.

'It's a good thing he's going out with Ruby, then, and not you,' Holly said.

Bobby snorted and pulled her blankets over her head.

Feeling deflated, Ruby got ready for bed and the others followed suit. She didn't feel like continuing the conversation with Bobby listening. As she curled up, trying to find a comfortable position on the lumpy mattress, some of her happiness faded. Of course Laurie had been vague. He'd apologised for it, hadn't he? She couldn't expect him to tell her everything about his brother. But now she couldn't help wondering if he would have explained himself at all if his mother hadn't told her about the bike ride.

It wasn't a nice thought and it kept her awake for hours before finally drifting into an uneasy sleep. Of course she fell into a heavy sleep not long before her alarm bell woke her, and she got up feeling heavy-eyed and exhausted.

She was fumbling with her tie, making a mess of the knot when Bobby sailed in, looking fresh as a daisy. She was in the habit of getting up early and going for a walk. 'You should try it,' she said to Ruby with a self-satisfied smile. 'There's nothing like a good walk first thing in the morning to set you up for the day.'

Ruby simply gave a smile that was probably closer to a grimace and said she'd think about it.

'Just say the word and I'll slip a laxative into her porridge,' Holly muttered.

Chapter Thirteen

Saturday couldn't come fast enough for Ruby. She was on an early shift on Friday and happened to see Laurie on her way to the hospital.

'I'm really looking forward to tomorrow night,' he told her, with a smile that she felt in the pit of her stomach.

'Me too.' She felt so breathless that she could only manage those two words.

'I'll pick you up at seven thirty,' he said.

She would have loved to stay and chat but she couldn't be late for her shift. So she said a hasty goodbye and carried on to the hospital.

Normally she enjoyed her work on the wards and wasn't prone to wishing it away. However if she could have sped up time she would have done so to get through her Friday and Saturday shifts and reach the moment when she would see Laurie again. The only thing that helped her through the agonisingly long hours was when Sister Macintosh told her that her request to hold the carolling fundraiser had been approved for the second Saturday in August and that the choir had agreed to help. She couldn't wait to tell Laurie.

Time did creep gradually towards seven thirty on Saturday evening, however, and at last she was looking at herself in the mirror, admiring the stylish victory rolls that Meg had arranged in her hair. 'My hair never usually looks that shiny,' she said, reaching to pat the rolls. 'How did you manage it?'

Meg batted her hand away. 'You'll spoil it if you do that. I used a little pomade,' she said, showing her the bottle. 'A lucky find in the NAAFI the other day.'

The finishing touch was a slick of lipstick, which also doubled up as rouge, and then she was dashing down the stairs to meet Laurie.

Laurie wasn't already waiting outside the door, which was unusual, for he had always been early before. Still, she didn't think anything of it, and strolled up and down the path while she waited, mentally rehearsing dance steps. The last time she had been to the dance, she had only danced with him once. But as they were going together this time she hoped they would dance every dance together.

Time ticked on and still there was no sign of Laurie. Other WAAFs going to the dance passed her in a cloud of Evening in Paris mingled with Californian Poppy. 'I'll see you there,' she called. Now she wished she had arranged to meet him there, because at this rate they were going to miss the opening numbers.

She was starting to feel a twinge of anxiety now. A glance at her watch told her it was a quarter to eight. He was fifteen whole minutes late. Earlier she had been convinced something had happened to delay him. Now she couldn't help remembering waiting for Dr Flint. Had she been taken in all over again? Was Laurie no better than him? Her ears buzzed and her throat felt uncomfortably tight. She couldn't cry, not out here where anyone could see her. She pressed her tongue against her teeth, willing the tears away. Surely he would be here at any minute, smiling that gorgeous smile, full of apologies for being late. He wouldn't leave her standing here without at least sending word.

Perhaps he'd had an accident? She comforted herself with the thought of him lying all alone with a twisted ankle until she decided she must be a horrible person if she would rather Laurie be injured or ill than standing her up.

At eight o'clock she knew he wasn't coming. Whether because something had happened or if he really was another Dr Flint she didn't know, but she couldn't stand out here any longer. Had he really said he would pick her up here or had he meant to meet her at the dance? She *thought* they'd arranged to meet at Poplar Court but maybe in her delight she hadn't paid attention to the arrangements and misheard? What if he was standing outside the Red Lion wondering where on earth *she* was?

Clinging to hope, she strode out, hoping her hairstyle wouldn't be completely out of place by the time she arrived. The thought of Laurie waiting, wondering where she was, lent her speed, and the Red Lion soon came into view. She couldn't see Laurie but he might have gone inside by this time. She could only hope he hadn't given up and returned to the Sergeants' Mess.

Hearing the lively music and laughter sent another wave of desolation sweeping through her. Although she hated going into pubs alone, she drew a deep breath and pushed open the door. The ballroom was packed and the dance floor was heaving with couples. Everywhere she looked, men and women were smiling and laughing as they whirled around the floor in their partners' arms. There was no sign of Laurie anywhere. Not on the dance floor – thank goodness – but neither could she catch a glimpse of his blond head in the crowd around the bar or at any of the tables encircling the room.

A hand tapped her shoulder. She spun round, catching her breath, then her heart sank when she saw it was Bobby.

'It's brave of you to come all alone,' Bobby said.

'I'm not here alone,' Ruby replied. 'Or, at least, I'm not supposed to be. I'm waiting for Laurie.'

Bobby's eyes opened wide. 'Didn't he tell you? I saw him at the Three Horseshoes earlier with his brother. When I asked if he was going to the dance he said he couldn't make it.'

Ruby couldn't reply. She had to get out of there as soon as possible. She fled for the door, and thankfully no one got in her way. A moment later she was on the street outside, tears running down her cheeks. Music followed her all down the street as she hurried for the safety of Poplar Court, mocking her for believing that Laurie could be different, that he wouldn't treat her as an object of amusement. That he wasn't like Dr Flint.

She only slowed down when she was nearly there, to give her time to wipe away her tears and compose herself before she had to face any WAAFs. Thankfully the hallway was deserted and she was able to keep fresh tears from falling as she went to sign in and muttered to the corporal on duty that she'd changed her mind and wasn't going out after all.

'Waste of a perfectly good late pass if you ask me,' the corporal called after her.

Ruby didn't reply but bolted up the stairs and was soon in the safety of her room, secure in the knowledge that at least Bobby wouldn't be there to sneer at her.

She found Holly, sitting cross-legged on her bed, darning a hole in her stockings. She looked up when Ruby burst in. 'What on earth are you doing here? You're supposed to be with Laurie.'

Ruby couldn't hold back the tears any longer. Her shoulders heaved as she managed to say in a strangled voice, 'He stood me up.' Between sobs she described what had happened, up to and including what Bobby had told her.

Holly scowled. 'I wouldn't take her word for it.'

'But he definitely wasn't there. I know it was crowded but I'd have seen him. And what reason does she have to lie? It's not as if she's after Laurie herself. She's always going on about her wonderful fiancé.'

'I don't know. But something doesn't ring quite true about this perfect man. We always see her writing letters to him, but has she ever had one back?'

'If he's serving overseas, his letters might take a long time to arrive.'

'I suppose so. It still doesn't feel right, though.'

Ruby pulled the pins out of her hair and dragged a comb through it, wincing when the comb snagged on a tangle. 'Whether or not Bobby's telling the truth is beside the point. Laurie didn't turn up and he didn't even have the courtesy to send me a message. He can't like me as much as I thought.' A thought struck and she groaned.

'What?' Holly asked.

'I've just remembered I'm on air ambulance duty tomorrow. On his crew. How can I face him now?'

She still hadn't answered that question to her satisfaction the next day when she was sitting in the cabin of the Oxford, looking out at the land far below. She had yet to speak to Laurie properly, having arrived at the crew room just in time for the briefing. It had been so different from other flights when she had arrived early so that she could spend as much time as possible with Laurie before it was time to depart. She had been professional enough to concentrate while Laurie explained that they were going to RAF Linton-on-Ouse in Yorkshire where they would be collecting a patient who had been in an air crash and needed transferring to the orthopaedic hospital in

Oswestry. However, when, at the end of the briefing, he had approached her, a question in his eyes, she had made a dash for the latrine. On reflection, not the most dignified of exits but it had been the only way she could think of avoiding him. When she had returned to the crew room she had lingered by the lockers, fiddling with her gear until Laurie left, then crossed to the Oxford deep in conversation with the wireless operator to ensure Laurie wouldn't have a chance to speak to her before it was time for him to begin the preflight checks.

Was she being childish? Perhaps, but it was hard enough not to dissolve into tears as it was, let alone if she argued with Laurie. Until she had seen her patient safely delivered to Oswestry she needed to stay as calm as possible, and that meant pretending she didn't have a care in the world. Easier said than done, of course.

As to what she would do or say when her patient was out of her hands, she didn't know. In her imagination she had delivered a magnificent speech, first withering Laurie with a single look, then telling him exactly what she thought of men who broke their word. Laurie had been reduced to a quivering wreck, apologising brokenly and begging her for another chance, but she had snubbed him, sailing away with her nose in the air. She doubted she would be able to carry that off in real life, though. In all likelihood, she wouldn't be able to get more than five words out before the tears started, and she couldn't bear the thought of crying in front of Laurie. She didn't want him to know how much he had hurt her.

The trouble was, her loss of confidence over Laurie had done nothing to boost her faith in her nursing abilities. Interspersed with her thoughts regarding Laurie came needle-sharp jabs of worry about being in charge of her patient. From what she had learned at the briefing, Flight Sergeant Kerry had broken both his legs, with a compound fracture of his left tibia. He had already undergone surgery to stabilise the fracture and stop the bleeding but would need another operation to set the bone properly. Although she had helped transport several seriously ill or injured patients by now, this would be the first time she would take charge of someone so recently out of surgery. What if complications arose while they were in the air? How would she cope? Her doubts refused to be silenced.

All in all, she was a mess of nerves by the time they were circling the airfield just outside York. And she wouldn't have a moment to compose herself, for she could already see a boxy vehicle with a red cross painted on the roof turning into the aerodrome. The ambulance was arriving.

As soon as they landed, she opened the hatch in the fuselage and climbed out. The ambulance pulled to a stop nearby. Telling herself that at least having to take care of the patient meant she didn't have to talk to Laurie, she went to meet the ambulance drivers so they could hand the patient over to her care.

Flight Sergeant Kerry was awake and smiling when he was unloaded from the ambulance although he looked very pale. Ruby tried to hide her anxiety while she listened to the driver explain what medication he had received before leaving hospital and what he could be given should he require more pain relief before the end of the flight.

She knew she mustn't let Kerry see her anxiety so she smiled at him as they crossed to the Oxford. 'I'm LACW Morris, but you can call me Ruby.'

The patient held out a hand for her to shake. 'Call me Jim,' he said. His handshake was weak and Ruby didn't press too hard, not wanting to cause him any more hurt.

'Well, I'm going to take good care of you, Jim, and we'll have you safely in Oswestry before you know it.'

Laurie came to help them load Jim into the Oxford; Ruby stood on the other side of the stretcher, using it as a barrier between her and Laurie. Once Jim was safely on board, Laurie caught her arm. 'Ruby, I'm sorry about—'

She cut him off. 'Save it for later. My patient needs me.' And she climbed into the cabin before Laurie could say anything else.

Jim had clearly picked up on the tension between the two and when Laurie climbed into the pilot's seat, Jim craned his neck to first look into the cockpit and then back at Ruby. 'Lovers' tiff, eh?'

'Everything's fine. Nothing to worry about,' she said and bent to rearrange his pillow. 'Tell me about yourself. Have you got a wife?' Jim looked like he was in his mid-thirties, so she wasn't surprised when he nodded.

'I've been married for ten years to my Polly. She's the love of my life.'

'How wonderful. Where is she now?'

'She's in Wales. We were living in London when we married but when the Blitz started she took the children to live with her aunt in Mold.'

'That's not too far from Oswestry.' Thanks to her flights around Britain, her geography had greatly improved. 'Maybe she'll be able to visit.'

'I hope so.' Jim glanced out of the window. 'The pilot had better get a move on. Looks like there's a storm brewing.'

Ruby followed his gaze but could only see white clouds. 'It looks calm to me.'

'Trust me. I've got a feel for the weather.'

The navigator must have heard the conversation, for he called to Laurie, who was preparing to start the engines.

'What's the latest weather forecast? Our patient reckons there's a storm on the way.'

Laurie shook his head. 'I just radioed the Watch Office and they say the pressure's dropped a little but nothing to indicate a storm.'

'There you go,' Ruby said to Jim. 'Nothing to worry about.'

The engines roared into life, and Ruby needed to give her full attention to Jim to make sure he was comfortable and the jolting of the craft as it taxied to the head of the runway wasn't causing him any discomfort. As she worked, she was able to push her unease at taking care of a patient in Jim's condition to the back of her mind. However, once they were in the air and on course for RAF Rednal in Shropshire, her fears resurfaced. Jim seemed distressed and complained of pain in his left leg, the one that had needed surgery. Ruby checked the dressing and was able to reassure him that there was no bleeding but he still insisted it didn't feel right.

Ruby felt helpless. This was precisely the sort of situation she felt unprepared for. 'I can give you some pain relief,' she offered, but Jim refused, saying it made him feel sick. He looked pale, though, so she put him on oxygen and was relieved to see his colour improve after a while.

She squeezed his hand. 'You're looking better now, at any rate, and it won't be long before we reach Shropshire. And every mile is a mile closer to Mold and your family.'

He smiled at that and squeezed her hand back. Then he closed his eyes and slept.

It was only then that it dawned on Ruby that Laurie was having a conversation with the navigator, and it sounded urgent.

'I want to stay well clear of that,' Laurie was saying. 'Plot a course to keep us at least twenty miles to the south.'

'Righto, Skipper.'

To the south of what? Ruby glanced out of the window and her mouth went dry. A column of black clouds loomed up ahead. It looked horribly like a thunderstorm. She glanced at Jim to make sure he was still asleep and moved forward to speak to Laurie. It no longer mattered that she wasn't speaking to him; the safety of her patient was her only concern, and she needed to know if there was going to be a delay.

'What's happening?' she asked, bracing herself on the back of the navigator's seat. 'Are we heading into a storm?'

Laurie answered without turning his head. 'Looks like it. We're going to fly around it to be on the safe side, which will add another ten minutes or so to our time. It might get bumpy.'

The navigator called out a bearing then, and they banked. Staggering back to her patient, Ruby saw the storm clouds shift towards the starboard side of the aircraft or, rather, the aircraft was turning south.

When she got back to Jim she saw his eyes were open. He pushed away the oxygen mask. 'What's wrong?'

Doing her best to keep her concern from her voice, she said, 'Nothing. The pilot is going round a patch of bad weather. It might take us a bit longer to get to RAF Rednal, that's all.'

The furrow between Jim's eyes deepened but he said nothing. A moment later, however, when the aircraft jolted, his eyes flew open and he groaned through his teeth.

Ruby was instantly by his side, bracing herself against another bump. 'What's the matter?'

He answered through gritted teeth. 'My leg.'

'Your left one?'

He nodded and groaned again when the Oxford hit another patch of turbulence.

Her heart thumping, she lifted the blanket to inspect the dressing on his left leg. A red stain was spreading over the dressing.

She drew a breath. *Don't let him see how scared you are.* Somehow she managed to force her features into a smile. 'It is bleeding a bit, probably caused by this jolting. I'll put another dressing on.'

Grabbing her medical bag, she pulled out a dressing and applied it over the top of the one that was already there. Making herself sound like she was doing nothing more serious than putting a plaster on a child's grazed knee, she said, 'This is going to hurt a bit,' and then she applied pressure to the wound. Jim cried out then, mercifully, fainted. With her free hand, Ruby affixed the oxygen mask back over his mouth and increased the flow. She could only pray she was doing the right thing. She had never felt so helpless in her life. This was exactly why she had left nursing – she had never wanted to hold a patient's fate in her hands.

That was when the bottom seemed to fall from the world. She hovered, weightless, and her stomach swooped. An instant later she crashed back to the floor and something struck the side of her head. She heard someone cry out and it took her a moment to realise it was her. For a moment she couldn't work out what was happening, and then she remembered her patient. Pulling herself to her knees, she leaned over the stretcher and pressed hard upon the bloodied dressing. Blood welled between her fingers. Jim's leg was bleeding badly.

Chapter Fourteen

Her hearing returned. It was like surfacing after being underwater. Laurie was snapping orders to the navigator, and in the background was the rapid metallic tapping of Rhys the wireless operator frantically sending a signal. When he finished, she asked, 'What's happening?'

'We can't make it through the storm so the skipper's turned us around. We're going to try landing at RAF Bircotes.'

'Where's that?'

'Near Doncaster.'

She nodded, thinking fast. 'The patient's bleeding. I think the jolting did some damage but I daren't remove the dressing to look. He needs to be transferred to hospital as soon as we land.'

'I'll request an ambulance.' Rhys bent over the wireless. More tapping then, 'What about you? You took a nasty bash. How bad's that cut?'

'What cut?'

'On your forehead.' Rhys tapped his own forehead, indicating the place he meant.

She put her fingers of her free hand to the spot, belatedly aware that it was stinging, and they came away covered in blood. She gazed at them in bemusement. 'I don't think it can be too bad. I didn't notice I was bleeding until you pointed it out.'

The Oxford lurched again, and her bag flew across the cabin. Ruby couldn't go after it because she didn't dare stop applying pressure to Jim's leg. She thought the bleeding might be slowing yet without another medic to help, all she could do was keep applying pressure until they met the ambulance.

'Hang on!' Laurie called back. 'We're caught between two storms. Things are going to get bumpy for a few minutes.'

'Understatement of the year,' Ruby muttered, fumbling in her pocket with one hand to find her handkerchief so she could wipe away the blood that still trickled down her face.

Another jolt. Somehow Ruby managed to brace herself against the stretcher. It was a good thing Jim had lost consciousness because she couldn't bear to think of the pain he would suffer being bumped around like this, let alone from her pressure on the wound. Her medical bag slid back within reach, and she grabbed it and wedged it down the side of the navigator's seat. Rain battered the window, and the aircraft now rattled so hard she was growing alarmed. Unbidden, memories rose to the surface of her mind of hearing about aircraft that had broken up from the stresses of flying through a storm.

With an almighty crash, the flap in the fuselage burst open. Icy wind howled around the cabin, tearing at her clothes and hair. There was no way she could reach to close it without leaving her patient so all she could do was lean over Jim to protect him from the rain as much as possible and stare in horrified fascination at the black clouds surrounding them.

She tore her gaze from the view to focus on Jim. Despite her best efforts, the dressing was soaked in blood. There was another in her bag so she inched it towards her, praying they didn't hit more turbulence that would send it flying out of the aircraft. She had to search by feel and gasped with relief when her fingers encountered the dressing. Somehow she managed to unwrap it and press it to the wound with only the briefest reduction of pressure. Then she hung on for dear life when they were shaken by another pocket of turbulence.

Then a moment later all was calm. The rain stopped pouring into the cabin and the Oxford sailed smoothly through the sky. Ruby drew deep lungfuls of air, unable to believe the conditions could change so fast. Looking out now she could see the ground and, unbelievably, it was bathed in sunshine.

'Is everyone all right?' Laurie called, having to shout to be heard, for the wind still howled through the open doorway.

Ruby replied along with the others that all was well.

'We're approaching RAF Bircotes now, and I'm in contact with their Flying Control. I've already requested an ambulance for Jim. Anything else we need?'

'Please ask their MO to meet us,' Ruby said. 'Jim's bleeding and needs treatment before we move him.'

'Will do.' And Ruby heard him speaking over the radio.

'Ruby needs treatment too,' Rhys called. 'She's cut her head.'

In the battle to keep pressure on Jim's leg while simultaneously trying to stop herself being flung around the cabin, she had forgotten her head but now it throbbed. Miraculously she had kept hold of her handkerchief so she dabbed the cut again and saw it was still bleeding.

The ground was fast approaching now, and she could see the landing strip ahead with an ambulance already parked nearby. As though to make up for the rough flight, Laurie managed one of his best landings ever, and the wheels touched the ground so smoothly she hardly felt it.

They had barely stopped when Rhys made for the door. 'I'll fetch the MO,' he said.

Thankfully the MO must have been waiting, for Rhys was soon back, accompanied by the doctor, a kindly looking man with greying hair and gentle brown eyes. 'You look like you've been in the wars,' he said to Ruby after only one glance.

'I can wait,' she said. 'My patient needs help. He had surgery on a compound fracture before we collected him and he started bleeding during the flight. I've been applying pressure but he's still bleeding.'

'Let's have a look.' The MO bent over the still unconscious Jim. 'Right. I've got him. You can let go now.'

She had spent so long struggling to maintain pressure that her fingers were cramping and it took a moment to relax her grip enough to pull back her hand. Then she slumped into Rhys's vacated seat and watched the doctor while he worked.

A few minutes later, he glanced at her over his shoulder with a smile. 'Well done. I've managed to stop the bleeding now, and we can transfer him to the hospital in Doncaster. But if you hadn't had the presence of mind to apply pressure he would probably have bled to death before you got here.'

She had done the right thing? Suddenly it didn't matter that she had been scared half to death and her head was really starting to throb now. All she cared about was that she had been in charge of a patient during an emergency and had not lost her head but had taken the correct action. She gave a beaming smile. 'Thank you. That's good to know.'

'Now, let's take a look at your head.' He tilted her face to the light and frowned as he examined the wound. 'Not too bad but you'll need a couple of stitches.'

'I won't have to go to the hospital, will I?'

'No, we can do it here in Sick Quarters. I'll request another ambulance to take you there. Stay here while we get the patient into the ambulance.'

He left the aircraft. A moment later he returned with the ambulance drivers. Together they disconnected Jim from the oxygen and then manoeuvred his stretcher outside and to the waiting ambulance.

Ruby leaned back in her seat and closed her eyes. Although her head hurt, her overwhelming feeling was of pride. She had been faced with a patient haemorrhaging and in need of urgent care, and the doctor had told her that she had saved his life. She knew she would no longer fear the responsibility of being in sole charge of a patient.

She heard a step as someone came through the door and thought it must be the doctor. She opened her eyes reluctantly, thinking it must be time to stand and leave the Oxford only to see Laurie hovering over her.

'How are you feeling?' he asked.

'Not too bad. The MO said I needed a couple of stitches but I'll be fine.'

'Good. We're going to have to stay overnight because I'm not going anywhere until the weather clears and I've asked the ground crew to fix any damage to that door.' He shuffled his feet, and Ruby wondered if he was going to apologise for standing her up. If that was his intention, he'd left it too long, for the MO returned, announcing there was an ambulance waiting to take Ruby to Sick Quarters.

'Take care of her,' Laurie said to the MO then, turning to her, he added, 'I need to sort out our billets. I'll come and find you in Sick Quarters when I know where we're staying.'

Ruby followed the doctor to the ambulance feeling half relieved and half disappointed that there had been no mention of the dance.

An hour later, Ruby was feeling much better. The MO had stitched her wound and then let her rest on the bed in the treatment room while she waited for Laurie. A short while later, a nursing orderly arrived with a steaming mug of tea and a rock cake.

'Fresh from the NAAFI van,' the nursing orderly told her. 'We thought you'd earned it after all you've been through.'

She had just finished the rock cake when Laurie arrived. 'The station CO's arranged for us to stay at a nearby farmhouse,' he told her. 'You'll be sharing with a group of land girls.' After a pause he added in a lower voice, 'I hope you don't mind about last night.'

Maybe the old Ruby would have told him to forget it, hating the thought of conflict. But today she had flown through a storm and saved a patient's life. She was done with being afraid, and especially done with being afraid to speak her mind. 'I do mind, actually. I waited for ages. Why didn't you let me know if you couldn't make it?'

'I did!' Laurie was so indignant, Ruby had no doubt he was telling the truth. 'I sent a message.'

'I didn't get it.'

Laurie shook his head. 'I don't understand. I wrote a note and gave it to Bobby.'

'Well, she didn't give it to me.' And if he was going to break a date, why did he have to send a message through Bobby of all people?

'Oh. Well, I'm going to have words with her when we get back. But then I need to apologise to you. I'm really sorry I couldn't make it, and I'm doubly sorry I left you hanging around.'

Ruby still wasn't happy with his apology. He hadn't offered a reason and if he was going to stand her up with no or little notice, she didn't want to go out with him any more, no matter how much it hurt to think of breaking up with him. If there had been more time, she would have asked for an explanation but a WAAF driver arrived to take them to their billets. They went to join the others in the car and Ruby was given the seat beside the driver while the men crammed into the back seat.

The farmhouse turned out to be a large redbrick building with a higgledy-piggledy roof and looked as though successive generations had added to the original building. A young woman with flyaway fair hair, wearing overalls and wellington boots, strode into the farmyard to greet them.

'I'm Mrs Oldthwaite,' she said. 'Come along into the kitchen.'

Soon they were sitting round an enormous oak table that was so scratched and dented it looked like it had been in use for centuries. A large copper saucepan stood upon a cast-iron range from which a divine savoury scent was rising. Ruby's stomach rumbled. She hadn't realised until then how hungry she felt.

'You're lucky I got the phone call telling me you were on your way before I'd finished serving lunch to the land girls, or those gannets would have polished off the lot. I managed to save you plenty.'

They were each presented with a brimming bowl full of vegetable soup and a slice of crusty brown bread.

Ruby had been through so much that day, it was hard to believe it was still only early afternoon. She tucked in with enthusiasm. 'This is heavenly,' she said. 'So much better than anything we're served at our canteen.'

'Maybe you should rethink your calling if you could eat like this as a land girl,' Laurie quipped.

The others laughed and so Ruby forced a chuckle even though she didn't feel it. Was he saying he wouldn't miss her if she left the WAAF? After the high of realising that she had handled an emergency as well as anyone, Laurie's comment left her feeling deflated.

'Well, you certainly wouldn't find yourself flying through a thunderstorm,' Mrs Oldthwaite remarked. 'I couldn't believe it when I heard what you'd been through.' She peered at the dressing on Ruby's forehead. 'And you were hurt, too.'

'We managed to avoid the storms but we got too close for comfort,' Laurie said. 'I thought we were doing well to avoid the first one, then another storm brewed out of nowhere, and I couldn't escape the turbulence.' He looked at Ruby. 'I'm sorry you got flung around. I feel awful that you hurt your head.'

Ruby would rather have had as heartfelt an apology for standing her up, but she supposed that was too much to ask for in front of the whole group. 'You couldn't help that. It's hardly your fault that there was an unexpected storm. I'm just glad you got us through in one piece. It was scary, though, and when the door flew open it gave me a right shock.'

'I nearly peed my pants,' Rhys declared. And suddenly they were all laughing and talking nineteen to the dozen, their high spirits dispelling the lingering effects of shock.

It was mid-afternoon by the time they finished their meal, and Ruby would have liked to go for a walk to stretch her legs. However the tail end of the storm had now arrived, and rain lashed down the window panes. Mrs Oldthwaite had work to get on with but she showed the crew to their rooms – Ruby would be sharing with two land girls, who were still out working in the fields, and the men were to sleep in the playroom upon truckle beds.

'I would give you our sons' room,' Mrs Oldthwaite told the men, looking troubled, 'only they sleep in bunk beds and I doubt you'd fit.'

'This is far more than we could expect at such short notice,' Laurie assured her. 'I thought we'd have to sleep in a barn.'

'It's very kind of you to say so, but it goes against the grain to put you up on camp beds after all you RAF boys have done for us.' Mrs Oldthwaite brushed the hair from her eyes. 'Well, I'll just fetch the sheets and make up your beds, then I'll leave you to it.'

'We can make our beds. It's one of the first things we learn in the RAF. I know you must be busy. Please don't put yourself to any more trouble.'

'Well, I *do* have a lot to get on with. If you're sure?'

'We are,' Ruby told her.

Some of their hostess's worry lines eased. 'Well, I don't mind admitting that would be a big help. Oh' – she looked them up and down – 'I don't suppose you have any night things. I'll see what I can rummage up.'

She disappeared and returned a short while later with an armful of bedding, a faded floral nightdress for Ruby and three shapeless nightshirts that looked like they had been made in Victorian times. 'They used to belong to my husband's grandfather. We inherited the farm from him, and I never felt quite right throwing away his things. Bill – that's my husband – won't touch them, though.'

Ruby could see why. It was exactly the kind of nightwear she pictured Ebenezer Scrooge wearing. The only things missing were the pointed night caps. She took her bedding and the nightgown and made a bolt for her room before she burst into laughter.

As she tucked a sheet around the thin mattress on her camp bed, she heard Mrs Oldthwaite's parting words. 'We have high tea at six in the kitchen. Feel free to come and go as you please – we don't lock the doors around here. We usually sit in the kitchen of an evening, and you're welcome to join us. That's where we keep the wireless. The Dog and Duck is a fifteen-minute walk across the fields, and they'll give you a good welcome. If any of you want a bit of peace and quiet after the day you've had, you're welcome to sit in the parlour. We don't tend to use it, so you won't be disturbed. There's a gramophone in there.'

Ruby finished making her bed and tucked the nightdress under the pillow. Now she was alone she finally allowed herself to think of what Laurie had told her. He had sent a note via Bobby? Something inside her shrivelled at the prospect of having to challenge Bobby about it. It had been Bobby who had told her that she had seen Laurie at the pub with Adam, so why hadn't she handed over the note? It wasn't as if Bobby could be jealous of Ruby and Laurie, for she was always going on about her fiancé. Yet while Bobby could be annoying and was undeniably spoiled, she had never struck Ruby as having the kind of nasty streak one would need to deliberately withhold a letter and put Ruby through the humiliation of being stood up.

She decided to forget about Bobby's involvement for now. There was still the fact that Laurie had now cancelled a date twice. As much as she liked him, she didn't know if she could continue going out with him if she couldn't rely on him, family problems or not. The question was, should she simply turn him down if he asked her out again and leave it at that or did she want to try again? Could she risk her heart, risk being treated the way Dr Flint had treated her?

The twist in her chest told her she was already falling for him and, deep down, she knew he was nothing like Dr

Flint. But she also knew she didn't want to lose her heart to a man who was going to be unreliable. If she wanted a relationship with Laurie, she needed to challenge him about why he continued to back out of dates. Even if Bobby had delivered the note, it still wasn't good enough. Either Laurie let her in or she would protect her heart and break it off now.

She smoothed down the blankets with a heavy heart. She hated conflict, had always found it difficult to speak up for herself, but if there was any hope of an equal relationship with Laurie, she had to learn to speak her mind. Could she face it?

She straightened. Of course she could. She had faced her deepest fear today and triumphed. If she could save a man from bleeding to death while being flung about by a violent storm, surely there shouldn't be a problem giving voice to the words on her heart.

Chapter Fifteen

Hearing the heavy tread of the men's boots on the stairs, she prepared to follow them down. A quick glance in the mirror revealed her pale face with a bruise blossoming around the dressing. Her hair was a mess, not surprising considering she hadn't given it a thought since being flung around the cabin. She removed the grips and combed her fingers through it, wishing she had some lipstick to make her look more presentable. Then again, she had to spend the evening dressed in her unflattering slacks and jacket, so a bit of lipstick was neither here nor there. In future, she resolved to always pack a comb and emergency toiletries in case of an unexpected overnight stay.

Finally, satisfied she looked as good as possible in the circumstances, she made her way downstairs to where a grandfather clock stood in the hall, noting the passing seconds with ponderous tocks. Guided by the sound of masculine voices, she pushed open a solid oak door on the other side of the hall from the kitchen and found herself in the parlour. Sash windows on two sides of the room rattled in the wind and rain. The heavy clouds outside made the room dark but as her eyes adjusted she saw the three men gathered around a table. Rhys was shuffling a deck of cards.

'We're about to play a game of rummy. Want to join in?'

She shook her head, saying goodbye to any chance of having a quiet talk with Laurie, and retired to an armchair by the window. There was a stack of magazines on a small table nearby and, selecting an old issue of *Britannia and Eve* magazine, she settled down to make the most of an unexpected afternoon of leisure. Soon she had lost herself in a tale of intrigue at sea.

She was brought back to earth abruptly when Mrs Oldthwaite tapped on the door to let them know high tea was ready. They trooped into the kitchen to find it full with not just Mr and Mrs Oldthwaite and their two young boys but also three land girls. The table was spread with what looked like a sumptuous feast to Ruby's eyes: a selection of pies, salad dishes and a steaming loaf of freshly baked bread. 'My goodness! We must be eating you out of house and home, and we don't even have ration books.' Usually, if staying away on leave, they would be issued coupons to cover the period they would be away. But this unexpected overnight stay meant they were unable to compensate the Oldthwaites for the food they would be consuming. She glanced at her fellow crew members, who were clustered around the table, looking awkward. And hungry. 'Perhaps we should go into Doncaster and find a place to eat?' She was tired, hungry and her head throbbed, so a trip in the rain was the last thing she wanted, but it felt wrong to accept such lavish hospitality when rationing had tightened its grip on the country.

Mrs Oldthwaite waved away her concerns. 'Don't worry about it. We've billeted people from the base before now, and it's all in hand. Sit down and enjoy your meal. Besides,' she added with twinkling eyes, 'we've got a large kitchen garden and keep our own hens, so we're much better off than the poor folk in the cities. There's plenty to go around.'

Reassured, Ruby was soon tucking into the best meal she'd had in a long time. The men were the centre of attention, with the two young Oldthwaite boys pestering Laurie with all sorts of questions about flying, eager to know if he had piloted a Spitfire and whether he had flown in the Battle of Britain. Ruby didn't pay much attention to his replies because she was painfully aware of the land girls shooting Laurie covetous looks, making her quite jealous. Laurie didn't seem to notice, however, and the girls eventually transferred their regard to Rhys and Neil. Ruby was overlooked, but she didn't mind.

At the end of the meal, everyone helped to clear the table and wash up. When the last plate was stacked upon the dresser, one of the land girls looked at Laurie and said, 'The rain seems to be clearing. We're going to the Dog and Duck in a while. Fancy coming with us?'

'No thanks,' Laurie said. 'Got to keep a clear head for the flights tomorrow. The others might want to join you, though.'

The two other men both said they would like to go. Ruby, seeing her chance to finally get Laurie alone, declined, saying she was too tired. 'I'll sit in the parlour and read for a while,' she said with a glance at Laurie. 'Then I'll get an early night.'

'We'll try not to disturb you when we get back,' the land girl told her.

Ruby made her way back to the parlour, feeling distinctly jittery. Please let Laurie take the hint and join her. She picked up the magazine again but was unable to concentrate, and instead mentally rehearsed what she wanted to say. It was clear, logical and made it plain that she deserved a full explanation for why he had cancelled two dates with little notice. When she heard a step outside the door she thought her heart would leap from her chest and then the door opened and Laurie entered. She promptly forgot everything she had intended to say.

'What are the plans for tomorrow?' she asked, then kicked herself for not having the nerve to plunge in and demand an explanation.

'Oh, that's right, I forgot you were in Sick Quarters while we arranged everything.' Laurie dropped onto the sofa and propped his elbows on his knees. 'A driver's coming to collect us at eight tomorrow morning. The ground crew should have checked over the Ox-box by then, but I'll give it a once-over myself and then we'll take a look at the weather forecast.'

Ruby snorted, interrupting him. 'Fat lot that did for us today.'

'I know. But it's better than nothing. Usually. Anyway, if we're clear to fly, we'll arrange for an ambulance to fetch the patient and hopefully we'll get all the way to Shropshire this time without running into any storms. If all goes well, I aim to take off at 0930.' Laurie slipped into the military style of telling the time now he was talking of their schedule. 'It's only a short hop to Oswestry from here, so if all goes to plan we'll be back in Starsden in plenty of time for lunch. I telephoned Starsden while you were getting your head seen to, to let them know we wouldn't be back until tomorrow, so our duties have already been rearranged.'

'That's good. I was worried I'd be put on jankers for being out all night.'

There was a pause then, and Ruby gathered the courage to say what she had planned. 'We need to—'

'Ruby, I—'

They both stopped.

'Go on,' Laurie said.

Ruby was tempted to ask Laurie to have his say first, because now the moment had arrived she didn't trust herself to say what needed to be said. It would be so much easier if she just let Laurie apologise – for she was certain that was what he had begun to do – and then they could carry on as before.

Carry on as before? But that was exactly what Ruby needed to avoid. Doing her best to remember the exact words she had mentally rehearsed, she drew a breath and said, 'I need to explain why I've been avoiding you today.'

'I thought it was because you were cross with me for standing you up.'

'I was. I *am*.'

'But I explained. I don't know why Bobby didn't give you my note, but—'

'I know. It's not that. Please,' she added when Laurie looked like he was about to speak again, 'let me have my say. I promise I'll hear you out when I've finished but I've got to get this out before I get all muddled.'

Laurie nodded and she took a moment to gather her thoughts. 'Of course I wouldn't have been so upset had Bobby handed me the note,' she said at last. 'A lot of the reason I was so upset was because I was left hanging around outside, feeling like a prize chump. It was humiliating. I even went to the Red Lion in case I'd misunderstood and you were waiting for me there.'

Her voice shook as the embarrassment and humiliation came rushing back, forcing her to pause and swallow, fighting tears. Great. This was not how she had seen it going. She expected Laurie to leap to his defence but to his credit he remained silent, his face a picture of concern.

Once she had her voice under control, she tried again. 'That's not what this is about, though. Not really. You see, before I joined the WAAF I was a student nurse and there was this doctor who stood me up several times. He always had a reasonable excuse and it wasn't until I caught him out that I saw that he was just toying with me for his own amusement. I know you're nothing like him,' she hastened to explain, not wanting Laurie to think that she was likening him to Dr Flint, 'but when I was left standing outside Poplar Court last night it brought back all those feelings. And the thing is, I really like you. I want to go out with you again, but I need to be able to trust you. And that means understanding why you keep cancelling our dates. If there's something wrong with Adam then I understand. Of course you have to put him first. But I also don't want to be treated like someone who can be dropped at short notice with no explanation.'

She stopped, out of breath. There was probably more that she should say if only she knew how to express the emotion churning within. But she was already annoyed with herself for not being able to explain herself as clearly as she would have liked and saying more would likely only confuse the issue even more.

'Thank you for hearing me out,' she said when she could speak. 'It's your turn now.'

—

Laurie had listened in growing horror while Ruby explained about the cruel doctor. How could anyone treat another human being as though they had been put on this earth solely for their amusement? Worst of all, though, he couldn't bear that his treatment had brought back Ruby's pain. Now he wished he had taken Adam's advice and explained what was going on. In trying to protect his brother he had hurt Ruby, and he couldn't forgive himself for that.

It was time to make amends. 'You're right, Ruby. I've treated you badly and I'm really sorry. I will explain why

I keep cancelling on you, but I want you to know that it's not an excuse and I don't blame you for being angry and upset. All I can do is promise to treat you with more respect from now on. I should have told you this before. Adam said I could, but I was trying to protect him. I didn't mean to hurt you in the process, though. You see, Adam's been getting these letters.'

As he went on to explain about the poison pen letters he kept his gaze fixed on Ruby's face. Her expression grew steadily more outraged.

Finally she burst out, 'This is awful. Poor Adam! You should go to the police.' Then she clapped a hand over her mouth. 'Sorry. I shut you up and now I can't even hear you out in silence myself.'

He shook his head with a faint smile. 'It's all right. I'd just about finished anyway. And I would go to the police only Adam won't let me. He doesn't want to upset our parents.'

'I suppose that makes sense. I'd probably feel the same way.' Ruby's face was creased with distress. 'I can't believe someone would do such a horrible thing. Have you any idea who it is?'

'Not a clue. Everyone around Starsden knows Adam was in the army. They all saw him when he first came home, thin as a rail and looking like he'd be blown away in the slightest breeze. So for anyone to call him a coward is horrendous. Everyone knows that he's fought for his country and suffered for it.' As ever, when speaking of Adam's sacrifice he felt a twinge of shame. He was already feeling embarrassed at the attention lavished on him by the Oldthwaites' sons. They had treated him like a hero, had breathlessly asked if he had flown in the Battle of Britain. Although common sense told him not all pilots could have taken part, that some had been needed to protect Britain's fleet, it was always difficult to admit that he had been posted elsewhere.

'He must be feeling awful.'

'He is.' Laurie made an effort to forget his own feelings of inadequacy and focus on Ruby. If there was any way he could mend their relationship, he was determined to try. 'That's why I took him out for a bike ride that day. He looked haunted and I thought a change and some fresh air would do him good. He needed to spend the day somewhere he knew he wasn't going to get another letter.'

'I do understand.' She touched his sleeve. 'Thank you for trusting me.'

He dared to place a hand over hers and his heart skipped when she didn't pull away. 'I didn't mean to turn this into a discussion about Adam, no matter how much this business is weighing on my mind.'

'But it's part and parcel of what happened.'

'I know. And that's why I told you about the letters. Yet the important thing right now is that you understand how much you've come to mean to me.' He swallowed. He was unused to giving voice to his emotions. He was a firm believer in expecting people to work out how he felt from his actions. But he hated to think what Ruby's impressions of him would be judging from his behaviour so far. Her eyes were fixed on his, her lips pressed together not quite tightly enough to hide the faint quiver. It was time to tell her exactly how he felt so there were no further misunderstandings. 'I've never felt this way about anyone before and maybe that's why I'm making such a mess of it. But I'm sorry that the way I acted made you feel like you don't matter. Because you do matter. Very much. And although I can't promise not to drop everything if Adam needs me, I can promise that I'll do my best to tell you in person or, if that's not possible, to get the message to you via someone reliable.'

'Not Bobby, in other words.'

'Definitely not Bobby.' Thank goodness she was smiling.

She turned the hand he was covering palm up and entwined her fingers with his. Electricity fizzed through his flesh.

'I'm so glad you've explained. I was terribly confused, wondering if I had done anything wrong. The time we've spent together has been precious, and now I know why you had to cancel our dates I completely forgive you and I can be patient if you have to do it again. As long as you let me know why, of course.'

'Definitely.' Laurie's chest didn't feel big enough to contain his heart. She forgave him! She thought the time they had spent together was precious! He had hardly realised until now how heavily her distress had weighed on him until it was gone and now he felt giddy with relief. He tightened his grip upon her hand and then touched the bruise on her forehead with gentle fingers. 'I'm sorry about that, too. Does it hurt?'

She leaned her head against his shoulder. 'Not really. And don't go apologising for things beyond your control. The storm wasn't your fault. Unless you really are a Norse god.'

'A what?'

She sat up, her face flaming. 'I can't believe I said that. Please forget it.'

'Not likely.' He couldn't prevent a smile. 'You think I look like a Norse god?'

Her answer was muffled, coming as it did while speaking with her face buried in her hands. 'Nooo! Promise you'll never mention it again.'

'I don't know if I can.' He was enjoying himself immensely now. 'What with being a capricious Norse god.'

She peered up at him. 'You're never going to let me live this down, are you?'

'Well, that depends.'

'On?'

'On whether you'll consider coming into London with me on Thursday. You do have the day off then, don't you?' He tried not to look like he had memorised her schedule.

The embarrassment faded from her face. 'I'd love to. As long as you're sure Adam won't need you.'

'One of his army friends is home on leave, and his family lives in Devon. He invited Adam to stay for the week, so Dad's given him the time off. No chance of any letters reaching him there.'

'Good. Then that's settled. We'll spend Thursday in London.' To Laurie's joy, she snuggled against him. 'I'm so glad we sorted this out.'

'Me too.'

They remained like that for a while, not speaking. Laurie hugged her closer and drank in the peace and quiet.

Then the door burst open and Rhys bounded in. Laurie and Ruby sprang apart.

'Oops, sorry!' Rhys said, looking not at all repentant. 'I was just going to let you know we're leaving for the pub, in case you'd changed your minds and decided to join us. But I guess you'd rather stay here. Alone.'

If Laurie hadn't been so happy he'd have been tempted to wipe Rhys's cheeky smile off his face. As it was, he just said, 'Run along!' as though he were speaking to a child who had asked permission to go out and play.

Rhys withdrew from the room only to lean back in and add, 'Oh, Mrs Oldthwaite asked me to let you know she'll be serving breakfast at seven.' And then he was gone.

Ruby had risen and was now studying the records stacked in the shelves beside the gramophone. 'Let's put on some music. What do you fancy?'

'Something soothing after the day we've had.'

'How about this?' Ruby pulled a record from its sleeve and placed it on the turntable. A moment later the mellow notes of Duke Ellington's 'Clarinet Lament' filled the room.

'Perfect.' He swung Ruby into his arms. 'I do owe you a dance, after all.'

She leaned into his embrace. 'I think you'll find you owe me several.'

Chapter Sixteen

Ruby would never have dreamed of being so brazen before, but maybe it was the relief at having faced up to Laurie and spelled out exactly why she had been hurt that gave her courage. That, and her joy at his admission that she meant a lot to him. She had been shocked and dismayed on Adam's behalf when Laurie had explained about the poison pen letters, and at least now she could understand why Laurie had needed to cancel their date, even if his choice of messenger had been questionable.

She rested her head against his shoulder, enjoying the comfort of his arms around her. No matter that the music didn't have the easiest rhythm for dancing, it felt good to be in his arms swaying on the spot. After the humiliation of the previous night, followed by the alarm of the storm and the emergency with her patient, she let the music wash over her. Gradually the tension of the day drifted away and all that mattered was the mellow clarinet and Laurie's fingers running up and down her spine.

When the music ended, inspired by her new-found courage, she raised herself onto tiptoe and pressed a kiss on his lips.

Then a thought struck and she giggled, drawing away slightly.

Laurie looked down at her with an intensity in his eyes that made her catch her breath. 'I hope you weren't laughing at my kissing technique.'

'I wouldn't dare! No, I was suddenly convinced that Rhys was going to burst in again.'

'I think we're safe but maybe we should play a game of cards in case one of the Oldthwaites decides to come in.'

A few minutes later they were absorbed in a game of two-player whist. At least, Laurie was absorbed. Ruby's thoughts kept drifting to the poison pen letters, and she missed winning a couple of easy tricks as a result.

Finally she flung down her cards. 'I'm sorry. I can't concentrate. I keep thinking about those awful letters. There must be a way of finding out who sent them.'

'I know. I thought the same. That's why I asked Adam to give me any more letters that arrive in case there's anything about the handwriting or paper that might give the writer away.'

'And?'

Laurie shook his head. 'Nothing really. For a start, the letters are very short, and although they're handwritten, they're written in block capitals, and I'm pretty sure the writer has taken pains to eliminate any individuality from his writing.'

'His? You think it's a man, then?'

'Sorry. Force of habit. It could be a man or a woman.' He rearranged the cards in his hand before adding, 'The only thing that stands out is the quality of the writing paper. It's much firmer than the flimsy stuff we get nowadays. So whoever is sending them must have a large stock of notepaper from before the war.'

'And they must be well off.' When Laurie raised an enquiring eyebrow, Ruby explained, 'It's someone who doesn't think twice about using expensive paper that you can't get for love nor money these days. If I had any notepaper like that, I would treasure it and only use it on special occasions. I certainly wouldn't waste it on a vicious poison pen letter.'

'That's true.' Laurie played a card.

Ruby, however, hadn't finished yet. 'Please let me help. I hate that Adam's going through this. I understand why he doesn't want to involve the police, but this is serious.' She had felt ill when Laurie had told her about the letter telling Adam he deserved to be hanged, and she burned with the injustice of it all. She left her cards face-down upon the table, refusing to resume the game until Laurie answered her.

Laurie made a helpless gesture and flung down his own cards with a sigh. 'What can you do? And I'm not suggesting that you have nothing to offer. It's just that I've been thinking about little else for weeks yet there is so little to go on.'

'Maybe not, but I can't bear to think of you going through this alone. Let me help.' Laurie was right, though. There *was* very little to go on. If she was to convince him that she could be useful, she needed to offer him a suggestion right now.

As she grappled for inspiration, the first glimmer of an idea formed in her mind. She hurried to speak before he could come up with an objection. 'Look, these letters are delivered by hand, so it must be someone living or working in the neighbourhood, right?'

'It makes sense.'

'Has it occurred to you that they might be sending them to others in the area?'

'I did wonder at first, but then the messages got so personal I thought the writer must be targeting him.'

'That doesn't necessarily mean he's not targeting others too.'

Laurie raked his fingers through his hair. 'Why didn't I think of that?'

She hastened to reassure him. 'Why would you? Your whole attention has been on Adam. But it's possible that others are getting letters too and, like you, not reporting them. You said yourself that Adam feels ashamed even though he has absolutely no reason to feel that way. Why wouldn't others feel the same?'

'You could be right, but if that's the case, how would we find out?'

'That's where I come in. I'm going to these fundraising meetings, remember?'

'Yes but I still don't see how that helps. You can hardly ask for a show of hands from anyone whose menfolk are receiving poison pen letters.'

'I can be more subtle than that. I'll think of a way. Oh, I know – I can pretend I've got a friend who's on sick leave and has been on the receiving end of the kind of comments that Adam got during the air raid. I don't have to mention letters at all, just see if anyone has a husband, son or brother going through the same thing.'

Laurie's face cleared. 'That might work. Then you could approach anyone with a similar story in private and sound them out about the poison pen letters.'

Ruby beamed at him, glad that they had a plan and also relieved that he wasn't throwing out any more objections to her help. 'Then I'll try that. And I promise not to mention Adam at all.'

'Good. Don't forget my mum goes to those meetings too, and Adam made me promise not to breathe a word to her or Dad. So if you're going to do this, I have to ask you to keep her from finding out.'

'I promise. But it would help if I could tell Holly and Meg.' She hoped he wouldn't object because she would find it difficult not to mention something so huge to her two best friends. 'They're out and about in Starsden a lot when they're off duty so I could recruit them to keep their eyes and ears open.'

Laurie drummed his fingers on the table in an obvious show of reluctance.

'I'll make them promise not to breathe a word to anyone. They're completely trustworthy. I've known them for ages.'

'Fine,' Laurie said eventually. 'As long as you can be sure they won't mention it to anyone else.'

'They won't.'

'It's not that I don't trust them,' Laurie said. 'It's more that...' His eyes slid out of focus and he seemed to be holding an inner debate. 'Oh well, in for a penny, in for a pound,' he said finally. 'You see, I rather suspect Adam has a crush on Holly. He'd probably be horrified if he knew she'd found out about the letters.'

Ruby stared at him in surprise. 'I had no idea.' She thought back to the few times she had seen Adam and Holly together. In retrospect, maybe Adam had paid more attention to Holly than to her or Meg. And of course Laurie knew his brother so much better than she did, making him more likely to notice any partiality. 'Holly hasn't said anything about it, though. She often mentions a man she met before she joined the WAAF and they're still writing to each other, so I don't think Adam stands much of a chance, I'm afraid.'

Laurie pulled a face. 'Perhaps I'd better mention this man to Adam. Before he gets hurt.'

'It might be a good idea. Oh dear, I hope he won't be too disappointed.'

'He'll be fine, I'm sure. To be honest, it's good to see him develop an interest in her. He was always going out with girls before the war, although I don't think he was ever in love. Hopefully his feelings for Holly aren't serious.'

And what about Laurie's feelings for her? Ruby wished she could ask. If his brother had enjoyed flirtations, was Laurie the same? Was what he felt for her nothing more to him than a pleasant way of passing the time? She didn't think so. When she had danced in his arms, she had sensed that his feelings for her ran deep. She wished she could have confessed that she felt she was falling in love with him. But he hadn't mentioned love. He had said she meant a great deal to him, and she had waited with bated breath for him to say more but he hadn't. Perhaps if Dr Flint's actions hadn't wounded her so deeply, she might have dared to confess her feelings but she just didn't trust Laurie enough yet. No, that wasn't quite right. It wasn't that she didn't trust Laurie but she didn't trust her own judgement. She had been taken in by a smooth-talking man once before, and could she really be sure she wasn't being taken for a ride again?

Chapter Seventeen

'So everything is all right again between you and Laurie? I'm so happy for you,' Meg said.

It was the following evening, and Ruby had finally been reunited with her friends after two blessedly uneventful flights, first to Oswestry and then back to Starsden. She had found Holly and Meg alone in their room, so she had curled up on her bed and told them her tale. They had listened wide-eyed while she had described the terror of how she had struggled to stem her patient's haemorrhage during the storm and they had applauded her handling of the crisis. When she had gone on to explain about the poison pen letters, they'd shared her outrage at the vitriol being directed towards a former soldier who had nearly lost his life at Dunkirk.

'I'm happy for me too,' she told Meg now with a soft smile. No need to mention the lingering shadow of mistrust. That was her problem and something she needed to work out herself. 'But now I can't stop thinking about the letters and what we can do to help.'

'It's hard to believe anyone would do such a thing,' Holly said, looking up from her task. She was sitting cross-legged on her bed with her best tunic spread upon her lap. She was polishing the brass buttons, using Silvo – the girls' favoured polish as they liked the silvery gleam that this gave to their buttons. The bottle of Silvo was open upon the chest of drawers, filling the room with its pungent smell. 'It must be someone not quite right in the head.'

Meg sat up straight, her eyes blazing. 'You're right.' She jabbed the air with one of her knitting needles to punctuate her pronouncement. 'And we've already seen someone like that. Someone who has lost everything.'

'Of course!' Holly cried. 'The woman who yelled at Adam during the air raid.'

Ruby looked from one to the other, certain they were right. 'I can't believe I didn't think of her before.'

'I dare say you had other things on your mind,' Holly said with a grin.

Ruby felt her cheeks redden. She and Laurie had never finished their game of whist, having abandoned it to play more music and dance. She had, indeed, quite forgotten about the letters in her happiness at being in Laurie's arms again. 'It just goes to show that I was right to ask Laurie to let the two of you into the case. We can ask about this woman when we're out and about in Starsden. Do either of you remember her name?'

'Jean,' Holly said. 'I never heard her surname.'

'I didn't hear her surname either but her first name was definitely Jean,' Meg said. 'I'd say she's our number one suspect.'

'On a list of one person,' Holly added.

'Maybe but it's a start.' Meg glared at Holly over her knitting. 'You can count on us, Ruby. We're in and out of Starsden most days and you know how the ladies in the tea rooms love to gossip. It should be easy to casually ask after this Jean character.'

'You're stars, both of you,' Ruby said. 'I can try getting into conversation with women at the fundraising meetings too. But remember just because Jean flew off the handle at

Adam it doesn't make her the poison pen writer. Keep open minds, both of you.'

'That's true,' Holly said. 'It could be anyone. Why, it could even be Bobby. She's always writing letters, and I bet she only ever uses the best notepaper. I mean, she claims to be writing to her fiancé, but who knows what she's really writing?'

The others laughed, and Ruby said, 'Admit it, you want it to be her in the hope of getting her transferred elsewhere so you can have her bed.'

'Maybe. But it's really unfair that she gets the one by the window.'

Ruby put her plan into practice the next day at the next fundraising meeting. Although there had been other meetings since the first one, she hadn't been able to attend them. As she was behind with the progress made by the other women, she was content to sit in silence through most of the meeting and catch up with what the others had achieved. She was pleased to find that the collection tins left in the local shops and businesses had already raised a fair amount and there seemed to be a good deal of interest in the proposed jumble sale and concert.

'I'm delighted to report that a choir from RAF Starsden has offered to take part in the concert,' Mrs Copeland said with a smile in Ruby's direction when the meeting turned to the concert. 'Sister Macintosh from the hospital has been in touch to inform us. Of course, we have Leading Aircraftwoman Morris here to thank for the interest the RAF base has taken in our fundraising efforts. Perhaps you'd like to update us on the progress you've made?'

'Oh, yes.' Ruby rose and gathered her thoughts. She had been so busy looking around the gathered women that she had quite forgotten that as representative of RAF Starsden, she would be required to make a report. 'Well, as Mrs Copeland has already mentioned, the choir are looking forward to taking part in the concert. I've also spoken to the lady in charge of the NAAFI and she has agreed to allow us to keep a collection tin there, so if you have one spare, I can drop it in after the meeting.' She went on to explain about the plans for the 'Carols in Summertime' event.

When she finished and sat down a murmur of approval rippled around the room.

'You've made wonderful progress,' Mrs Copeland said. 'And the date is perfect timing – the start of the autumn term is going to be an expensive time. I must congratulate you and ask you to pass on our thanks to all involved. We appreciate your support.'

As unprepared as she had been to make her report, Ruby was glad she had been called upon, for it meant several women approached her when they were enjoying refreshments after the meeting. As Laurie's mother was deep in conversation with Mrs Copeland, she was able to steer the conversation around to Adam's situation without drawing Mrs Foster's attention to it. After discussion with Holly and Meg, they had decided upon an approach they thought might draw out useful information.

'I must say,' she said, hoping her speech didn't sound too rehearsed, 'how friendly and welcoming everyone has been in Starsden. I've recently heard from a friend of mine from back home who's on sick leave. He was walking down the High Street when a woman stormed up to him and demanded to know why he wasn't fighting for his country.'

This elicited a general murmur of sympathy.

'Where is home for you?' asked a woman with her dark hair styled in a sleek bob. Ruby groped for her name and seemed to remember it was Mrs Cotton.

'High Wycombe,' Ruby replied. 'But—'

'Oh, I know Wycombe quite well,' another woman exclaimed. 'I have a cousin who lives there. On Suffield Road. Whereabouts do you live?'

'Kitchener Road,' Ruby replied. 'I—'

'Wycombe's ever so hilly, isn't it?' the woman said before Ruby could attempt to turn the conversation back to her imaginary friend. 'I always get exhausted going for walks with my cousin.'

'Yes, it is rather.' Ruby resigned herself to a conversation about her hometown. Hopefully later she would be able to get back to local attitudes about young men who weren't fighting.

Then another woman spoke up. 'I'm sorry about your friend,' she said. 'I heard about something similar around here. It happened the night the school was bombed, actually.'

'Oh?' Ruby said, her senses quivering. Surely this could only be the verbal attack on Adam.

The woman's next words confirmed it. 'Yes, my husband told me all about it. He was at the pub that night and apparently a woman flew into a rage at poor Adam Foster. That's our Mrs Foster's son,' she said with a jerk of the head towards Lettie, who, thankfully, was still deep in conversation and not looking their way.

'Yes, I heard about that too,' Mrs Cotton said. 'Dreadful business. Of course we locals all know what Adam Foster has been through, so it was shocking to hear how Mrs Basset singled him out. Although, of course, she's not from around here.'

'Mrs Basset?' Ruby asked hastily before the conversation could turn into a diatribe on outsiders. 'She's the woman who attacked Adam?'

'That's right. Mr Draper's sister.'

If Ruby hadn't been so intent on the story she would have been amused at Mrs Cotton's way of assuming Ruby knew everyone she was talking about. As it was, she just kept quiet and concentrated on every word, determined not to miss any vital information.

'Terrible, what happened to her.' Mrs Cotton shook her head sadly yet Ruby could also detect a ghoulish glee. 'She lost her whole family in the Blitz. Mr Draper brought her here to live but you can tell that the whole dreadful experience has affected her mind.'

'Yes, but I thought she was getting better,' put in the woman who had first mentioned Jean Basset's attack on Adam. 'Until the air raid, at any rate. She seemed to be taking more interest in life. Even started helping out with the WVS. I think hearing the planes and the bomb must have set her off.'

'Poor thing,' Mrs Cotton said. 'I hope she's all right.'

'I hope Adam Foster has got over that night too,' the first woman said. 'It can't have been pleasant.'

'Have you seen Mrs Basset since that night?'

'Once or twice,' Mrs Cotton replied. 'I saw her in the queue at the butcher's the other day but she was very quiet and didn't speak to anyone. I think she's embarrassed at her outburst.'

'Maybe I'll pop in for a visit tomorrow,' the first woman said. She seemed to be a little kinder than Mrs Cotton – more concerned about the people involved and less taken up with the sensation of spreading shocking news. 'Let her know nobody blames her for being frightened. I dare say

I'd fly off the handle at the drop of a hat if I'd been through what she has.'

The conversation moved on, inexplicably, to the Duchess of Kent's new baby. Ruby murmured an excuse and drifted to a new group. By the time the meeting broke up, she had mentioned her fictional friend to all the women she had managed to speak to, and the conversation had inevitably moved to Jean Basset's verbal attack on Adam. She had studied everyone carefully as they had aired their opinions and, as far as she could tell, there was general sympathy expressed for both Mrs Basset and for Adam.

'Unless the Poison Pen is an incredibly talented actor, I don't think it's any of them,' Ruby said to Meg and Holly when she met them in the NAAFI that evening. She had related all the conversations in minute detail, confident that she wouldn't be overheard over the rattle of crockery and the general hum of conversation. 'No one seemed to agree with what Jean Basset said.'

'That does make Mrs Basset the most likely candidate,' Meg observed.

'I agree. I feel sorry for her, though.' Ruby propped her elbows on the table and thought back over everything she had heard. 'I can't begin to imagine what losing your whole family must do to you. Apparently the bomb shelter she and her children were in had been hit. She survived but her children were with their friends at the other end of the shelter, which was the side that collapsed. Then when she went home she found that had been destroyed too, so she even lost the photographs she had of them. I think it's amazing she's sane at all.'

'What should we do about her, though?' Meg persisted. 'If she sent the letters, I mean.'

Ruby thought about it. 'I suppose the first thing to do is to prove she really did send them.'

'How?'

'By catching her in the act.'

Chapter Eighteen

It was one thing to decide to catch Jean Basset in the act of sending a letter, quite another to actually do it. Ruby, Holly and Meg discussed it from all angles but failed to arrive at a workable plan. The main problem was that they had no idea what time the letters usually arrived. They also didn't know where Jean Basset lived, scuppering Holly's idea of lurking outside her house and following her when she emerged. Yet even had they known, there was a bigger problem. They were on duty for long hours and only had limited time to carry out their plan.

So far Ruby had resisted Holly's suggestion of them requesting a precious forty-eight-hour pass and using the time to stake out Starsden for the Poison Pen. She was nursing the idea of taking leave at the same time as Laurie and taking him to Wycombe to meet her parents and didn't want to waste her precious leave by spending it in the same place where she'd been working for weeks. However, she was still wary that her relationship with Laurie was in its early days and didn't feel ready to make such a suggestion.

In the meantime, she was looking forward to their day out in London. She had only seen him once since their last date and that was at the first singing practice. He had shot her an encouraging smile when she had stood in front of the group with trembling knees to explain about the

'Carols in Summertime' fundraiser and then given her an enthusiastic thumbs up when she gratefully handed over to the choir leader. After that, they had stood in separate sections of the choir – her with the sopranos and Laurie with the tenors – and hadn't had a chance to speak before the end of the practice. Their respective duties since then meant they hadn't had a chance to meet. So frustrating, especially considering her growing dread that he would stand her up again. Even though she understood that if he did it would be because Adam needed him, she wished he would put her first just once. She hated feeling that way but couldn't seem to stop herself.

The day of their trip dawned. By this time she had become so convinced that Laurie would find an excuse not to go that she didn't take any extra care with her appearance that morning. She simply rolled her hair around a ribbon to keep it off her collar and wore her usual dusky rose lipstick.

She left Poplar Court at the appointed time, sure he wouldn't be there, and so although she was disappointed, she wasn't surprised to find the porch unoccupied.

'Morning, Ruby.'

She jumped then her heart set off at a gallop when Laurie's handsome face peered at her from around the corner.

'It's such a beautiful morning, I thought I'd wait out here. Are you ready to go?'

It *was* a beautiful morning. It was a spectacular morning. Until now Ruby had never noticed what a wonderful place Starsden was. She had never looked beyond the somewhat dingy shopfronts and rows of brick houses and seen the way the sunlight sparkled upon the windows and heard the sweet chattering of the sparrows that flocked in the gardens.

Laurie offered her his hand, and when she took it, she felt a jolt like an electric shock zip through her flesh. She was almost ready to forget her lingering misgivings. Almost.

'How's Bentley?' she asked, saying the first thing that came into her head to distract from her confused feelings. 'Did he cope all right without you when we had to stay in Yorkshire?'

'He's fine. Squadron Leader Norton took care of him. He doesn't like to admit it, but he's just as fond of Bentley as everyone else.'

Talk of their mascot helped Ruby relax, and soon she was able to forget her doubts and chatter away as easily as ever. They took the Underground to central London, emerging at Piccadilly because Ruby expressed a desire to see the famous street.

'I can't believe you grew up so close to London yet never visited,' Laurie remarked as they strolled hand in hand past renowned shops such as Fortnum & Mason and Hatchards. It didn't matter to her that there were sandbags piled around the windows and the offerings on display were depleted thanks to rationing and paper shortages. She was finally walking down the street that she had longed to see for as long as she could remember.

'My mum and dad both worked so hard there was never much time for days out. And my dad works in a furniture factory so when he has time off he prefers to breathe the clean air in the woods and hills rather than going into a smoky town like London. If we wanted to go to a city we would always go to Oxford. That's why it made sense for me to do my nursing training in Oxford instead of London, because I was nervous of going to a city that I didn't know at all.'

'Tell me about Wycombe. I've never been there.'

'The town itself is nothing special, although I love it because it's home. But it's surrounded by beautiful hills and woods which are within easy reach. From where I live, it's only a short walk to Tom Burt's Hill, and from the top you can see along the valley all the way to West Wycombe.' As they continued their walk, she told him all about West Wycombe with its caves and shocking tales of the Hellfire Club.

'It sounds like a wonderful place to visit.'

'Oh, it is.' *Stop being a chicken and ask him to visit!* But something held her back and she couldn't get the words past her suddenly tight throat.

Then the road opened out and they were in Piccadilly Circus. In the centre boards were arranged in a rough cylinder around the plinth where the famous statue of Eros had stood in happier times. Now all that could be seen were posters urging her to buy war bonds.

'So here we are at the magical Piccadilly Circus.' If Laurie was disappointed not to get an invitation to meet her parents, he didn't show it. 'What do you think?'

'It's still magical, even without the lights and statue.' It was magical because she was here with Laurie. Why couldn't she tell him that?

Perhaps he understood anyway because he squeezed her hand. 'I hope we can come back here together when the war's over and everything's back to normal. You should see it at Christmas. There's nothing quite like it. It's a spectacular sight.'

A strange fluttering started in her chest. She tried to speak but no words would come out so she gave a vigorous nod of the head instead. He must be serious if he could speak of still being together after the war.

But then she remembered Dr Flint and the way he had always hinted at feelings and a future together without ever putting them into words that could be construed as a promise. Some of the joy faded from the day.

Her stomach chose that moment to give a loud gurgle, reminding her it had been a long time since breakfast. 'Oops. Sorry!' She clutched her stomach, feeling her face flaming.

Laurie laughed. 'I was about to ask what you wanted to do next, but I think we should eat. Let's go to the Lyons Corner House. My treat.'

Possibly her rumbling stomach saved the day, for the tightly wound tension snapped, and she found herself laughing back. 'Sounds like a good idea.'

It's still early days, she told herself as they headed for the corner house. *Just because I've met Laurie's family, it doesn't mean he's expecting to be introduced to mine. I've only met the Fosters because they live so close. And it's too soon for Laurie to speak about love.*

She'd almost managed to persuade herself of that by the time she was handed a large bowl of vegetable soup accompanied by bread and butter.

As they ate, she told Laurie what she had discovered about Jean Basset. 'Do you think she might be the Poison Pen?' she asked finally.

—

Laurie put down his spoon and gazed at Ruby in amazement. 'I can't believe I didn't think of her. It would certainly make sense. I wish I'd thought of her before.'

Ruby's eyes shone. They had been shown to a table in the window with Coventry Street spread out below them. The view was wasted on Laurie, though, for he couldn't drag his gaze from Ruby's beautiful face. He found himself fascinated with the curve of her cheeks, the shadow of her long lashes sweeping across them. Even the healed scar and fading bruise seemed impossibly attractive on her. He was overcome with a sudden urge to lean across the table and kiss it better.

Only belatedly did it dawn on him that she had spoken and was waiting for a reply. 'I'm sorry, I was miles away. What did you say?'

'I was saying that Holly, Meg and I were talking it over and we realised we need more information before we can come up with a plan of action.'

'What information?'

Ruby sat a little straighter. 'For a start, do you know what time the letters are delivered? I remember you saying they were delivered by hand. It might help if we could see the Poison Pen was following a routine.'

'We've been thinking along the same lines. The letters have been delivered to the shop. The trouble is, we don't know exactly when they've been arriving because Adam has always found them when he arrives at the shop or when he collects the post and finds a letter for him at the bottom of the pile. So all we know is they are being delivered some time after the shop closes in the evening but before the post is delivered in the morning, at around eight thirty.' He forced himself to concentrate on the conversation and stop trying to think about how much he would enjoy kissing her. He was more than grateful that Ruby had taken Adam's plight to heart and that her friends were also eager to help. With the four of them working together, plus anything Adam himself could discover, of course, they were bound to uncover the culprit.

'What do you think about Jean Basset, then?' Ruby asked.

'I agree she seems the most likely person. She's lost so much, and I have nothing but sympathy for her. If it is her, I'm glad Adam wouldn't let me go to the police. Whatever we do, I want to make sure she gets whatever help she needs. But I do want her to stop her campaign against Adam. It's wearing him down.'

'When did you last see him?'

'Yesterday evening. He hasn't had any more letters, thank goodness, but I can tell the ones he's had have been preying on his mind. He knows he's not fit enough to fight any more but I can see he feels guilty all the same. I—'

He stopped himself just in time. He had been poised to blurt out his feelings about flying an air ambulance when other pilots were risking their lives flying dangerous missions over Europe. There was no way he was going to burden Ruby with that. 'I wish I could get through to him that he's already done more than enough,' he said instead.

Ruby nodded, looking thoughtful. There was silence while they finished their soup before it went cold.

Laurie's thoughts drifted back to the moment when they had stood in Piccadilly Circus. Ruby had gazed around, her eyes alight, and even though he had seen it many times before, he found he was seeing it through her eyes, drinking in the sights and sounds, gazing up at the tall buildings surrounding them on all sides. Even a poster advertising shoes had looked exciting and exotic when viewed in that frame of mind. He had felt an urge then to tell her that he was falling in love with her but something had held him back. It was something to do with what the Oldthwaites' sons had said when they had bombarded him with questions. When they had found out he was a pilot, they had been full of all they had read about fighter and bomber pilots. They had wanted to know how many enemy aircraft he had shot down and whether he had flown into Germany. While they had listened with rapt attention while he had described some of the dogfights from his Coastal Command days, he had sensed their disappointment when he had explained that the farthest he had flown recently was to Orkney.

He was being ridiculous, he knew. Yet he couldn't completely silence the voice that told him that Ruby would only stay with him until someone more deserving came along. And so he protected his heart by not revealing the full depth of his feelings. Because when she left him, he didn't want her to pity him for his love being unrequited.

—

The happiness of the London trip still enveloped Ruby like a cosy shawl when she made her way to the crew room the following morning. The sky was clear blue, and the early morning sun bathed everything in a golden glow. Even the sparrows seemed to have picked up on Ruby's mood, for they sang their hearts out as they fluttered among the hedgerows. Nothing could happen to spoil her joy, especially when she learned that Laurie would be her pilot that day.

When he entered the crew room he shot her a smile that set her pulse hammering then addressed the whole crew. 'Get your gear. We're picking up a patient from RAF Harrowbeer. He's going to the Royal National Orthopaedic Hospital in Stanmore for specialist treatment.'

It didn't take Ruby long to gather her jacket, boots and bag. She had only refilled her medical bag the day before but even so she gave it one last check to make sure there were no missing supplies. While they waited for the navigator to return with his charts and the latest weather forecast, Laurie sat beside her. 'Will you be all right today?'

She knew what he meant. This was her first flight since the horrific flight through the storm. 'I'll be fine.' She touched her forehead with a rueful smile. While the bruise had now faded to yellow, she was still a little self-conscious of the injury, even though she'd now had her stitches removed. The nurse who had done it had assured her the scar would quickly fade. 'Anyway, don't they say it's best to get back on the horse as soon as possible?'

Someone up there seemed to be testing her to her limit, though, for her new patient was a disturbingly similar case to Flight Sergeant Jim Kerry. Flying Officer Tomáš Pavel had survived a crash landing, and Ruby winced as the ambulance driver recited his list of injuries. It would be quicker to say which bones hadn't been broken. Just like Jim Kerry, there were compound fractures which had already been stabilised in surgery. He had been sedated for the flight and Ruby hoped for his sake that he would remain unconscious for any movement would be agony.

When Laurie came to help carry the stretcher into the Oxford, he shot her an enquiring glance. She gave him a smile and a nod. How had she ever doubted him? It was obvious he cared for her.

The glow of happiness persisted through takeoff and as Ruby saw to her patient. She busied herself checking the oxygen flow and ensuring the patient's dressings remained free of fresh blood.

Rhys grinned at her from his post at the wireless set. 'I can't believe you're taking this in your stride so soon after the storm.'

Two weeks ago she wouldn't have believed it either, but now she could treat Flying Officer Pavel without a qualm.

'It's strange,' she said, 'but I did so many flights dreading the worst. Yet when it happened, I was too busy doing my job to give the fear a chance to take hold. Now I've been through that, I know I can face anything. Still' – she grinned back at him – 'I'll be happy if I never have to face anything like that again.' Although Rhys had been talking about taking another flight so soon after her injury, Ruby was thinking of her fear of harming a patient. Flying through a storm with a haemorrhaging patient had been a baptism of fire but considering she and her patient had survived, she was glad it had happened. She would never again fear the responsibility of her job.

They were still about twenty minutes away from Starsden – the ambulance would drive the patient to the Royal National Orthopaedic Hospital in Stanmore from there – when Flying Officer Pavel stirred. His face creased in pain, and when Ruby took his hand and spoke to him in soothing tones, he gripped her fingers painfully.

'You're in the air ambulance,' she told him. 'Not long before we land.' She gently extricated her hand from his grip. 'I'll give you some morphine. You'll feel better soon.'

Thanks to the meticulous organisation of her medical bag, she could put her hand straight on one of the morphine syrettes. She had practised this many times during training yet this was the first time she would be using this on a real patient. There was no fear, however, and the instructions she had memorised came to her as clearly as if she had Sister Macintosh beside her, talking her through each step. First she counted Pavel's respirations. *Never administer morphine if they are breathing under twelve times a minute.* Then she removed the cap and pushed down the wire ring at the top of a length of wire that was threaded through the hollow needle. Once she felt the wire break through the tube's seal, she pulled it out. Now for the injection itself.

'Just a tiny scratch,' she said, positioning the needle at a shallow angle to the man's upper arm. Without giving herself a chance to question if she was doing it correctly, she pushed in the needle and squeezed the tube to deliver the drug. Thankfully the Oxford didn't hit any turbulence, and the injection was over in an instant.

'All done,' she said. 'You'll feel better soon.'

She took Pavel's hand again. It took about twenty minutes for the morphine to start working, so although it would help him through the landing and the short ambulance ride, she would need to help him endure the rest of the flight. 'The ambulance driver told me you're from Czechoslovakia,' she said.

A slight nod. 'Are best pilots,' Pavel said, and his pain couldn't erase all the pride from his voice.

'Tell me about your home.'

'I am from Znojmo. Is very beautiful.' And in a voice that grew increasingly slurred, he spoke of a high castle, of a river winding through a valley far below and of slopes lined with vineyards. He finally drifted to sleep as they circled around Starsden.

'How do you feel now?' Laurie asked once they had seen their patient safely loaded into the waiting ambulance.

'Even better than before.' Ruby couldn't seem to stop smiling. If she'd had any lingering doubts about her ability as a medic, they were well and truly gone. The incident with Jim Kerry hadn't been a fluke. She'd done all the right things and helped another patient through his distress. And to cap it all, she had no more doubts about Laurie.

She drew a deep breath. She had hesitated before but she couldn't hold back now. 'In fact, there's something I've been meaning to ask. Would you like to come to Wycombe with me? My parents would love to meet you.'

Chapter Nineteen

'What did he say?' Meg bounced in her armchair, eyes shining. It was evening, and Ruby was with her friends in the common room. She had told them all about the flight, concluding with her asking Laurie to visit Wycombe with her.

'He said yes! Can you believe it?'

'Course we can. He was never going to say no to you.'

'He thinks the world of you,' Holly put in, then added, 'I find it harder to believe that you invited Laurie to come away with you. You brazen hussy!' But she was laughing.

'I know. If you'd told me a week ago I'd do that, I'd have laughed in your face. But it was like everything had gone right on the flight and I was just overcome by confidence.'

'Well, it suits you,' Holly told her. 'I've always thought you should have more faith in yourself.'

'So you two are getting serious then?' Meg asked.

'Yes. I think so. Everything feels... right.' She'd finally put all her doubts about Laurie behind her.

A thought struck, and she glanced at Holly. 'You don't mind, do you?' For as Holly had no family to speak of, besides an aunt and uncle that she loathed, she usually arranged to take leave at the same time as Holly and invited her to stay with her parents. Meg would have done the same but as her parents had a houseful, there wasn't room for a friend.

'It's fine. Anyway, I'm sure your parents will be wanting to meet Laurie. You've talked about him enough in your letters.'

Ruby grimaced. That was certainly true. No matter how much she tried to tell herself it was early days with Laurie, she found she mentioned him in just about every paragraph she wrote to her parents. It didn't help that he was one of the air ambulance pilots so even when she wrote of her work more often than not he was involved. She wouldn't be surprised if her parents were expecting her to announce their engagement at any day. Perhaps when they met him they would realise they hadn't been stepping out for long.

'Anyway, you must be looking forward to showing him around.'

'I really am.' Ruby drifted into a blissful world filled with walks through the beech woods hand in hand with Laurie.

Her daydreams were interrupted by Meg saying, 'Are you sure he won't back out at the last moment? He did stand you up before.'

'I'm sure. He already explained that, remember?'

'Yes, but what if Adam gets another one of those letters?'

Holly leaned forward. 'It's up to us to stop that happening by catching the Poison Pen. We've got a pretty good idea who it is now, haven't we?'

'I suppose so. Laurie thought it was probably Jean Basset as well.' After a pause, Ruby admitted, 'Well, he didn't exactly say he thought it was her but he said he couldn't believe he hadn't considered her. That's practically the same thing.'

'Then if we keep an eye on her we're bound to see her delivering a letter sooner or later. It's worth a try, isn't it?'

'Absolutely.' Ruby tried to remember what she already knew about the Poison Pen. 'Laurie says the letters are delivered to the hardware shop between the time when the shop closes and the post arrives.'

Holly frowned. 'That's a big window.'

'We can probably cut it down, though,' Meg said. 'I doubt Mrs Basset would want to wander around alone in the blackout, so she would either deliver them between closing time and sunset or between sunrise and when the post arrives. Did Laurie mention what time the post usually arrives?'

'Around eight thirty. If she delivers the letters in the morning, it would have to be well before then. Before seven, I'd say. Otherwise there would be too many people out and about.' Would Mrs Basset realistically be able to leave the house that early? Ruby tapped her lips a few times while she pondered the question. 'I reckon she posts them in the evening. She's living with her brother, remember. Her mornings are bound to be busy with making the breakfast and getting ready for whatever she does during the day. I expect she has a job somewhere. Anyway, we know she sometimes goes out in the evening because she was at the pub that night.' She frowned at Holly. 'What are you thinking – that we should follow her around all evening? She'd be bound to spot us.'

'I don't know. I wondered about asking Laurie if he could get us into the shop after his dad and Adam have gone home.'

Ruby shook her head. 'I've never been in but I've passed it once or twice and it wouldn't work. The windows are boarded up, so while we might see when the letter arrives, we wouldn't see who had posted it. By the time we got the door open, the culprit would probably have blended in with the other passersby. It's on a busy street.'

Holly groaned. 'There goes a perfectly good plan. Do we really have to lurk around the streets of Starsden all night?'

'Maybe we won't have to. Do either of you know where Mrs Basset lives?' Meg asked. When the others shook their heads she said, 'Look, I'm not on duty until tomorrow afternoon. Mrs Basset must go to the shops so I'll have a wander around and if I spot her I'll follow her home. Once we know where she lives we can make a plan.'

Ruby and Holly were in the common room the following evening when Meg returned from her shift in the hospital.

'Did you see her?' Ruby asked.

When Meg nodded, they retired to a quiet corner where they wouldn't disturb the others in the common room who were all listening to the wireless.

'Come on, then,' Holly said. 'Spill the beans.'

'I was quite lucky really because I spotted her right away, going into the Cosy Nook Tea Rooms on the High Street. I followed her in and got a table at the back so I could keep an eye on her without it being obvious. I had to make a pot of tea last for ages! It's a good thing I thought to pay the bill in advance because she left quite suddenly, and I might have lost her if I hadn't been able to follow her out straight away.'

Ruby listened impatiently, wanting to hear if Meg had seen Mrs Basset do anything suspicious but Meg seemed to be enjoying being the centre of attention for once and drew out her tale.

'I managed to follow her around the shops although it was tricky. She queued at the bakery and the butcher, and of course it would have looked strange if I'd joined the line.'

Holly snorted. 'You'd have had a job explaining why you'd wanted to queue at the butchers for ages when you don't even have a ration book.'

'I know! But I went into the haberdashery and bought some darning yarn. I had to spend ages pretending to dither over the right shade. Anyway, even after I'd paid, I had to act like I was enraptured by a display of crochet hooks. It's a good thing Mrs Basset came out of the butcher's when she did because I was running out of things to look at, and the shop assistant was giving me some very peculiar looks.'

Ruby's patience ran out. 'Are you going to tell us where she lives before I die of old age?'

Meg grinned. 'If you had waited for just a few more seconds I was about to say that she went straight home after that. She lives at number 65 Midsummer Way.'

Ruby frowned. 'I don't know where that is.'

'That's the good bit. It's one of the roads bordering Ashgrove Park. And number 65 is directly opposite a park bench.'

Ruby caught on. 'So anyone wanting to keep watch on her house need only sit on the bench and pretend to be reading a newspaper until she comes out.' She thought about it. 'Still, it would probably be best for two of us to watch at a time. It might look odd for a WAAF to be sitting on a park bench in the evening all alone.'

They compared their off-duty hours and worked out that two of them would be able to work together every evening with the possible exception of Thursday. Ruby was free that evening but Meg was working at the hospital and Holly was on air ambulance duty.

'I'm sure I'll be back by then, if we're flying at all,' Holly said. 'But even if you have to start off alone, I can always join you later.'

'Wait. I thought of something. How will we know Jean Basset is at home when we get there? We can't possibly keep an eye on her all day, but what if she's out? She could be lurking near the shop to post the letter when she sees Adam and Mr Foster leave, then go home. Until we saw her arrive at the house, we wouldn't know she was out.'

'Lucky for us, I already thought of that.' Meg looked like the cat who had got the cream. 'When I saw her in the tearoom, I was worried I was following the wrong woman. I only saw her in that dim cellar, after all. So before I followed her out, I asked the waitress who she was. I didn't ask right out, of course. I asked if she was the woman who worked in the book shop because I wanted to ask if they had any books about nursing. The waitress said I must have the wrong woman because Mrs Basset works every afternoon at Dolcis shoes.'

'Nice work! So all we have to do is hover around Dolcis and keep watch on her from there.'

'I just hope we're in for a spell of sunny weather,' Meg commented. 'We'd look jolly strange sitting in the park in the rain.'

Fortunately the next day was the perfect summer's day, and there were plenty of people strolling around the High Street when Ruby and Meg arrived, even though the shops were closing up. In an attempt to look inconspicuous, they stationed themselves outside a jeweller's which was conveniently located opposite Dolcis and pretended to be admiring a selection of brooches while actually watching the shoe shop in the reflection.

'I hope she's there,' Meg muttered. 'I won't feel so pleased about my detecting abilities if it turns out today's her afternoon off.'

She needn't have worried. Only a few minutes later, Ruby grabbed Meg's arm and pointed at the reflection. There was Mrs Basset, leaving the shop with another woman. The two women chatted as they lowered the shutters with a rattle that could be heard across the street. Then they waved goodbye to each other and set off in different directions.

'Come on,' Ruby ordered. 'That's our cue.'

Careful to trail a good twenty yards behind, they followed Mrs Basset up the street. Ruby's heart thumped when she turned into George Street, where the ironmongery was located. 'You don't suppose she's going to post it now?' She quickened her pace.

But their quarry strode past Foster's Ironmongery without a glance.

Ruby tried not to feel too disappointed. 'I suppose it was too much to hope for.'

'I should have warned you that this is the quickest route to Midsummer Way,' Meg said. 'It would have been marvellous to catch her red-handed right at the start, though.'

Midsummer Way turned out to be a ten-minute walk. Ashgrove Park was little more than a glorified square, forming a rectangle bounded by four roads. At one end was a clump of ash trees, swaying in the light breeze. The rest of it had probably been dedicated to flower beds and pathways before the war, but it now housed an air raid shelter and allotments. The vegetable beds bustled with activity.

'I didn't think about the people working on the allotments.' Meg cast an uneasy glance at a man with his shirtsleeves rolled up who was pulling up weeds. He regarded the friends with frank admiration. 'There wasn't anyone working here when I came by yesterday. They might think it odd to see us hanging around. WAAFs don't usually come this way.'

'Let's just stick to our plan for now. Ah, she's gone inside.' For as Ruby had been speaking, Mrs Basset had gone through a gate and disappeared through a blue doorway. 'Where's that bench you mentioned?'

Meg led them across the road and into the park. They followed the path leading around the park's perimeter, heading for a line of benches. Other paths led to the shelter in the centre and a public lavatory.

'They'll be useful if we end up stuck here for a long time.' Ruby pointed to the lavatories.

Meg wrinkled her nose. 'Let's hope it doesn't come to that. I can smell them from here. Anyway, here's the bench. Oh.'

The bench was indeed opposite number 65, but the girls were obliged to sit with their backs to the house.

'I'm an idiot,' Meg groaned. 'I was so excited to see the bench, it didn't even occur to me that it faced the wrong way. But of course people wouldn't want to sit with their backs to the park. Now what are we going to do? It will look jolly suspicious if we keep twisting round to look at the house.'

'Hang on.' Ruby rummaged in her pocket. 'I've got my compact. Let's see if we can sort something out.' She pulled out her face powder and opened the lid, angling the mirror inside towards the street. 'Yes, this will do. I can see the door. If Mrs Basset leaves we won't miss her.'

Meg chuckled. 'Anyone looking at you will think you're the most vain woman that ever lived.'

'I can live with that as long as we stop her sending those letters. But look, if you open the newspaper, I can hide the mirror behind it.'

Meg unfolded the newspaper she had been carrying under her arm. After some trial and error, they managed to place the mirror so nobody would be able to see it unless they walked directly behind the bench. For some minutes they kept their gazes fixed on the house. Ruby was tense with expectation: Mrs Basset was bound to emerge at any moment. However, as the minutes became half an hour and then three-quarters of an hour, her enthusiasm waned.

'I know it was unrealistic to expect to catch her at it within minutes of seeing her, but I didn't fully grasp what we were letting ourselves in for until now,' she confessed.

'Same here,' Meg said. 'And even if we do follow her to the shop and see her posting a letter, what should we do – tackle her there and then?'

This was something else Ruby hadn't really considered. She swapped the mirror into her other hand, for her arm was aching, then continued to gaze at the stubbornly closed blue door. 'I don't think we should approach her,' she said eventually. 'I mean, I feel awful for her, for what she's been through. I don't think accusing her in the street is going to help. She needs to be treated with care.'

'Then what should we do?'

'Tell Laurie what we've seen and check that whatever she posted really was a poison pen letter. Remember she's innocent until proven guilty. For all we know, she might be posting an order for some new fifteen-amp fuses. If she really does turn out to be the culprit then we should leave it to Adam and Laurie to decide what to do. Adam's the one most affected, after all.'

'You're right. Anyway, I feel happier knowing we don't have to tackle her ourselves.'

The evening passed with agonising slowness. One by one the workers on the allotments picked up their tools and left, carrying baskets of produce. The sight of the fresh vegetables reminded Ruby painfully that she hadn't eaten yet. When the sun finally disappeared behind the houses, she rose stiffly. 'I don't think she's going anywhere tonight. Let's go to the chippy. I'm starving.'

Chapter Twenty

Ruby tried not to become discouraged after their first evening on watch. 'After all, we were unlikely to strike lucky on our very first time,' she said to Holly when they reported to her the next morning. 'We should think of last night as a trial run. We now know roughly what time she leaves the shoe shop and we also know we need to bring a mirror and newspaper.'

'And probably some knitting,' Meg put in with a wry smile. 'Be prepared for a dull night.'

Ruby and Holly endured a similarly disappointing watch that evening and by the time they returned, Ruby wasn't looking forward to a third evening spent on the hard park bench. The next day she had a long, tiring shift on the wards and trudged back to Poplar Court not at all enthusiastic about having to loiter on the High Street and then follow Mrs Basset all the way home. However, as the time approached for her to leave, she had a fresh worry, for Holly had not yet returned from her air ambulance duty. She had happened to be looking out of the window from her ward that morning and seen the Oxford take off so she knew Holly had been flying but she would have expected her back by now. Either she'd had a long journey, like Ruby's trip to Orkney, or the Oxford had been delayed by weather or a technical fault. Still, they had previously arranged that she should go alone if necessary so she set off for the High Street, hoping nothing serious had caused her friend's delay.

As before, she had no difficulty following Mrs Basset back to Midsummer Way. She took up her post on the bench, preparing herself for another long, dull watch. However, only about fifteen minutes had gone by when the blue door opened and Mrs Basset appeared. At last! Ruby's hand quivered, making the tiny reflection blur. She couldn't bear it if Mrs Basset was just putting out a note for the milkman. When her quarry walked through the gate and down the road towards the shops, Ruby could have cheered.

After hastily folding the newspaper under her arm, Ruby pocketed her compact and followed, every nerve in her body fizzing with excitement. Was she finally going to witness Jean Basset posting a letter at the ironmongery? She almost skipped along the road, her head filled with images of reporting the good news to Laurie. If she was lucky, he would be so pleased with her that he would take her in his arms and tell her how much he loved her.

It was therefore a nasty surprise when Jean didn't go down George Street and past the ironmongery but took a route that would bring her to a point lower down the High Street. Even so, she still didn't give up hope. Maybe Jean Basset simply wanted a bit of a walk and would circle round to George Street. But when she turned the wrong direction down the High Street and started walking out of Starsden in the direction of the base, Ruby had to admit that it didn't look like she was going to deliver a letter. Still, she wasn't going to give up now. Wherever Mrs Basset was going, she would have to return home before dark and maybe she would deliver the letter on the way back. She slowed down to increase the distance between them. There were fewer people out on the streets now, and if Mrs Basset turned she couldn't fail to notice her. However, she needn't have worried; the woman strode out with a purpose, never looking back.

When Ruby saw they were heading towards the Three Horseshoes an inkling of the truth dawned, which was confirmed when Mrs Basset went inside. She quickened her pace but then lingered outside, hesitating. For a start, Ruby wasn't in the habit of walking alone into a pub. What if there was no one she knew inside? The pub was a place you went to be with friends and she would stand out like a sore thumb sitting there alone. Maybe she could stand outside and pretend she was waiting for friends. There was a problem with this, however. For the pub had two entrances – the main one that Ruby and her friends always used and another one that led into a yard from which you could get to a different street. If Mrs Basset left that way, Ruby would never see her.

'Pull yourself together, Morris,' she muttered and opened the door.

Her courage wavered when the noise from the public bar hit her. What if Mrs Basset was in there? Going into the snug alone was bad enough, let alone the rowdy public bar. It was a relief when she glanced in and saw a sea of blue uniforms and not a woman in sight. Feeling somewhat better but still nervous, she walked through to the snug. She could only pray that she recognised someone there who wouldn't object to her intruding on them because she didn't feel brave enough to stay on her own. It really wasn't the done thing for a woman to go to the pub alone, and she wondered why Mrs Basset had done so.

She saw her quarry straight away. She was sitting at a table with a man in RAF uniform. Ruby vaguely recognised him as someone she had seen around the base but as he wasn't anything to do with the air ambulance or the hospital, she had never spoken to him and didn't know his name. He was older than Ruby, in his late thirties, she guessed. From the way they both leaned across the table, their faces almost touching, it looked like they were on a date.

Now Ruby was in a quandary. The couple looked like they were settled for the evening, and delivering poison pen letters was a million miles from Mrs Basset's mind. Could she return to Poplar Court? It didn't look like Mrs Basset would be delivering any letters that evening. But what if the date ended early and she posted it on the way home? Ruby would never forgive herself if she missed it. She was also painfully aware that Holly might be looking for her at this very moment.

She glanced around the snug to see if she recognised anyone, and only then noticed Laurie and Adam in the corner. Their heads were close together and they looked like they were speaking of something serious. Bentley was lying under the table with his head resting on his paws. She hesitated to disturb them but Laurie chose that moment to look up and met her gaze. The transformation of his expression from deep concern to happiness had Ruby's heart performing a polka in her chest. When he beckoned her over, she indicated that she was on her way then went to the bar to order a shandy. Armed with her drink, she went to sit with Laurie and Adam, remembering just in time to sit with her back to the wall so she could still keep an eye on Mrs Basset.

'What brings you here?' Laurie asked.

'I was—' Ruby stopped herself, remembering just in time that she didn't think Laurie had told Adam that she knew about the letters. 'I was just having a bit of a walk and I thought I'd see if there was anyone in here that I knew.' She leaned down to pat Bentley.

Understanding dawned in Laurie's eyes. 'Well, it's lovely to see you.'

She nodded over at Mrs Basset and lowered her voice. 'Isn't that the woman who yelled at you during the air raid?' she asked Adam. 'I'm surprised she dares show her face here after that night.'

Adam pulled a face. 'There was a bit of a stir when she walked in but maybe she felt she had to brave it. It's not as though she could shut herself away for ever. Anyway, after word got around of what happened to her family, everyone understands why she lost her head during the raid. I don't know the man she's with, though, but they look cosy.'

'It's Flight Lieutenant Groves,' Laurie said. 'He's got a sad story himself. Lost his wife when Birmingham was bombed. If anyone can understand Jean Basset and what she's suffered, it's him.'

Shortly afterwards, Adam excused himself and headed for the Gents. Ruby seized the opportunity to update Laurie on what she had been up to. She leaned closer to Laurie and said, 'Holly, Meg and I have been taking it in turns to keep an eye on Jean Basset in the evenings.'

'Oh? And where was she last night?'

'At home.'

'Then she's not the Poison Pen,' Laurie said heavily. 'Adam found another letter this morning. It must have been delivered yesterday evening because he was at the shop at the crack of dawn.'

Ruby looked at him in dismay. 'So I've been spending hours on an uncomfortable bench all for nothing?'

'It looks that way.'

Ruby struggled to accept that she had wasted all that time. 'But we've only been watching her until it gets dark. Maybe she slips out at night?'

'Can you really see her going out alone in the blackout?'

Her shoulders slumped. 'No.' While Starsden was safer than many areas of London, it was well known that criminals were taking advantage of the unlit nights. The newspapers had carried several stories recently of muggings carried out in the darkness, and no respectable woman would risk going out at night alone. 'I suppose it's back to the drawing board, then.'

Laurie took her hand. 'I do appreciate all you've done for Adam.'

She smiled, a surge of happiness overcoming her disappointment. 'It's the least I can do.'

'I do have some good news. I've managed to get a forty-eight-hour pass for the weekend after next.'

All her disappointment was forgotten. 'So you'll come to Wycombe?'

'Try and stop me.'

'I can't wait to tell my parents!'

—

Ruby didn't stay long after she had finished her drink. Laurie felt bad that she and her friends had given up so much of their precious free time. It hadn't been entirely in vain, he had tried to persuade her before Adam returned. They had managed to eliminate their prime suspect so at least they wouldn't waste any more time following Mrs Basset. Although Ruby hadn't looked convinced, he hoped she would come to realise the value of what they had learned.

Once Ruby had gone, Adam asked, 'She didn't leave on my account, did she? I could have left you two alone.'

Laurie shook his head. 'Don't worry.' Thinking fast, he invented a story to give a reason for her sudden appearance all alone. 'She said she only came in because she thought she saw a friend of hers come in and only realised her mistake when she got to the bar. I think she was relieved to see us but she probably wants an early night.'

'She was looking happier when she left, anyway.'

'That's because I told her I got leave the weekend after next. She invited me to meet her parents.'

Adam looked genuinely happy for him. 'I'm really glad things seem to be working out for the two of you.' He fiddled with his beer glass, and Laurie could guess what he was thinking about. Or who.

'If you like Holly, you should ask her out,' he said. 'Maybe she's tired of this bloke she's been writing to and is waiting for you to speak up. I'm sure she likes you.'

'She might like me, but does she fancy me?'

'Isn't that what you discover by going out with her? You won't know unless you ask.'

But Adam shook his head. 'I don't think I can. Not right now.'

'What have you got to lose?'

'Hope!' He spoke so sharply that Bentley sat up and whined.

'What do you mean?' Laurie asked.

Adam ruffled Bentley's ears with a sigh. 'Sorry, boy. I didn't mean to startle you.' He didn't reply to Laurie's question until Bentley shook himself and settled back down at his feet. 'I nearly plucked up the courage to ask her out last time I saw her but I'm glad I didn't now. What if she had turned me down? Thinking of her is the one bright spot in my life now, especially with all this business with the poison pen letters. I need to hold onto the hope that one day Holly and I might be together. Without that, I'd be lost.'

'So what are you going to do – spend your life admiring her from a distance? What happened to the Adam who was out with a different girl every night?'

'That Adam died at Dunkirk. Sorry. I know that sounds over-dramatic, but I don't feel like the same man I was before I was injured. To be honest, I don't want to go back to being the Adam who couldn't decide which girl he wanted to go out with that night. Maybe it's just that I'm older now but I'm after a serious relationship. I can't give up on Holly yet.'

'But how do you know she doesn't feel the same?'

'I don't. And that's why I have hope. Look, maybe when all this business with the Poison Pen is over, I'll be able to ask her out and deal with the let-down if she doesn't feel the same way. But right now I need the hope and I'm not prepared to let it go just yet.'

'I suppose I can understand that. So we'd better get our act together and work out who's sending these letters. Did you bring the note you got this morning?'

Adam nodded and handed over an envelope made from the same high-quality paper as all the others. The note inside was as short and to the point as the others too.

YOU DON'T DESERVE LIFE.

Laurie scowled. 'Whoever is sending these isn't right in the head. I really think you should change your mind about not going to the police. This person needs help.'

'You know what I think about that. Maybe I'd think differently if Mum and Dad weren't bound to find out but…' Adam tailed off.

Laurie wished there was a way around it but the moment the police started asking questions, it would set tongues wagging locally and their parents would be bound to hear. 'Fine. We have so little to go on, though, I don't know how we're going to get to the bottom of this. Are you sure it couldn't have been delivered this morning?' He had been so sure the Poison Pen was Jean Basset it was hard to give up the idea.

'I'm certain. I got to the shop at five this morning because I'd promised Dad I'd get all the new stock priced up and on the shelves before opening time. Can you seriously see anyone getting there before that?'

'I suppose not.' Thanks to Double Summer Time, it would only have been twilight at that time in the morning, and he was sure Mrs Basset wouldn't have left the house before then. If Ruby had been correct, and he had no reason to think she had been mistaken, then she couldn't be the Poison Pen because Ruby would have seen her leave the house. He sighed. 'Well, you'll be glad to know that the woman who harangued you during the air raid is in the clear.'

Adam's eyebrows rose in surprise. 'Mrs Basset? Why would you think it was her?'

'Because the letters accuse you of cowardice and she said you should be in uniform.' Laurie spoke slowly as though he was a teacher spelling out a concept to a slow child.

'Yes, but she wrote me a letter afterwards, apologising. Didn't I tell you?'

It took all Laurie's self-control not to grab his brother by the lapels. 'No. Why didn't you tell me?'

'It didn't occur to me. I mean, I had no idea you considered her a suspect or I would have said something. And, before you ask, it was written on the very flimsiest of notepaper and she didn't even use an envelope, just folded it and wrote my name on the blank side. Oh, and although it was hand delivered, she sent it to the house.'

Laurie finished his drink, sending a silent apology to Ruby and her friends for wasting their precious time. 'That does sound conclusive.' After a moment's thought he added,

'Come to think of it, it's strange that the Poison Pen is sending the letters to the shop. Most people around here know where you live.'

'I don't know. Maybe that was true before the war but there's been a lot of coming and going these days. There are plenty of people around here now who know me as the person who serves them at the shop but don't know me personally. Starsden has changed a lot since we joined up, or hadn't you noticed?'

'I suppose I hadn't really thought about it, but maybe you're right. This is the first time I've been home properly since I joined the RAF.' He decided to take a different approach. 'What do you think about the Poison Pen? Have you any ideas?'

'Not really. Unless it's one of the women who've stopped me on the street demanding to know why I wasn't in uniform. No one who knows me would do that because they know I've been injured.'

'That makes sense. So it's probably someone who has seen you in the shop but is fairly new to the area. I don't suppose you recognised any of the people who said that you should be in uniform?'

Adam shook his head. 'I'm sure I would have recognised them if they'd been regular customers.'

Laurie wanted to howl in frustration. There was so little to go on. At least when they had thought it was Mrs Basset they had been able to watch her house. Now he had no idea what to try next.

Chapter Twenty-One

The following days dragged by, partly because Ruby couldn't wait for her weekend away but also because her duties coincided with Bobby's and they were both assigned to the same ward. The nursing orderlies were supposed to assist the trained nurses, and in most of the hospital the nurses treated them with respect and were grateful for their help. Sister Allen, however, treated the presence of the nursing orderlies on her ward on the same level as a cockroach infestation. While Ruby had previously done stints on Ward Five, it had been with one of her friends. But Bobby, although an efficient worker, wasn't supportive. While Ruby could never pin down how it happened, Bobby always seemed to be occupied with something else when the worst jobs needed doing.

By the end of the first week, Ruby was tired and out of sorts. The only things keeping her spirits up were the prospect of her upcoming weekend home and rehearsals for the singing fundraiser, which was taking place the Saturday after Ruby's weekend away.

'You took your time,' Sister Allen grumbled when Ruby returned from the sluice room having scrubbed and disinfected a stack of bedpans. Ward Five was for patients recovering from surgery and therefore mostly bed-bound.

'I'm sorry,' Ruby said, 'I'll try and be quicker next time.' Even though she had already worked as fast as she could.

'Make sure you do. Just because you get to fly with the air ambulance, it doesn't make you better than those of us who have to work here every day.' This was the first time she had mentioned air ambulance duties and it gave a hint as to Sister Allen's resentment of the nursing orderlies.

Later, when she and Bobby were making a bed and Sister Allen was on the telephone, she told Bobby what Sister Allen had said. 'I don't know why she's complaining, though,' she said as they folded the draw sheet. 'We spend more time in the hospital than we do in the air ambulance, and we all work our socks off.'

'Maybe she would have liked to work with the air ambulance too,' Bobby replied. 'Admit it, you thought it was exciting and glamorous when you first volunteered.'

'I suppose I did,' Ruby said, not wanting to confess that she had found it more terrifying than exciting at first. And, after all, Holly and Meg had wanted to join because they thought it sounded glamorous. 'But she should try doing what we do for only a few extra pennies for each day we fly.' For it was a sore point among the nursing orderlies that they were among the poorest paid trades in the WAAF. She decided to change the subject. 'I can't wait to introduce Laurie to my parents. They're dying to meet him. Will you be seeing your fiancé soon?'

Bobby smoothed the sheet to ensure there were no creases then tucked it under the mattress before replying. 'It depends on when he can get leave. You know how it is.'

Ruby nodded. 'I suppose I'm lucky, serving in the same place as Laurie.'

Sister Allen strode up as Ruby was tucking in the last corner. 'Really, you girls are taking your time. The laundry's being collected in ten minutes and it hasn't even been sorted yet.'

'I'll go.' Bobby dashed off.

Ruby stared at her departing back with surprise. Checking the laundry for items that had become accidentally tangled in the sheets was not the most pleasant job, and Bobby tended to avoid it when possible.

It was only two days later, when she was on air ambulance duty, that she got an inkling of the reason behind Bobby's behaviour.

Ruby had flown to RAF Dyce in the northeast of Scotland, only to be grounded by high winds.

'Looks like we'll have to stay the night,' Squadron Leader Norton, their pilot, told the crew when he returned from a trip to the Met Office. 'The wind isn't forecast to drop until the early hours. Good job the patient's still in the hospital, or he'd have had to endure an ambulance trip to the aerodrome for nothing.'

Luckily for Ruby, the WAAFs in the hut where she had been billeted for the night were a friendly bunch. They accompanied her to the canteen for a meal then invited her to join them in their common room for the evening. When they introduced her to the other WAAFs already present, one of them, a tall, elegant girl, looked at her with interest.

'Do you know Bobby Jones?' she asked.

'Yes, I'm sharing a room with her,' Ruby replied. 'How do you know her?'

'I went to school with her and we've kept in touch ever since. I was surprised when she said she was joining the WAAF because I thought she was training to be a nurse.'

'Maybe nursing didn't suit her,' Ruby said, intrigued. 'I started nursing training too but it wasn't for me. I have to say, I wasn't too pleased when I joined the WAAF and they made me a nursing orderly, but it worked out well in the end.'

'Perhaps, but I've always thought it was more to do with what happened to her fiancé.'

'What—?' Ruby began but was interrupted when a WAAF sergeant put her head around the door.

'Maltby, Section Officer Kendall wants to see you.'

Ruby's companion pulled a face. 'Excuse me,' she said. 'Probably wants to tear me off a strip for not making my bed properly.' And she was gone before Ruby could ask what had happened to Bobby's fiancé.

Burning with curiosity, Ruby stayed in the common room for as long as possible in the hope that Maltby would return and explain her cryptic remark but she didn't come back. Although she looked out for her at breakfast, there was no sign of Bobby's old schoolfriend and, as the wind had died down, she had no further chance to speak to her.

'I can't get it out of my head,' Ruby said to Holly in the early afternoon when, having delivered her patient to a nearby hospital, she returned to base and met her friend at the canteen. 'I wonder what happened to Bobby's fiancé.'

'Whatever it was, he must be fine now because he's posted overseas,' Holly pointed out.

'I know but aren't you even a little bit curious? It might have been the reason why Bobby gave up nursing. I never even knew she had started training, did you?'

'No, but that's not surprising. It's not as if we're best friends. She might have failed her exams or something and be too embarrassed to tell anyone.'

'I suppose you've got a point.'

'I am curious to know about her fiancé, though. She's always writing to him and makes sure we know it.'

Ruby scraped up the last of her mashed potato. 'It's so frustrating that Maltby got called away when she did. I was just about to ask what she meant.'

Holly shrugged. 'She might not have told you. I mean, from what she said, it sounded like she thought you already knew. She might have clammed up when she realised you didn't.'

'Maybe you're right. She seemed a decent sort. Probably wouldn't have wanted to gossip.' Ruby rose and picked up her tray.

Holly followed suit. While they were rinsing their eating irons, she remarked, 'You should ask Bobby. You're on duty together at the moment. It's the perfect opportunity to get to know her better.'

'Maybe I will.' Ruby pulled a face. 'Anyway, I'd better go and report to Ward Five. See you later at singing practice.'

Sister Allen was most put out that Ruby's air ambulance duties had caused her to miss a morning's work.

'I'm ever so sorry,' Ruby said, feeling as though the bad weather had been her fault, 'but we were stranded near Aberdeen for the night and then we still had to take the patient to Cambridge this morning.' She didn't know why she was saying all this. Sister Allen would already have been informed and a replacement sent to cover her work that morning.

Sister Allen shook her head. 'I said that this was the sort of thing that would happen when the air ambulance was first suggested. But did they listen to me? Oh no.'

Ruby let her complain without trying to defend herself or the Air Ambulance Service. In Sister Allen's eyes, the whole system seemed to have been set up without consideration on how it would affect her personally. Pointing out that there were people still alive who might well be dead now if they hadn't received a prompt transfer to a specialist hospital wasn't going to change her mind. Sometimes she wondered how a woman like Sister Allen, who seemed to lack all compassion, had got so far in the profession.

When the sister finally finished and set her to work, Ruby caught Bobby's eye. There was solidarity in her expression, and for a brief moment the two women were united against their superior's unfairness. In that moment, Ruby made up her mind to try and draw Bobby out about her fiancé.

Her opportunity came when they were tasked with making up a bed for a new patient who was due out of surgery later that afternoon. It was always more efficient if two workers could be spared to make the beds, and as the ward wasn't particularly busy, Sister Allen asked Ruby and Bobby to do it.

Ruby decided to start with a casual approach. 'I met an old school friend of yours yesterday,' she began. 'LACW Maltby. I never caught her first name.'

'Oh, you must mean Penelope Maltby. She was a good friend of mine at school, and we still keep in touch.' Bobby seemed to have forgotten her usual air of superiority and looked pleased. 'I remember her writing to tell me she was being posted up in the wilds of Scotland. How is she getting on?'

'We didn't talk long because she was called away not long after we met. She only spoke to me because she heard me say I was from Starsden and wanted to know if I knew you.' Ruby, encouraged by Bobby's interest, dared to add, 'Actually, she said she'd been surprised when you'd joined the WAAF because you were training to be a nurse.'

'Oh. Did she?'

Ruby couldn't interpret the note in Bobby's voice. Was that embarrassment? She hastened to reassure her. 'Oh, don't worry. I gave up nursing too. I didn't enjoy it at all. I was always too scared of making a mistake.'

Bobby drew herself up to her full height. 'I wasn't scared. I would have made a good nurse.'

'Sorry. I didn't mean you wouldn't. In fact, Maltby said she wondered if it was to do with your fiancé.'

'Did she now?' There was no mistaking the chill in Bobby's tone this time.

'Oh, she wasn't gossiping. She didn't say what had happened with your fiancé. She just—'

But Bobby, with jerky movements, completed her task in silence, making a precise envelope corner at the foot of the bed that looked like it had been made with a protractor. She dropped her end of the mattress and straightened her uniform. 'I'm sure you had wonderful fun discussing me and my fiancé but I'd rather you kept it to yourself, thank you very much.' And she stormed off, her arms full of the sheets they'd stripped from the bed.

'I feel awful,' Ruby said to Holly and Meg later when she'd told them what had happened. 'Now Bobby thinks this Penelope Maltby and I were gossiping all about her when it wasn't like that at all.'

'Am I the only one who's dying to know what Maltby meant about Bobby's fiancé, though?' Meg asked.

'Well, no,' Ruby was forced to admit.

Holly shot her a grin. 'Face it – the thing you feel most awful about is not finding out. If Penelope Maltby hadn't been called away, you would have happily gossiped about her. I know I would.'

Ruby felt her face flaming. 'You're right. Does that make me a horrible person?'

'It makes you human,' Meg said firmly. 'Anyway, Bobby's always going on about him. Don't you think it odd she never mentioned this terrible thing that happened?'

'We don't know it was terrible,' Ruby pointed out. 'As far as I remember, Penelope Maltby said something along the lines of her being surprised Bobby gave up her nursing training but she supposed it was something to do with what had happened to her fiancé. For all we know it was something good.'

Holly looked sceptical. 'Like what?'

Ruby thought fast. 'Maybe he unexpectedly came into a lot of money.'

'Ooh!' Meg's face was aglow. 'He might have inherited a fortune from a long-lost uncle he never knew existed.'

Holly snorted. 'Steady on, Charlotte Brontë. This is real life we're talking about. That sort of thing only happens in books. Anyway, I get the impression from Bobby that her fiancé is already well off. Didn't she say his father's an earl?'

'Yes but if he's a younger son he might not have had any money of his own so inheriting the fortune made him independent for the first time. Then Bobby would have left nursing to marry him.' Meg was clearly not giving up her romantic dream so easily.

'Then why didn't they marry?'

'Maybe the army sent him overseas before they could arrange the wedding. I mean, he's obviously out of the country now.'

Ruby shook her head. 'No. I know I said what happened to him wasn't necessarily bad, but the more I think about it there was something about the way Maltby spoke that sounded like it was.'

'Like being injured?' Meg asked.

'That would make sense,' Ruby replied. 'She might have given up her training to take care of him. Then when he recovered she joined the WAAF.'

Meg nodded. 'That sounds likely.'

'Or' – Holly's eyes danced – 'he was arrested following some dreadful scandal and Bobby retired to the country to recover from the shame.'

The girls' shrieks of laughter rang out, and they thought up ever more incredible reasons for Penelope Maltby's cryptic remark as they made their way to singing practice. But while Ruby joined in the laughter she couldn't forget Bobby's fury when she had tried to ask what had happened. She was hiding something, that was for sure.

Chapter Twenty-Two

The cheery jingle of the ironmongery doorbell didn't at all match the expression on his brother's face when Laurie walked in with Bentley at his heels.

'Where's Dad?' he asked.

Adam gave a jerk of the head towards the stock room. 'Out back. Why – do you need to see him?'

'No, I wanted to see how you are.' His duties had kept him away from his family for some days and, considering the last time he had seen Adam he had received another letter, the worry had weighed on his mind. 'I thought we could have lunch together. What time can you have a break?'

Adam glanced at his watch. 'I can probably stop now. Hang on, I'll check with Dad.'

He slipped into the stock room and emerged a few moments later with their father just behind him.

'Haven't seen you for a while,' his dad said. 'RAF keeping you busy?'

'I've been flying most days,' Laurie said.

'I've been reading up about those Lancaster bombers. Any chance you'll get to fly one of those?'

'I doubt it. I'd need to retrain and the air ambulance work is keeping me busy.' Laurie did his best to ignore the twinge of envy. He *was* doing important work. So what if the press kept going on about the brave men who flew Lancasters, Spitfires and Hurricanes? He was helping to save lives and should be proud of what he did. Should be. 'Anyway,' he said, making an effort to appear cheerful, 'is it all right if I take Adam off your hands for an hour? It's my day off and I thought it'd be nice for us to have lunch together.'

'By all means. I was about to close for lunch.'

Adam had to dart into the storeroom to collect his jacket, and while he was gone Laurie's father leaned across the counter and lowered his voice. 'And if you can persuade him to go back to veterinary college, that would be grand.'

'Why – has he said something about it?'

'No but it's obvious he's not happy here. And, frankly, there isn't enough for him to do. The customers are hardly flocking here. Everyone's struggling for money at the moment and people have got better things to spend their money on.'

'You should have said.' Laurie was aghast. 'I can spare you some more money. I'll sort it out right away.' He already arranged to have a proportion of his pay sent straight to his parents but he could cope with less.

His father shook his head. 'You already do enough. And we'll get by. We always do.'

Adam returned at that point so all Laurie could do was nod at his father as he left but he made a mental note to arrange to send more of his pay home as soon as he was back on the base.

Mindful that he would need to economise more, he happily agreed to Adam's suggestion that they eat at the local British Restaurant. This was a canteen set up in the church hall where they could get a substantial three-course meal and a cup of tea for just over a shilling. More importantly in Laurie's opinion, they allowed well-behaved dogs inside. They didn't talk on the short walk to the hall but once they had paid for their tickets and then collected a tray each of thick lentil soup, corned beef hash and jam sponge and found a free table at the back of the hall, Laurie went on the attack.

'What's been happening since I saw you last? Have you had any more letters? Dad said you've been moping around with a face like a wet weekend.'

'I doubt those were his exact words.'

'Well, no, but I can imagine.' Laurie watched as Adam shook salt and pepper over his soup. 'So what's the problem?'

Adam placed the salt and pepper pots in the centre of the table, making minute adjustments to follow an alignment only he could see. Only when they were placed to his apparent satisfaction did he reply. 'I did get another one. I suppose I hoped that whoever was sending them would get bored and stop. But they keep on coming, and we have no more idea who's doing it than when the first one arrived.'

Laurie sighed. 'I hate to say it, but I'm stumped. I'm not giving up, though. What does the latest one say? Have you got it on you?'

'Here.' Adam fished in his pocket. 'You don't think I was going to leave it lying around for Mum or Dad to find, do you?' He handed over an envelope.

Laurie took it with a sense of foreboding. He'd come to hate the sight and feel of these expensive envelopes so he could only imagine how Adam felt. 'When did it arrive?'

'Yesterday morning. Dad picked it up. I nearly had a fit when he handed it to me. Honestly just the thought that he might have opened it by mistake gives me the screaming heebie-jeebies.'

'He can't have opened it or he would have told me about it,' Laurie said. 'He's worried about you but he has no idea what's wrong.' He briefly considered tackling Adam about veterinary college again but realised he was putting off reading the contents of the note.

But when he read it he wished he hadn't.

> MEN LIKE YOU ARE PARASITES, LIVING OFF THE SACRIFICE OF OTHERS.

'Short and sweet,' he said, trying to lighten the atmosphere. 'Honestly, I've had some Valentine's Day cards like that.'

'I'm not surprised, seeing the way you treat your girlfriends. If you think the Three Horseshoes is a good place for a date, I'm surprised Ruby doesn't give you the push.'

Laurie examined the letter while Adam, apparently feeling better now he had handed it over, fed Bentley a piece of corned beef. The paper and writing looked exactly the same as before, and he wondered who would waste expensive paper on such sordid notes. 'Mind if I hang onto it? I should show Ruby.' After the awkward meeting with her at the pub, he had thought it best to explain to Adam that he had told Ruby about the Poison Pen. Adam had been upset at first but had understood after Laurie had explained how the secrecy had threatened to damage their relationship.

'Be my guest. It'll give her inspiration for next Valentine's Day, assuming you two last that long.'

He had to agree it was hardly the most romantic gesture, to show one's girlfriend a poison pen letter, but considering he had nearly lost her by keeping them a secret, he wasn't going to repeat his mistake.

What with Ruby being grounded overnight in Scotland, he hadn't seen her for a few days and he was practically hopping from foot to foot while he waited for her at the appointed time outside Poplar Court that evening. His heart gave a jolt when she emerged and waved enthusiastically when he caught her eye.

She flew into his arms and he enjoyed a leisurely kiss until the jeers of the other WAAFs around forced him to reluctantly release her.

'It feels like ages since I last saw you,' she said, taking his hand and falling into step with him. 'Where are we going?'

'It's a lovely evening. Fancy a walk?' He couldn't forget Adam's jibe about the pub being an unromantic place for a date.

'Sounds perfect. I spent the morning cramped up in the Ox-box then all afternoon on the ward under Sister Allen's beady eye. I could do with being out in the fresh air for a while.'

'Let's go to the common.' Starsden Common lay on the opposite side of the RAF base from the town, sandwiching the aerodrome between them. As a child, he had played there with his brother, splashing in the brook and making camps in the thickets, but since his return to Starsden as an RAF pilot, he hadn't often gone there, preferring to spend his free time in the pubs or cinema. Today, however, he couldn't believe he hadn't taken Ruby there sooner. Once they had crossed the road and climbed the stile, it was like they had left the world behind and emerged into a place where war and hatred couldn't reach them. The bounds of the common were marked by a narrow strip of woodland. As they strolled along the path, shaded from the sun by the branches arching overhead, they spoke of what they had been doing since they had last met.

'I'm glad your overnight stay in Scotland wasn't for any dramatic a reason,' he said when Ruby had finished her account. 'Not like our flight through the storms.'

'Me too. I don't want to repeat that in a hurry.' Then she shot him a sideways glance that set his pulse racing.

'Although I wouldn't mind repeating the evening in the farmhouse living room.'

Laurie swallowed, remembering the wonderful feeling of peace, holding Ruby in his arms and swaying in time to the tinny gramophone music. He should tell her that he loved her, and what better location than this beautiful common? When the time was right, he would tell her what was in his heart.

First, though, he wanted to get the news about Adam's latest letter out of the way. He put it off for as long as possible, not wanting to spoil the atmosphere, but when they came to the end of the woods and were strolling through hummocky grass dotted with buttercups and daisies, Ruby asked, 'What else have you been doing today? It was your day off, wasn't it?'

'I had lunch with Adam.'

His tone must have given him away, for Ruby turned to face him, her expression grave. 'He's had another letter, hasn't he.' It wasn't a question.

—

Ruby felt as though the sun had disappeared when Laurie nodded, even though there wasn't a cloud in sight. 'What did it say?'

'I can show you.' He pulled out the letter from his pocket. 'Let's sit down.'

They found a spot on the banks of a narrow brook, and Laurie spread his jacket for her to sit on. At any other time this would have been an idyllic moment, sitting shoulder to shoulder with Laurie and listening to the water gurgling over its pebbly bed while the sun warmed her back and she breathed in the scent of clover. But when she took the envelope, although she felt distaste and anger as she braced herself to read the contents, she was also aware of the familiar stomach-clenching sensation of unwanted responsibility. What did she think she was doing? How dare she give Laurie and Adam false hope by claiming to be able to help? Hadn't she already made a mess of things by falsely accusing Mrs Basset and then being proved wrong? She should never have suggested helping Laurie investigate. Typical. Just when she thought she had got over her fear of making a mistake, it sprang up in another part of her life.

Doing her best to suppress the unwelcome feelings, she read the note. It didn't take long for anger to overcome all other emotion. 'The only parasite round here is whoever is sending these,' she said. She resisted the urge to fling the letter into the brook, instead holding it close to her face to examine it more carefully.

It was handwritten in bold, inked block capitals that appeared to have been formed with care to avoid any quirks that might reveal the sender. 'I wonder why the Poison Pen doesn't use cut-out letters from the papers,' she said. 'I mean, look how precisely each letter is formed. Whoever wrote this took a lot of care to disguise their handwriting. Why not just stick cut-out letters onto the paper? That's how poison pen writers usually work.'

'They probably don't want to face a hefty fine for wasting paper.'

'Maybe. But doesn't it strike you as odd that someone who would go to the risk of sending poison pen letters would worry about running afoul of salvage regulations?'

Laurie shrugged. 'The newspapers are cutting down on pages, and the only letters big enough to use on an anonymous letter are the ones in the headlines. It could just be that there aren't enough of those available.'

Ruby didn't reply immediately yet she wasn't convinced. She thought of her family home, which arranged its paper salvage like every other household, thanks to the number of leaflets and articles telling them what to do. There was a salvage basket where her parents stored read newspapers and magazines while they waited for the Scouts to come and collect them. There would be more than enough letters of the right size to cut out and paste onto a letter.

Then it dawned on her. 'The problem with cutting out letters could be with hiding the evidence from others. If the Poison Pen was someone like my mother, who is alone at home while my dad is out at work, she could make the letters during the day, then use the cut-out pages to start a fire or bury them deep in the salvage basket so that no one else could see what she had done.'

Laurie shifted to face her. 'So you're saying that the Poison Pen isn't someone like Mrs Basset, who has a house to themselves at times, but perhaps someone living in shared accommodation who doesn't get enough privacy to mess about cutting up paper?'

'Maybe. I haven't thought it through properly but don't you think they would use cut-up letters if they could?'

'Or a typewriter. No, wait. I think I read a book once where the criminal was discovered by having a letter or will or something traced back to his typewriter.' Laurie raked his fingers through his hair. 'I wish I could remember.'

'Well, that's not important, considering this poison pen isn't using one. But it makes sense that whoever it is lives somewhere that lacks privacy. I mean, if anyone in Poplar Court was cutting letters out of newspapers, we would know about it.'

Laurie nodded. 'You've got a point. It would be impossible in the Sergeants' Mess too. So are you saying the Poison Pen lives on the base?'

'Or a boarding house or someone who's with other people all the time. Sorry. I haven't exactly narrowed it down, have I?'

'You've still helped. And I think you're right. I hadn't really wondered why the letters were handwritten, but you might have hit upon the reason.' He shifted sideways again until he could wrap an arm around her. 'And I'm sorry, too, that we're spending all our precious evening on these letters again. It's not the most romantic of dates.'

Ruby leaned her head against his shoulder. 'I don't know. It feels pretty special being out here on a warm summer's evening.'

Laurie drew breath as though he was about to say something, but at the same moment she happened to glance at the letter just as the paper was caught by the sunlight. She stiffened and sat up, holding it up to allow the sunlight to stream through. 'Well, that's something I didn't notice before. A watermark.'

Laurie peered at it. 'I can't believe I never thought to check. Of course paper this quality would have one.'

Ruby gazed at the image of the coat of arms and below it the words 'Basildon Bond'. 'Well, we know something at least. Whoever it is owns a Basildon Bond notepad.'

'That *is* progress. So all we have to do is search every room in Starsden until we find a Basildon Bond notepad.'

Ruby ignored his sarcasm and looked at the pale watermark a moment longer, then peered at the paper more closely. What were those marks at the top of the page? Her pulse raced and not just because Laurie had pulled her closer. 'I don't believe this.' She handed the paper to Laurie. 'Can you see the imprint of writing here?' She pointed to the top right-hand corner.

Laurie squinted at it. 'It might be. I can't make it out, though.'

'Nor me. But we could try scribbling over it with a soft pencil. Have you got one on you? I know I haven't.' She had emptied her pockets before leaving Poplar Court, conscious that having full pockets didn't show off her figure to its best. Now she regretted it because she distinctly remembered taking out a pencil and putting it in her bedside cabinet.

'I might have.' Laurie patted his pockets and pulled out a pencil with a triumphant flourish. 'We're in luck! Hang on. I've got a notebook too. We'll need it to make a smooth surface.'

He pulled the notebook from the inside pocket of his jacket and placed it on the ground between them then smoothed the letter on top. Ruby watched with bated breath as he ran the pencil lightly over the spot where she had seen the etched letters. As she watched, handwriting appeared on the paper, white against the grey background of the pencil. The layout looked familiar.

'I don't believe it,' she breathed. 'It's an address. Right in the place where someone would write their own address if they were writing a letter.'

Unfortunately it was not completely legible, but holding it to catch the light in exactly the right way, Ruby could make out a line that said 'RAF Starsden'.

'I don't believe it,' she said again, and from the look of shock on Laurie's face, he felt the same. 'The Poison Pen is one of us.'

Chapter Twenty-Three

Ruby hardly knew how to behave towards anyone on the base in the days that followed. Whether it was the WAAF who ladled lentil stew onto her tray at the cookhouse, the officer who handed over her wages at Pay Parade or even Sister Allen at the hospital, whenever she spoke to or saluted someone at RAF Starsden she wondered if that person wrote their letters on Basildon Bond notepaper. The only people she could wholly trust were Laurie, Holly and Meg and she sought out their company as much as possible.

'It's awful,' she said one evening two days before her much-longed-for visit home. They were on their way to singing practice, and the evening sunshine warmed their backs as they walked through the base. As this was the first time she had been out of earshot of anyone else, it was her first chance to speak openly of what she and Laurie had discovered, and her voice had shaken with suppressed anger as she had filled them in. 'I hate suspecting everyone I see,' she concluded, 'but I can't help it, knowing that someone on the base has been sending those letters.'

'I can hardly believe it.' Holly looked distraught. 'It was bad enough knowing someone in Starsden was thinking such things about Adam, but one of us...' She tailed off, shaking her head.

'That's exactly how I feel,' Ruby said.

'Have you got anywhere since then?' Meg asked. 'I mean, if one letter has imprints from another, you might find more on the others.'

'No such luck.'

Meg and Holly's groans that greeted her news was how she and Laurie had felt when they had excitedly inspected the other letters.

'That was the first thing we thought. I was so excited, thinking that we might find a signature or at least a clue to whereabouts on the base they worked, but none of the other pages had any indentations.' Ruby scowled. 'We really thought we were onto something. The Poison Pen must usually either tear each sheet from the notepad before they write a letter or slip a piece of cardboard or blotting paper under the page they're writing on. I suppose they must have forgotten when they wrote the last one.'

'Then maybe they'll forget again and we'll catch them,' Meg said.

'I hope so. It's so frustrating finally finding a clue and then having it not help much.'

Ruby drew a deep breath then released it slowly. There was still more she wanted to say, but they had reached the hut where they held singing practice – the classroom where she and her friends had done their training. 'Come on,' she said, pushing open the door. 'If I don't get the descant right this time in "Early One Morning", I'm going to die from embarrassment.'

Once the whole group was assembled – sadly minus Laurie, who was late returning from his day's flights – Ruby stepped to the front of the group. 'Thank you all for coming,' she said. 'I've managed to finalise the programme, so if Sister Macintosh doesn't mind, I'll go over it now.' Sister Macintosh, who had kindly agreed to act as choir mistress, gestured for Ruby to continue.

'It's good news,' Ruby went on. 'Matron and the NAAFI manager have both agreed to our suggestions.' This was met with a murmur of approval from the group. 'So the programme is as follows: first we'll sing in the nurses' sitting room; next we do a repeat performance in the NAAFI then we finish the evening in the hospital grounds.' Ruby went on to cover the timings. She concluded with, 'Remember to tell all your friends. We want to collect as much money as possible.'

She handed back to Sister Macintosh, the tension draining from her shoulders. It would be a relief when the event was over and she could cross it from her list of worries. Still, the singing was fun, and she threw herself into the rehearsal with gusto. This time she even hit the high notes with ease.

'I thought we all sounded wonderful,' Ruby said when they left the hut at the end of the evening. Her head still rang with interweaving harmonies. 'If we sing like that on the night, we'll raise loads.' Then she sighed. If only they could have the same success tracking down the Poison Pen.

'I know that sound,' Holly said. 'You're still thinking about those letters, aren't you.'

'Can you blame me?'

'Of course not. I want to catch the culprit as much as you but worrying yourself sick isn't going to get you anywhere. Give yourself a break.'

'I suppose you're right.' Ruby made an effort to think of a different subject. 'What have you two been up to?'

Holly and Meg shared their news of air ambulance flights and difficult ward sisters, and gradually Ruby felt her tense muscles relax. She laughed along with the others when Holly described the escapes of Corporal Danny Lewis, a patient in her ward who had both his arms in plaster. Apparently he had persuaded his friends to break him out of the ward one night and take him to the Three Horseshoes. 'They all thought they were terribly clever, getting him out without the ward sister noticing but I think she turned a blind eye because she wanted a night away from him constantly asking her to scratch his nose.' Holly chuckled. 'Of course, he couldn't drink without someone holding the glass for him, but he still managed to have a hangover the next day. Sister Norris knew exactly what was wrong with him and deliberately made a load of bangs and clatters when she was serving breakfast.'

'I suppose that's one person we can cross off our list of suspects,' Ruby said when Holly had finished. 'Corporal Lewis obviously can't have written any letters with his arms in plaster.'

'That's the spirit!' Holly said, taking her arm. 'We'll find the Poison Pen, even if it takes months to eliminate all the innocent people one at a time.' She gave Ruby a nudge. 'Anyway, you don't need to worry about it for a while. Aren't you off to visit your parents with Laurie on Friday? I thought you'd be more excited.'

'I am. I really am. I've just had so much else to think about, what with the Poison Pen and the singing event.'

'Well, you can forget about all that for a few days and enjoy your weekend,' Meg said. 'There's nothing so important it can't wait until Monday.'

Ruby gazed up at the sunset and made a conscious effort to savour the moment. Meg was right – everything could wait. The second she came off duty on Friday, she would think of nothing but enjoying every moment with Laurie. This was going to be the best weekend ever.

When she met Laurie in the NAAFI the next day, he was full of the trip. 'I can't wait to get out of Starsden,' he said, breaking off a chunk of rock cake. 'It will be good to see somewhere new for a couple of days.'

Ruby laughed. 'What do you mean? You're always flying all around the country.'

'Yes but I usually only ever see the aerodrome, wherever I am. I mean somewhere I can explore.'

'You do know we're only going to Wycombe, and it's not much more exciting than Starsden.'

'That's not what you said when you were trying to persuade me to go.'

'Yes, but now the visit's only a day away, I feel I ought to warn you. I love it because it's my home but I have to admit there are prettier places.'

'If you love it then I'm going to love it,' Laurie told her.

Was now the moment when he was going to announce that he loved her? But the conversation moved on with no great declaration. Still, tomorrow evening they would be on their way to High Wycombe and a whole weekend of opportunities for him to share his feelings. It would be more special to hear him say 'I love you' in her hometown. She couldn't wait.

Laurie glanced at his watch. 'Got to dash or Squadron Leader Norton will have my guts for garters,' he said. 'Oh, and I promised I'd pop home tonight so I won't see you until tomorrow.' They arranged the time and place where they would meet and then he was gone.

It was time for Ruby to return to the ward so she gathered up her things and set off for the hospital. Yet although she was kept busy all afternoon, her thoughts kept drifting back to Laurie. How would he tell her? Would he say something as soon as they were on the train? Or maybe he would wait until they were on a romantic walk. The weather had better stay dry. It would be awful if they had to spend the weekend shut in the house with her parents.

'Mind what you're doing, Morris!'

Ruby jumped and saw that the glass she was filling with water was overflowing, and Sister Allen was scowling at her.

'I'm sorry, Sister. I'll fetch a cloth.'

'And keep your mind on your work from now on,' Sister Allen snapped.

Ruby hastened to clear up the water on her patient's bedside cabinet. Although she forced herself to concentrate on her work for the remainder of the afternoon, her thoughts inevitably returned to Laurie every now and again. How could they not when she was so sure he returned her feelings? It didn't matter whether he told her at the top of a hill or curled up together at home, listening to the radio. The important thing was that he loved her and it was only a matter of time before he confessed his feelings.

Chapter Twenty-Four

Laurie walked down the path to his parents' front door, whistling a cheery ditty. Bentley trotted beside him, his tail wagging and ears pricked. Laurie knew how he felt — life was good, and this time tomorrow he would be with Ruby, on his way to meeting her parents for the first time. Ever since their London trip he had been waiting for an opportune moment to tell her he loved her. He would have done so on the common, only the discovery of the watermark and imprinted address on Adam's latest letter had scuppered his plans. One way or another, the Poison Pen had managed to get between him and Ruby quite enough. If he ever found himself face to face with the writer, he would give them a piece of his mind.

He breezed into the living room then stopped dead when he saw his parents, sitting side by side on the sofa, looking like stern figures carved in stone. The wireless was off, and neither of them was reading or even speaking. The look they gave him took him back in time to when he was a boy and they had found out he had sneaked out at night to go to the fair with his friends. This time, though, he didn't know what he had done wrong.

'Something the matter?' he asked, knowing full well there must be. He sank into an armchair.

His father pointed to an object on the table between them. 'That.'

Laurie looked and his heart gave a lurch. It was an all-too-familiar envelope. Laurie would have bet his life savings that the paper inside had a Basildon Bond watermark. 'Oh.'

'I take it you've seen one before.'

There was no point in denying it. Besides, Laurie hated lying to his parents. 'Yes. I noticed something was off with Adam a while back and he told me about them. I wanted him to go to the police but he refused.'

His father closed his eyes briefly, looking suddenly very old. 'So this isn't the first one. I was afraid of that.'

'No, and I had a fight to get him to tell me about them. Wait.' He looked around. 'Where is he?'

'At the shop. I made up a job that would keep him back late so I could speak to you alone.'

'You left him there alone after he'd got another letter? How is he?'

'He's fine. He doesn't know. I didn't show him.'

'Oh. How did you find out, then?'

His father sighed. 'I had to go in early this morning to—well, that doesn't matter now. But I thought I heard the post arrive and when I went to collect it, I found that. I only glanced at the name and thought it was for me. "Adam" looks a lot like "Alan". But when I saw what was inside…'

Laurie picked up the letter and opened it. As he'd already known, the paper was the same Basildon Bond notepaper the Poison Pen always used. The message was brief but devastating.

> YOU SHOULD HAVE DIED AT DUNKIRK

Laurie stared at it, feeling a chill creep through his bones. He only moved when he felt a cold, damp nose nudge his hand. Looking down, he saw Bentley gazing at him with such a mournful expression that he could have sworn the dog could read his mind. He petted him absently, trying to work out what to say. He hated to think what his father had thought when he'd first read it. It was to spare his parents the worry that he'd agreed to keep the letters secret and now they'd found out in the most horrible way. 'I'm so sorry you found out like that.'

He put down the letter and gazed at his parents. His mother was wringing her hands and her eyes brimmed with tears. 'I don't understand how anyone could say such a hateful thing,' she said, 'but most of all I can't bear to think that Adam's been going through this alone.'

'Not alone,' Laurie said. 'He's had me.' He thought it prudent not to say that Ruby and her friends also knew.

'And just how many of these have been sent?' His father pointed at the letter with a trembling finger. 'I thought he was hiding something when he insisted upon going to the shop so early each day. I should have forced him to tell me.'

'He didn't want to worry you. He only told me when I promised not to say a word to you.'

His mother dabbed her eyes with a handkerchief and then balled it in her fist. 'Well, I think we should report this to the police. Whoever is sending these letters needs to be punished.'

'But Adam doesn't want that and I think we should respect that.'

'I'll see about that.' His mother sprang up as though intending to march to the shop there and then.

'Please. Sit down and hear me out.' Having his parents up in arms wasn't going to help Adam at all. 'Let me make us all some tea and then we can talk it over and work out what to say to Adam without upsetting him any more than he already is.'

His mother looked like she was going to ignore him until his father tugged her back down beside him. 'Laurie's right, sweetheart. If we go charging in and try to take over, we'll only make things worse.'

It took some doing, but eventually his mother was persuaded to stay put. Laurie made them all tea and put an extra spoon of sugar into his parents' cups, rations be damned. He also found a tin containing a fruitcake and served them all a generous slice. Today was not the day to fret about coupons and points.

While his parents were eating and drinking, Laurie explained what he already knew. After a brief battle with himself he also confessed that Ruby knew about the letters too, hoping that his parents wouldn't be angry with her for keeping the secret. 'I had to tell her,' he told them, 'because I kept having to break dates and she thought I didn't care about her. Anyway, she discovered the most important thing.' And he explained about the watermark and the imprint from another letter. 'So we know the Poison Pen is based at RAF Starsden,' he said in conclusion. 'That's narrowed down our list of possible culprits a great deal, and I think you should leave it with us to sort out. Considering we both live there, we've got a better chance of finding the writer than the police.'

His mother nodded. 'I suppose you're right.' She looked at her husband. 'What do you think, Alan?'

'I agree we should leave it in Laurie's hands for now. But if this business drags on for much longer then I still think we should go to the police.' He turned to Laurie. 'You've got a month. If you can't find the Poison Pen by then, I'll go to the police myself.'

Laurie sank back in his chair. He could tell from the set of his father's jaw that there was no sense in arguing but he hoped he would be able to change his mind later. 'Then I suppose I should get started.' A thought struck him. 'Wait. You heard the letter being delivered? That's important. We haven't been able to pin down the time other letters have arrived. When was it?'

His father scratched his head. 'It must have been around six thirty. Does that help?'

'It might.' Laurie was thinking fast. All personnel leaving the base had to sign in and out at the gates. He remembered Ruby telling him that she was glad the nursing orderlies lived at Poplar Court because, being outside the station, it was easier to enter and leave unobserved. They were supposed to sign in and out too, of course, but there were ways around it. Also, as they worked shifts, they were coming and going at all hours. It made sense that the Poison Pen lived outside the base. He should focus on personnel, like the nursing orderlies, who worked shifts and lived outside the base. 'I think it does,' he said. 'I've got an idea and I'll have to speak to Ruby about it. I'll have plenty of time to discuss it over the weekend.'

'Oh no, if you think you're gallivanting off to Ruby's home this weekend, you've got another think coming.'

Laurie stared at his mother in dismay. 'I have to go. You can't believe how difficult it was for us to get a pass for the same weekend. She'll never forgive me if I back out now.'

His mother bit her lip. 'I know it's a lot to ask, but we still need to decide what to say to Adam. I'm sure he'll be upset with his father when he hears he opened the letter by mistake, and you're the only one he can really confide in. Please don't leave us hanging for the whole weekend.'

Laurie's shoulders slumped. He could never say no to his mother and she was right that Adam would be upset. He couldn't begin to imagine how he was going to react when he found out what had happened. It would be mean to leave him just when he needed his help more than ever. 'Fine. But it might be me who needs help when Ruby breaks up with me.'

—

'Today's the day!' Ruby cried, leaping out of bed.

Winnie, who had the day off, groaned and pulled the blankets over her head while the others got up with varying degrees of reluctance.

'Golly, I'm going to be late!' Holly, who was on air ambulance duty that day, grabbed her slacks and pulled them on, nearly tripping over in the process. 'I doubt I'll be back in time to see you off this evening, so have a good time.'

Bobby, who was already fully dressed, closed her lipstick with a snap and arched a brow at Ruby. 'Where are you off to?'

'Home for the weekend. High Wycombe.'

'Oh? There's a good girls' school there – Wycombe Abbey. Is that where you went?'

Judging from Bobby's smug smile, she knew full well Ruby's parents could never have afforded the fees for the exclusive school even if they had saved for a hundred years. 'No.' Not unless you counted looking through the gates with longing at the beautiful wooded grounds. 'I went to a council school.'

'I'm sure that was a good school too.' This was said in patronising tones that made Ruby's fists curl. 'My parents considered sending me to Wycombe Abbey but they chose Roedean instead.'

Holly rolled her eyes at her then took Ruby's arm. 'I've got to dash but have a good time with Laurie!' She fled, still buttoning her jacket.

'So Laurie's meeting your parents. It sounds like things are getting serious,' Bobby said. She sounded both curious and a touch patronising.

Ruby wished she could stand up to Bobby, who was so self-satisfied with her rich fiancé, and say that yes, things were serious and Laurie had declared his undying love. But all she could do was shrug and say, 'I think so.'

'Oh, you know he's crazy about you,' said Meg, who had just returned from the bathroom. 'You're going to have such a wonderful, romantic time.' She gave a wistful sigh, making Ruby forget her own hopes for the weekend and look at Meg in concern.

'Is everything all right?'

'Of course. It's just that seeing you and Laurie together makes me wish I had someone special in my life. But no one looks twice at me.'

'Don't be daft. You're a knock-out.'

Meg shook her head. 'You're just saying that. Anyway, come on. Let's grab breakfast before someone else finishes all the toast.'

At another time Ruby would have been more concerned for her friend and asked why she didn't believe she was attractive, but today her excitement over her weekend with Laurie won out and she followed Meg down to breakfast without a word.

For all she knew, he might declare his love this very evening. She hugged the thought to herself all through breakfast, not daring to give voice to her hope. Besides, even if he didn't say anything, the fact he was going at all must mean that he was serious. Surely he wouldn't want to meet her parents unless he meant this relationship to last. She couldn't wait for her parents to meet him, and she particularly wanted to hear her mother's opinion. She would be able to tell if Laurie was serious, Ruby was sure.

Her head was so full of dreams when she left for her shift at the hospital that she didn't notice Laurie waiting outside the house until he grabbed her arm. Her heart gave a little skip but then seemed to lurch to a halt when she saw his grim expression. 'What's happened?' she asked.

'Ruby, I'm really sorry but I can't make it this weekend.' He drew her aside from the group of WAAFs she had left the building with and lowered his voice. 'My parents found out about the letters.'

It was as though she'd been doused in icy water. This couldn't be happening. She searched his face for any sign that he was joking, but his expression didn't crack. 'But you can still come, can't you? I mean, it's awful about your parents finding out but—'

'I can't. I'd much rather be with you, but my mother's in pieces and I can't leave Adam on his own to sort it all out.'

But this was supposed to be the perfect weekend, she wanted to wail. 'Well, your family must come first, of course.' She had meant to sound sympathetic, but instead her words were snappish.

Laurie reached for her hand, but she snatched it away. He frowned. 'I'm really sorry. I was so looking forward to this weekend but I can't leave my family now.'

It was as though she'd been punctured and all her new-found confidence was leaking away. She was once again that crushed seventeen-year-old who had pinned her hopes on a man who regarded her as nothing more than a joke. She swallowed to clear the painful lump in her throat and said, 'No, of course you can't leave them all alone. Of course you'd rather spend the weekend with them instead of me.'

'That's not—'

But she was too fired up to hear him out. 'I feel sorry for Adam, I really do, but you can't keep doing everything for him. He's a grown man, and you should give him a chance to act like one.' Laurie took her arm, his eyes searching hers with concern, but she snatched it away. 'I have to go now before Sister Allen puts me on a charge and really makes my day.'

She was a fool to have let Laurie persuade her that he wasn't like Dr Flint. When it boiled down to it, all men were the same. They were looking for a woman to bolster their ego, make them feel good about themselves. But the moment you needed any kind of commitment or, heaven forbid, emotional support, they were off.

She drew a shaky breath and struggled to keep her voice steady. 'It's obvious your family is more important to you, so I think we should call it a day while we can still remain friends.'

Laurie stared at her, his brows knotted. 'You're saying we should end it?'

'It's the sensible thing to do.' She was using the same discipline that enabled her to regard a gruesome wound dispassionately. If it hadn't been for her training she would be sobbing by now and telling Laurie that of course she didn't want to break up, that she loved him. As it was, she was able to look him in the eye and say, 'It's better this way. I have no wish to come between you and your family.'

Without waiting for a reply, she marched off, her chin pointing defiantly up, painfully aware of Laurie's gaze burning between her shoulder blades. Her righteous indignation lasted all the way to the corner of the road, where she turned into the road where the hospital entrance was located. The moment she knew she was out of Laurie's sight, she slumped. She wanted nothing more than to curl up in a corner and cry, but she had a shift to endure.

Somehow she managed to get through her long shift. Her torment wasn't over, however, for she now had to face her family. While she'd worked, she had contemplated sending a cable to her parents, explaining that something had cropped up and she couldn't make it after all. Two things stopped her: firstly, the arrival of the telegram boy was a thing to be dreaded these days, and she didn't want her parents to suffer, no matter how briefly; secondly, she had a deep longing to pour out her heart to her mother and escape from Starsden, with all its reminders of Laurie, for the weekend. There would be time enough to face up to him when she returned but for now she wanted to retreat and lick her wounds.

In fact, once she left the hospital she was glad that she had this respite from Laurie to look forward to, not to mention her mother's sympathy and home cooking and her father's undemonstrative affection. If she saw him too soon she knew there was a danger that she would beg him to take her back. But that would be a mistake. She had been made to look a fool once before, and she wasn't about to make the same mistake again. Laurie had shown several times that he couldn't be relied upon. While she had every sympathy for Adam, she was starting to wonder if the letters weren't a handy excuse to prevent her from getting too close. She had been a convenient girl for him, there when he needed company but easy to forget when he had other things on his mind.

She signed out for the weekend as quickly as she could and collected her railway warrant and ration book. It was a relief to leave RAF Starsden behind, knowing she wouldn't have to face any awkward questions from her friends for a day or two. With luck, Holly and Meg would hear the news from Laurie himself before she returned so she wouldn't be obliged to break the painful news herself. Hopefully by then she would be able to speak about it without wanting to burst into tears.

She took the bus to Wembley and caught the train to Wycombe from there. As the train sped away from London and out through the leafy hills and valleys of the Chilterns, the wheels rattling over the tracks told her the same thing, over and over: *It's all for the best; it's all for the best.*

Chapter Twenty-Five

Ruby had hardly taken two steps through the old, familiar front door when she found herself enveloped in a lavender-scented hug.

'Welcome home, love,' her mother said. 'It's so good to see you at last.' Then she stepped back and peered over Ruby's shoulder. 'But where's your young man? Is he catching a later train?'

It was best to get it over with in one fell swoop, like ripping off a plaster. 'He's not coming. We broke up.'

'Oh no! I'm so sorry.'

And once again, Ruby was folded into a hug.

Hearing a step behind her, Ruby extricated herself from the embrace and turned to see her father hovering at her shoulder.

'Are you feeling all right?'

'Of course she's not all right, Malcolm. Her boyfriend's just broken up with her.' Her mother rounded on her dad, hands on her hips. 'Honestly, you don't have an ounce of sense!'

Ruby kissed her dad on the cheek. 'I'm fine, really. And for your information, Mum, *I* broke up with *him*.'

'But why would you do that? He sounded so lovely!'

Ruby picked up her bag and prayed that her smile would remain fixed until she reached her room. Perhaps coming here had been a mistake. It wasn't too late. She could escape and hide out in the woods, somewhere no one could ask awkward questions.

Then her mother patted her shoulder. 'Oh well, I'm sure you had your reasons. If you feel like talking about them, I'm here. Things have a way of sorting themselves out, just wait and see.'

And now Ruby remembered why she had longed to be home. She gave a weak smile. 'Thanks, Mum. I *would* like to talk about it. Just give me a little time.'

'Take all the time you need.' Her mother gave her a shrewd look, and Ruby knew she wasn't fooled by the brave face she had been putting on. 'Now, I expect you'd like to freshen up. Run along. Supper can wait until you're ready. The butcher heard you were coming home and he put aside some very tasty-looking sausages for us. What with the veg your father's brought back from the allotment, we're in for a feast.'

'Sounds lovely, Mum.' While Ruby wasn't hungry and would see to it that her sausages found their way onto her parents' plates, the prospect of opening her heart to them did make her feel better. Although her mother's confident assertion that things would sort themselves out didn't fill her with much hope. Laurie's unreliable behaviour had opened up all the old wounds that she thought had healed after her disastrous experience with Dr Flint, and she wasn't going to hang around getting more and more hurt every time he came up with an excuse for why he had to cancel a date.

—

Laurie went to his parents' house on dragging feet that evening. It was hard not to resent his parents for insisting he remain in Starsden instead of going away with Ruby. If only they had been more reasonable, he and Ruby would still be together.

When he got there, he found the house empty. Adam and his father must still be in the shop, but he was surprised to find his mother out. In the kitchen he found a note from her explaining that she had a last-minute meeting with the fundraising committee. With nothing else to do, he set about boiling water for tea and washing up the lunchtime dishes that were stacked in the sink.

As he worked, he found his resentment draining away, to be replaced by a dizzying sense of loss. Ruby had been the one bright spot in a world darkened by war. How was he to cope without her? And how were they supposed to carry on working side by side after she had ripped his heart to shreds?

By the time his mother arrived home, he had put away the dishes and had a pot of tea brewing.

'You didn't have to do that,' Lettie said, looking around the kitchen in surprise.

The last of Laurie's resentment disappeared when he saw how tired she looked. 'I wanted to,' he said firmly. 'Go and sit down. The tea's ready.'

'But I should start on the evening meal.'

'Let's get fish and chips tonight. My treat. You look like you could do with a break.'

Lettie put up only the most half-hearted of objections to this plan and sank into her armchair with a sigh that seemed to emanate from the depths of her soul. Bentley, who had remained in the living room while Laurie had been working in the kitchen, immediately went and curled up by her feet. Laurie regarded her with concern as he poured the tea. This resulted in him pouring more tea in his saucer than his cup, and when his mother didn't tell him off for carelessness, he knew things were bad indeed.

He waited until Lettie had drained her first cup and was halfway through the second before he ventured to ask, 'Has anything happened since last night?'

'No. No more letters, if that's what you mean. But Adam was very upset when he heard that you'd agreed not to go away with Ruby this weekend. He said wasn't it bad enough that he was having a hard time and couldn't we let you have some joy in your life.'

Laurie had to fight hard to school his features to prevent his mother from seeing how strongly he agreed. 'Let me talk to him. You know how sensitive he is about having us all hovering over him.' As he spoke, he couldn't help remembering Ruby's outburst. Was she right? Adam had complained many times about their parents treating him like a child. Was he guilty of doing the same thing?

He got his opportunity later that evening when Adam and his father returned home. His offer of fish and chips was met with enthusiasm, and Adam volunteered to go with him. They walked to Davy's Plaice in silence but when they had joined the queue that snaked around the corner, Adam said, 'I'm sorry that Mum and Dad made you stay this weekend. I hope it didn't cause any trouble with Ruby.'

Laurie hesitated. It was on the tip of his tongue to assure Adam that all was well and Ruby had understood, but then he changed his mind. Adam resented being over-protected just as much as he would were their positions reversed, yet if he told the easy lie, that would make him as bad as his parents. 'Actually she was really upset. She broke up with me.'

Adam looked horrified. 'I'm so sorry. Maybe she'll change her mind once she's had a chance to cool down.'

'I doubt it. It's not the first time I've cancelled on her. She had every right to be upset.'

'Wait – this isn't the first time you've messed her around?'
'Well, no.'

Adam's frown deepened. 'So the day you told me Ruby's schedule had been changed and we went cycling…?'

He fixed Laurie with such a piercing stare that Laurie was forced to admit the truth. 'Fine. We were supposed to go to London that day but then you had another letter and it was so awful I knew I couldn't leave you alone.'

'I can't believe it. I'm not a child, you know. I could have coped for a day without you.'

'You were in a state. You had no one else to turn to. Do you really think I was going to leave you to your own devices? Admit it – you needed me that day.'

Adam sighed. 'Maybe. I mean, I was grateful to you for getting me away from Starsden. And if that was the only time, I wouldn't mind. But it's clear from Ruby's reaction that there have been other times.'

Laurie mumbled that there had been other cancelled dates. 'But you have to understand how torn I felt. And when I eventually told Ruby why, she understood.'

'I bet she understood. She understood that she was never going to come first with you. Poor girl – every time the two of you made plans, she must have been waiting for you to break them. And for you to make her go away alone after you'd promised to spend the whole weekend with her, that was cruel.'

'She's not alone. She's with her parents.'

'Yes, her parents who were expecting to meet her boyfriend. Can you imagine how awful she must have felt, having to explain that you had broken up?'

Laurie squirmed. He wasn't used to being given a lesson on relationships from his younger brother. 'You know, when I told you Ruby had broken up with me, I thought you might be sympathetic.'

'I am sympathetic. With *her*. Now I know that you've been using me as an excuse to avoid getting close to her, I'm amazed she didn't finish with you sooner.'

'What do you mean, using you as an excuse?' Laurie was indignant. Adam had needed him!

'Work it out for yourself.'

'Oh yeah?' Adam's certainty that he knew best was starting to grate, making Laurie's temper flare. 'Well if you're so clever, why haven't you worked out who is the Poison Pen? Why did you ask me to solve it for you?'

'I didn't ask you to take over. I asked for your help. There's a difference. But you seem to have taken my request for help as a reason to take over and be the hero. Why – what are you trying to prove?'

Laurie wasn't at all happy with the turn this conversation had taken. Ruby had been the one to end the relationship so why was Adam trying to convince him it was all his fault? He was so occupied with thinking up a good answer that he didn't notice it was his turn to be served until someone tapped his shoulder. 'Your turn, mate. Get a move on. Some of us have homes to get to, not like you fancy Brylcreem boys.'

Face smarting, Laurie hurried up to the counter and gave his order. While he waited, the man who had called him a Brylcreem boy sauntered up to stand beside him while he waited for his own order to be prepared. 'You a pilot, then?' At Laurie's curt nod, he said, 'What do you fly – Spitfires? Or are you one of those bomber pilots?'

Laurie sighed inwardly. The general public only seemed interested in fighter and bomber pilots. 'No,' he replied. 'I fly Airspeed Oxfords for the Air Ambulance Service.'

'Oh. Fair enough. I suppose that's important too.' The man's gaze switched to Adam. 'What about you? You on leave or something?'

Laurie's irritation flared. The man was not much older than him so clearly of service age yet he wasn't in uniform either. What gave him the right to question Adam? He opened his mouth to say something of the kind but Adam got there before him.

'I was in the army,' Adam said, his even tone not betraying the discomfort he must be feeling. 'But I was injured at Dunkirk and I was discharged on medical grounds.'

The man shuffled his feet. 'Ah. Bad luck.'

Adam gave a small smile. 'It was worse luck for those who didn't make it back at all.'

Laurie, overcome with amazement, was lost for words. Where was the Adam who had been unable to stand up for himself when verbally attacked for being out of uniform?

There was a short pause then the man said, 'I tried to join up, you know, when the war started. But I couldn't get through the medical. Heart trouble.'

'It's all right,' Adam told him. 'You don't owe me an explanation.'

The woman behind the counter called Laurie forward to collect his order, and he paid and picked up the warm newspaper-wrapped packages and hurried out. The other man also collected his food and, to Laurie's relief, headed off down the street in the other direction.

Laurie turned to his brother, pleased to have something to talk about that wasn't his failure at relationships. 'You did well back there.'

'What did you expect – me to run crying to you?'

'No, but face it, you've always been upset whenever people have asked why you weren't in uniform before.'

Adam nodded, looking thoughtful. 'I think it was something Holly said the other day when I bumped into her in the pub.'

'Oh yes? What did she say?' Laurie resisted the temptation to tease him about Holly, too curious to know what she might have said to bring about this change.

'Well, it wasn't much really. Just that a uniform or rank doesn't define a man but what's in his heart. I've thought about it a lot since then, and she's right. I think when I was in the army, I hid behind the uniform, felt that it defined my worth. But it wasn't the uniform that made me who I am, and I'm not a lesser being now I no longer wear one. And that man back there, he's not lesser for being out of uniform either. I don't have the right to judge him any more than he can judge me. But when he was speaking to you about flying, I recognised his expression. I could tell he was feeling the same way I always had, and he felt inferior to you because you're a pilot. Which is ironic, because I know you always feel inferior to fighter and bomber pilots.'

'Don't be stupid. I never said that.'

'You never had to.'

This wasn't right. Adam was supposed to be the one needing help, not pointing out uncomfortable truths. 'I thought we were supposed to be speaking about Holly,' he said. 'It sounds like the two of you are getting close. It's obvious you like her. Why don't you ask her out?'

Adam gave a twisted smile. 'What a tempting offer that would be – a man plagued with poison pen letters. I do plan on asking her out but I want to wait until that's all sorted out first.'

'Well, don't wait too long. I think she likes you but she's not going to hang around for ever.'

Adam didn't reply, and Laurie hoped he was seriously considering his advice because he thought Holly would be good for his brother. She certainly seemed to know the right thing to say, judging from the way Adam had taken her words to heart. He also hoped that Adam was now too distracted by thoughts of Holly to criticise him about losing Ruby. Laurie was already hurting enough without his brother making matters worse by pointing out where he had gone wrong. He wished there was a way to put it right, but he couldn't see how. He also didn't know what Adam meant by using him as an excuse to avoid seeing Ruby. It didn't make sense but he wasn't going to give his brother the satisfaction of asking him to explain.

Chapter Twenty-Six

Once Ruby had got over the painful business of telling her parents she and Laurie were no longer together, she was able to take comfort in the familiarity of home. Summer was the perfect time to visit, for the town was nestled in a valley with wooded hills rising steeply on both sides. In the winter the beech trees overlooking the town would appear like stark sentinels, their skeletal fingers clawing the sky, but in the summer, their branches were heavy with leaves, and their rustling could be heard even in town on quiet evenings. Ruby enjoyed sleeping with her window open so that the sound could ease her into sleep.

Although all her old school friends were no longer in Wycombe, as they were dispersed all over the country doing war work, Ruby didn't mind keeping herself company on Saturday. She couldn't help thinking wistfully of Laurie when she walked up the High Street, picturing how proud she would have felt, pointing out the handsome Guildhall and the pretty area around All Saints church. Still it felt good to be walking along the familiar street, even though there were rather more people in uniform than she was used to seeing. There were also, she was interested to see, men and women in the uniform of the United States Army Air Forces. It was only when she left the High Street behind and wandered towards the Rye – the large park to the east of the town centre – that she saw the reason for this, for her route took her past the grounds of Wycombe Abbey School. Trucks bearing the American star markings were driving through the gateway, and she remembered hearing from her mother a few months ago that the school had been requisitioned at short notice to make way for a USAAF base. She smiled then, thinking of Bobby. It might interest her to know that the exclusive girls' school had obviously moved elsewhere.

Happy though she was to be home, she couldn't rid herself of the persistent ache she felt at not having Laurie by her side. She couldn't stop worrying over the reasons for ending the relationship and wavering between the conviction that she was right and the dread that she had made a terrible mistake.

Finally, remembering the offer to listen should she feel ready to talk about what had happened, she returned home and sought out her mother. She found her at the bottom of the garden, picking raspberries.

'Look!' her mother said, showing her the brimming bowl. 'We'll have enough to make a good supply of jam, and still have some left over for pudding this evening.' Then she frowned, peering at Ruby's face. 'Is anything the matter?'

Ruby joined her mother by the raspberry canes and picked some fruit before answering. 'Nothing new. But I think I'm ready to talk about Laurie now.'

'Do you want to go inside?'

'No. I want to help.' She gingerly eased aside a large branch, careful not to prick her fingers, and set to work retrieving the berries she'd uncovered. 'Do you remember what happened with Dr Flint?' she asked after a while.

'Do I ever,' her mother muttered. 'If I could get my hands on him, I'd have a thing or two to say.'

Despite herself, Ruby grinned. Dr Flint had been her first love, and she had poured out her heart to her mother when she had returned from Oxford, broken-hearted after finally realising he had never loved her. She would have loved to see her mother giving the arrogant doctor a piece of her mind. 'Well, I suppose I always worried that Laurie would treat me the same way as Dr Flint did.'

Her mother scowled. 'Why – is Laurie like that nasty piece of work, then? If I'd known, I'd have come up to Starsden myself to put him right.'

'Oh no! He's not like that at all.' Ruby couldn't bear to have her mother think ill of him. 'He's so lovely and kind. He'd never hurt me.'

'Then I don't understand. If he's nothing like that scoundrel, why are you afraid he'll treat you the same way? You're not making sense.'

'I know. I hardly understand myself.' Ruby inspected the berry she'd just picked. It was covered in mould so she threw it into the border with a shudder. Once she had gathered her thoughts, she explained, with much hesitation, about Laurie's frequent last-minute cancellations, ending up with how she had lost her temper and broken up with him.

'Hmmm, he does sound unreliable. I know you're hurt but you're better off without him.'

Ruby immediately leaped to defend him. 'He's not unreliable! He's been dealing with family problems – his brother. I can't tell you exactly what, because I don't want to break a confidence, but he always had a good reason for standing me up.'

Her mother stepped back from the bushes, shaking her head. 'Then why did you break up with him? All you've told me so far is that Laurie's a wonderful man who would never hurt you and only cancelled dates for good reason. What's there to worry about? Surely if you love him you can be patient and wait until he's free to give you his full attention.'

Put like that, Ruby couldn't think of anything to say other than mutter, 'I don't know. I suppose I worry that I'll never come first with him.'

'Are you sure that's all you're worried about?'

'Why?'

'Well' – her mother put down the raspberries and sat on the little bench beneath the kitchen window, patting the space beside her in invitation – 'I can't help remembering the state you were in when you gave up nursing.'

Ruby sat beside her. 'What do you mean?'

'I never believed that excuse you gave about needing to take care of me.'

Ruby shifted uneasily. Her mother had needed to have an emergency appendectomy just when she had known she couldn't carry on nursing, and Ruby had returned home to take care of her.

'My surgery went well, and I was making a good recovery when you announced you were coming home,' her mother continued, 'so I knew there must be another reason. I could see you were unhappy, so I wondered if you'd had trouble with a man. I was going to advise you to apply to move to a different hospital, but then you joined the WAAF and seemed happy with your choice so I held my tongue. But now seeing you making yourself unhappy over Laurie without being able to provide an adequate reason for why you can't go out with him, I wonder if there isn't a connection with what happened at Oxford.'

Ruby couldn't answer. She had never spoken to her parents about her fears of making a mistake with a patient. Instead, when they had wanted to know why she had squandered a chance at a promising career, she had said something about nursing not being for her. At the time she hadn't connected her decision with her humiliation over Dr Flint, but now she wondered if her mother had a point.

Her mother patted her shoulder. 'Well, I can see you've got plenty to think about. But there's one thing that might give you hope.'

'What's that?'

'The way you stood up to Laurie when he told you he wasn't coming this weekend. You know I've always been worried that you tried too hard to please your friends. But you showed real backbone by telling Laurie exactly what you thought. There's hope for you yet.'

'Great, so I've finally developed a backbone just in time to ruin things with the man I love.'

'If it's meant to be, things will sort themselves out. Now, are you going to help me make the jam? These raspberries won't keep long in this heat.'

Ruby spent the rest of the weekend pondering her mother's words. It wasn't until she was on the train back to London that it occurred to her that her real fear over harming a patient hadn't properly dug its claws in until after her humiliation over Dr Flint. Of course she had worried about making a mistake before then – all of her fellow students had confessed the same thing, and their teachers had told them that it was only human to have such fears and they probably made you a better nurse. But the dread that had crippled her had only started after her eyes had been opened to Dr Flint's cruelty. Why was that?

The first thing she did when she got back to Poplar Court was seek out her friends. She found Holly and Meg in the common room. She dropped onto the sofa beside her friends, who were untangling some wool.

'You're back!' Meg cried. She dropped the mess of wool and pulled Ruby into a hug that was so fierce, Ruby guessed that she already knew about Laurie.

When Meg sat back, she studied Ruby's face with sympathetic eyes. 'We saw Laurie in town yesterday, looking like he hadn't slept in a week. We'd thought he was with you, so we couldn't understand what he was doing there.'

'I marched up and asked him what he was playing at,' Holly put in. 'He said he'd stood you up again, and you'd broken up with him. Is that true?'

Ruby nodded, her lower lip wobbling shamefully before she could bring it under control. Once she felt able, she explained what had happened before going on to tell them what her mother had said and her thoughts on the return journey. She held nothing back. 'What do you think?' she asked finally. 'Do you think I made a mistake?'

Meg and Holly exchanged glances.

'You say it,' Meg said.

'No, you,' Holly insisted. 'You're more tactful.'

Ruby looked at them both in exasperation. 'One of you tell me!'

'Fine.' Meg heaved a sigh. 'Look, only you can know for sure, but I always thought you and Laurie were perfect for each other. I know it's been rough that he's stood you up a few times, but I always thought you accepted his explanation.'

'But only you know how you really feel about him,' Holly added. 'If you think you could never love him then we'll stand by you. Won't we, Meg?'

Meg nodded.

'But I do love him,' Ruby said. 'Being away this weekend has helped me see that.'

Holly scowled. 'That Dr Flint really messed you up, didn't he. If I ever meet him, I'd like to knock him into next week.'

Despite herself, Ruby smiled. 'You'll have to get in line. My mother's already vowed to teach him a thing or two.'

Then she sagged. 'I've been an idiot. I should never have broken up with him.'

'I hope you're talking about Laurie, not Dr Flint,' Holly remarked.

'Of course I am. I'll be next in the queue behind my mother if I ever see Dr Flint again. But I can see now that he shot my confidence to pieces. I didn't trust myself at all after that whole business was over. I think that's when I started to doubt myself as a nurse as well.' Ruby sighed. 'And now I've let it affect how I looked at Laurie. I let my fears get the better of me and imagine that it was all going to end the same way as it did with Dr Flint. No. That's not it. Well, it's true but not completely. I think the real issue is that I've lost faith in my own judgement. If I was taken in by Dr Flint, how can I trust my judgement of Laurie?' She looked at her friends, her heart twisting in anguish. 'I mean, I know that Laurie's nothing like Dr Flint but, deep down, I'm always going to be waiting for him to let me down. Will I ever get over it?' And even if she did, would Laurie take her back?

Ruby went to work at the hospital the next morning wishing she was on air ambulance duty instead. Then there was a chance she could speak to Laurie and put things right. Although how she could do that when she knew she hadn't worked out her own problems with trust, she couldn't say. What was certain, though, was that she owed him an apology.

Annoyingly she didn't know when she would get a chance to see him. Although she was on air ambulance duty on Thursday, Laurie was off duty that day and while they had a singing practice before that, it was too much to hope that Laurie would still attend now she had broken up with him. In the meantime, she was going to be busy on the wards and probably wouldn't get a chance to see him, not if he would be spending his off-duty hours with his family. She could hardly waltz up to his house and demand to see him when she had been the one to break off the relationship. His mother would probably send her away with a flea in her ear.

Sister Allen regarded her with a sniff when she arrived on the ward. 'Nice to see you've remembered you work here. You can start by making up bed five. We've got a patient on the way up from theatre. I would assign the other orderly to help but as she hasn't turned up yet, you'll have to do it alone.'

Ruby set to work without comment, knowing that when Sister Allen was in a bad mood, any attempt to explain oneself would be met with a tongue lashing. She felt sorry for whoever the other nursing orderly was. Not that she would be late for another ten minutes, for Ruby had reported for duty early. 'I won't bother next time, if this is all the thanks I get,' she muttered as she went to fetch clean sheets and blankets.

She had just set to work on the bed when Sister Allen's angry voice drifted down from the other end of the long ward. 'What time do you call this?'

Smoothing the bottom sheet across the mattress, Ruby glanced up and saw a confused-looking Bobby point at the clock. 'It's 0755, Sister.'

Sister Allen gave an impatient tut. 'Not according to my watch it isn't.' She tapped the watch pinned to her apron. 'I set it by the wireless yesterday morning, and it quite clearly says it's three minutes past eight.'

Poor Bobby had to stand there while Sister Allen lectured her at length about everything that was wrong about her, her uniform and the WAAF nursing orderlies in general. Even though she wasn't exactly Ruby's favourite person, Ruby took no pleasure in witnessing her humiliation.

'Nurse!' whispered the man in the next bed.

Ruby turned to him. All the patients called the orderlies 'nurse', and she had given up trying to correct them. 'How can I help?'

'I'd like a glass of water, please.'

She turned to pick up his water jug, expecting to find it empty, but it was half full. She poured his drink and handed it to him. 'Why didn't you pour it yourself?' For Corporal Bennet wasn't bed-bound and could have easily reached his own water jug.

'What, and miss this?' He was watching Sister Allen's diatribe with a rapt expression. 'A fine figure of a woman is our sister.'

Ruby suppressed a snort and went on making the bed before Sister Allen decided to tell *her* off. 'Takes all sorts,' she muttered.

Corporal Bennet was clearly in a talkative mood, for he carried on speaking to her as he worked, extolling Sister Allen's virtues. 'Pity she's wrong about the time,' he said eventually. 'Corporal Hunter changed it for a bet without her noticing when she was giving him a bed bath.'

Ruby glanced across at the patient in the opposite bed. He grinned at her and then gave Bennet a thumbs up. She mustered up the best severe frown she could manage. 'And when were you thinking of telling her?' she asked.

'Oh, we thought *you* could do that, Nurse,' Corporal Hunter said. Then he gave a feeble cough, not particularly convincing seeing as he was recovering from surgery on his shoulder. 'I'd do it myself but I'm not well enough.'

Great. The day was getting better and better. She spared Bobby a sympathetic smile when Sister Allen set her to work. Bobby didn't smile back – hardly surprising considering the unjust telling-off she had just endured. When she passed Ruby on her way to collect the breakfast trays, Ruby saw she pressed her lips in a tight line and knew she was fighting tears. For Bobby's sake she must tell Sister Allen about the changed watch soon. For her own sake, she would wait until the sister was in a better mood. Probably after the ward rounds – she was usually happier once they were over.

Sister Allen was always at her most officious when they were preparing for rounds. She insisted that the ward should be immaculately tidy, and this included the patients. Ruby and Bobby hurried around the ward, making the beds around each patient, tidying bedside cabinets and even straightening pyjama tops. Ruby had long ago realised that ward rounds were the nursing equivalent of a military inspection. She never knew what the fuss was about, though, for when the surgeon arrived, trailing his acolytes, he never appeared to notice the state of the ward. What she did know was that the ward sister would always be relieved when it was over, and even Sister Allen could occasionally manage a smile and appeared more relaxed once the surgeon had departed.

Bobby, however, didn't seem to be any happier. Although her work didn't suffer, she was pale and tight-lipped for the whole morning. Once, when Ruby passed her emerging from the sluice room, her eyes were suspiciously red-rimmed.

When the ward was at its most peaceful, Ruby approached Sister Allen at her desk and explained in a low voice about her watch.

'Honestly,' Sister Allen hissed, correcting her watch by the ward clock, 'these patients act like naughty schoolboys.'

The incident seemed to put her in a bad mood again yet she did approach Bobby and offer her a grudging apology.

Ruby was happy to make her escape when Sister Allen sent her on her break. It was a steaming hot day, and Ruby didn't feel hungry. Therefore, after grabbing a quick drink of water, she collected a blanket from the nurses' sitting room and went out onto the roof. The hospital had a flat roof, and now that summer had arrived, nurses and nursing orderlies used it to do a spot of sunbathing during their breaks.

As she had expected, she found several other nurses up there. Usually, Ruby would have joined them. Today having been particularly fraught, however, she searched for a quiet spot where she could collect her thoughts before it was time to return to the fray.

On the point of placing her blanket in a sunny spot behind a chimney stack, she heard a sniffle. She dropped the blanket and went to investigate. In the corner of the roof, her elbows propped upon the low wall, was Bobby. She had her back to Ruby and was gazing out across the aerodrome. At least, that's what she appeared to be doing at first, but then Ruby took in her hunched, shaking shoulders, and realised that she was crying.

Her heart twisted in sympathy. Forgetting her dislike of Bobby, she went to stand beside her. 'Bobby, what's wrong?'

Bobby gave a start and straightened up, rubbing her eyes. 'Oh, nothing really. Just Sister Allen, you know.'

'But Sister Allen's always picking on us. You've never let it get to you before.' She couldn't say exactly why she didn't like to leave Bobby alone considering the way she seemed to have taken delight in asserting her superiority over Ruby yet something about her forlorn droop of the head made her want to reach out and offer comfort.

'I know but' – Bobby gave an impatient huff – 'if you must know, it's not a good time for me at the moment. I'm having some… family difficulties.'

'Oh, I'm sorry. Is there anything I can do?'

'Yes, there's something you can do. You can stop sticking your nose in where it's not wanted.'

'I was only trying to help.'

But Bobby didn't reply. Instead she pointedly turned her back and leaned against the wall again.

Stung, Ruby retreated to another part of the roof.

Bobby's behaviour didn't improve in the days that followed. 'I understand her not wanting to talk to me,' Ruby said to Holly and Meg as they were on their way to singing practice on the Wednesday evening, 'but I wish she would let someone help her. I know we're not friends, but I hate to see her hurting.'

'It wouldn't be so bad if she didn't take her bad mood out on the rest of us,' Holly remarked. 'She had a right go at me this morning for dropping my hairbrush on the floor. Apparently the noise gave her a headache. Honestly, she's worse than the princess in "The Princess and the Pea".'

'Maybe she's not well,' Ruby said. 'Still, I've got a whole day without her tomorrow because I'm on air ambulance duty.'

Her thoughts had been so occupied with Bobby that she had temporarily forgotten about Laurie. She only remembered him when they reached the classroom where they did their singing practice and knew a moment of panic. What if he was there after all? She hadn't worked out what to say. It was therefore a relief to go inside and see he hadn't turned up. And as he had a day off the next day, there was no risk of running into him unprepared when she was on ambulance duty.

Her relief lasted right until she arrived in the crew room the next morning and saw that instead of Squadron Leader Norton as she had expected, her pilot was Laurie.

Chapter Twenty-Seven

A surge of pain hit Laurie in the chest when Ruby walked in. This was the first time he had seen her since she had broken up with him, and the pain was just as sharp now as it had been then. Yet he took no satisfaction at seeing the mingled confusion and upset in her expression.

'I didn't know you were flying today,' she said, stooping to pat Bentley.

'Norton's gone down with a stomach bug,' he told her.

'Where are we going?'

'Up near Aberdeen. RAF Dyce.'

'Oh, I went there the other week.' She paused then went on at a rush, 'I'm sorry for lashing out at you on Friday. I was disappointed but I shouldn't have said what I did. It must have been difficult having your parents find out, and I know you needed to be with them.'

No apology for breaking up with him, though. Or was she waiting for an apology from him now? Whatever she expected him to say, he was clearly too late, for she turned away and opened her locker, saying, 'I hope you don't mind that we're flying together today.'

'Of course not.' He paused, racking his brains for something intelligent to say. 'Weather looks set fair for the whole day.' *Oh, nice one, Laurie. That's exactly what she must have been dying to hear.* He just about managed to resist the urge to bash his head against the wall and went to his own locker instead and pulled out his flying jacket. What was wrong with him? Adam was right. He should have stood up to his parents and insisted upon joining Ruby for their planned weekend so why couldn't he say that to her? What was stopping him from attempting to make things right between them when he had ached from her absence all weekend?

The crew room door opened again and the rest of the crew arrived, preventing any further private conversation between him and Ruby even if he could have worked out what to say.

He and Neil Maitland, his navigator for the day, had already been briefed on their destination, and now he turned to Neil and asked, 'Got the route planned?'

'All sorted, Skipper, and ready when you are.'

'Right, then.' He quickly briefed Ruby and Rhys Powell, letting them know that they would be flying first to RAF Dyce to collect a WAAF who had been injured in a motorcycle accident. They were taking her to RAF Kidlington for her transfer to hospital in Oxford. From there it was a short hop back to Starsden. He finished with, 'Any questions?' When no one said anything he rose, saying, 'Let's get this show on the road.'

He cringed at his falsely hearty tone all the way to the aircraft. He had to give himself a stern talking-to to make sure he concentrated on the pre-flight checks. Why couldn't he act normally around Ruby or at least show her that he hadn't turned into a gibbering idiot since their breakup?

During the flight to Aberdeen he couldn't prevent his thoughts from drifting to Ruby. Did he want her back? Of course he did! He didn't need to ponder that question at all. But if that was the case, why hadn't he been able to apologise for letting her down so badly? Especially considering what she had told him about the doctor who had strung her along. He should have known that backing out of their weekend plans would bring back bad memories for her. And, after all, having been more than understanding about the other times he had cancelled plans, she deserved to be put first this time when she had made such big plans for the weekend. He could only imagine how difficult it must have been for her to arrive alone at her parents' when they had been expecting to meet him. So why did something keep holding him back when he had tried to apologise?

He thought of what Adam had said. Or, rather, refused to explain because, apparently, it should have been obvious. He had no idea what he had meant. Adam had said one thing, though. He had wanted to know what Laurie had been trying to prove by taking over the investigation of the Poison Pen. And something about him needing to play the hero.

Rhys spoke up, his voice sounding tinny over the intercom. 'There's a squadron of Spitfires on an intercept course, Skipper, at angels one five.' He gave the coordinates the courses were due to intercept, adding, 'The message came from RAF Church Fenton.'

At fifteen thousand feet, they were unlikely to collide, given that the air ambulances didn't fly above ten thousand feet. Still, there could be an issue if one of the Spitfires had to drop out of formation for any reason, so Laurie asked the navigator to plot an alternative course.

'On it, Skipper,' Maitland responded. A short while later he reported back giving a bearing.

As Laurie made the course correction, he felt a pang of envy thinking about the Spitfire pilots. He'd love to be in their shoes, flying one of the renowned fighter planes, doing battle one-on-one with enemy aircraft.

In that instant he had a flash of understanding and knew what Adam had been referring to. Adam, who daily faced people who accused him of shirking his duties because he was out of uniform, understood Laurie better than anyone. He knew that Laurie had longed to be a fighter pilot and, although Laurie had never told him so, would doubtless have guessed that Laurie felt somehow lesser to the men who were serving in the fighter squadrons. When Adam had asked him what he was trying to prove, he had meant that Laurie was trying to prove to Ruby that he was a hero. Because he felt that he wasn't good enough to be a fighter pilot and therefore not good enough for her.

In that moment, Laurie knew that was why he hadn't fought harder for Ruby. Because deep down he believed she deserved better. But how was he ever to overcome that feeling?

—

Ruby usually enjoyed the first flight of the day. As she didn't have any responsibilities until they picked up that day's patient, she was able to gaze out of the window at the countryside and clouds or chatter to the wireless operator if he wasn't busy. This time, however, she couldn't wait for it to end. No matter how many times she tried to enjoy the scenery, her gaze kept drifting to the back of Laurie's head and reliving their awkward conversation in the crew room.

Why hadn't he responded when she had apologised? She ran her words over and over through her mind. Should she have asked how his parents were? They were, after all, the reason why he had backed out of the Wycombe trip. Maybe she should have sounded more contrite? But however she tried to excuse it, there was no denying that he hadn't apologised for not going. Admittedly he had said he was sorry on Friday when he had made his excuses, but it had been a half-hearted apology, and he had seemed to take for granted that she wouldn't mind.

That was it — even though she had told him how Dr Flint's behaviour had humiliated her, he had still taken it for granted that she wouldn't mind being stood up, simply because he had told her the reason. But he should have known that it would bring back painful memories, and she wanted his apology to acknowledge that.

Yet more than that, she thought about her recent revelation regarding her inability to trust her judgement. She had hoped to be able to explain that to Laurie, but there hadn't been a chance. Perhaps if they had a wait for the ambulance at RAF Dyce, she would try again.

She was therefore disappointed when they found the ambulance already waiting for them when they landed at Aberdeen. Yet when she saw who her patient was, all thought of Laurie fled. It was LACW Penelope Maltby, Bobby's school friend. Maltby, it turned out, had been riding pillion with one of the station's pilots when his front wheel had struck a large pothole and flung both rider and passenger into a ditch. The driver had got away with minor injuries, but Maltby had damaged her back.

'It's not broken, thank goodness,' Maltby had explained as Ruby had got her settled in the aircraft's cabin, 'but it hurts like billy-o, and I've got to stay in bed for a while.'

'Do you have family near Oxford, then?' Ruby asked. 'Are you moving there to be close to them?'

'My parents live in Boars Hill, just outside Oxford.' Maltby winced when Ruby slipped a pillow under her head.

'I'm sorry. Would you like more pain relief?'

'No thanks. It makes me feel so sick I'd rather not. Anyway, I've never been up in a plane before, and I don't want to sleep through it.'

'Well, I'm sorry your first experience of flying isn't under better circumstances,' Ruby said with a smile. 'Is there anything I can do to help?'

'You can talk to me.'

'It would be a pleasure. What shall we talk about?' At least she would have something to keep her mind off Laurie during the flight.

'Give me a moment to think. Wait.' Maltby frowned up at Ruby. 'Haven't we met before?'

'Yes, not too long ago. I came to RAF Dyce a few weeks ago and had to stay for the night.'

'Yes, I remember now. You work with Bobby Jones.'

'That's right. I told her I'd met you, and I'm sure she would have sent her regards if she knew I was going to see you again today.'

'And how is she?'

'Oh, she's fine. In her usual form.' Ruby wasn't sure what to say here but certainly wasn't going to mention that Bobby had been weepy and out of sorts all week.

'That's good.'

By this time they were speeding down the runway, and Ruby didn't catch Maltby's next words over the roar of the engines. Maltby looked a little pale, so she placed her fingers on her wrist to take her pulse. With her mind occupied on counting, she simply nodded.

Maltby fell silent during takeoff, gazing out at the patch of sky visible from her stretcher. Once the Oxford levelled out, she carried on speaking of Bobby as though she hadn't stopped. 'I mean, I can't blame her. I don't think she's really come to terms with losing her fiancé, and he died two years ago this week.'

Chapter Twenty-Eight

Ruby never knew how she managed to control herself during the rest of the flight. Maltby soon steered the conversation in another direction, and Ruby had to make the appropriate responses without giving away her utter shock at Maltby's bombshell. She longed to ask more but didn't dare reveal to her patient that she had just given away her friend's secret. She would never forgive herself if Maltby became distressed and her pain increased as a result.

By the time she got back to Poplar Court that evening, she was dying to share her news, and thankfully Bobby wasn't there when she burst into the room and found Meg and Holly having a 'domestic' evening, along with Winnie. Meg and Holly were polishing their uniform buttons and Winnie was knitting. Even the open window couldn't dispel the pungent aroma of the Silvo polish Meg and Holly were using.

'You'll never guess what I heard today,' she said before flinging herself onto her bed.

Holly looked up briefly from daubing Silvo on a button. 'Umm… Squadron Leader Norton is having a passionate affair with Sister Allen?'

Ruby pulled a face. 'Eww! Don't be daft. Now you've made me picture them smooching in the cinema.'

Meg gave a mock shudder. 'You'd better tell us what you heard. Anything to get that image out of my head.'

'All right but actually it's rather sad, and I don't know what we should do about it.'

By the time she had finished, all three girls looked horrified. 'So all this time, her fiancé's been dead?' Winnie gasped. 'Then why's she been going on about him as though he was still alive?'

'Are you sure we can trust this Maltby girl?' Holly asked. 'You don't think she was pulling your leg, do you, or trying to stir up trouble?'

'No, she was genuine, I'm sure. For a start, she thought I already knew what she was telling me. And anyway, it all makes perfect sense, because Bobby has been upset all week. She wouldn't tell me why, just said something about family problems, but if this is the second anniversary of her fiancé's death, that would explain everything.'

'Except why she pretends he's still alive,' Holly said.

'Well, yes, except that.'

Meg moved her button stick over one of her pocket buttons, looking thoughtful. 'Do you think we should tell her what we know? It might help her to have someone she can confide in.'

'Or it might break her when she learns that her big secret is out,' Holly said. 'But why would she try and make everyone think her fiancé was still alive? It's not as if it reflects badly on her. It's just a tragedy that a lot of people can relate to these days.'

There was a pensive silence, broken only by the click of Winnie's knitting needles. Finally Ruby ventured to give voice to the thought that had been forming in her mind ever since she had said goodbye to Maltby at Kidlington. 'I wonder if she doesn't want to face up to his loss? By pretending he's still alive and writing him all those letters, she doesn't have to live in a world where he's no longer there. And have you noticed that she never goes home? Most people jump at the chance to go home on a forty-eight-hour pass, but she's been telling us she's waiting for when her fiancé gets leave. I think it's because her family know he's dead, so if she goes there she can't carry on believing he's just serving abroad.'

Meg stared at her, an opened can of Silvo in her hand. 'That doesn't sound... healthy. What should we do?'

'I don't know. If we tell her we know the truth, we'd be pulling the rug from under her feet in a jolly brutal way but if we carry on as if nothing has changed, we're probably making things worse for Bobby in the long run. Because I agree this pretence can't be healthy.' She thought a moment before carrying on. 'I suppose what I'm saying is that we shouldn't do anything in a hurry. Let's carry on as before but look out for opportunities where we might gently hint that we know the truth.'

Winnie put down her knitting. 'You're forgetting one thing. This Penelope Maltby girl is a friend of Bobby's. She might realise she dropped a brick and confess to Bobby in a letter.'

'That's a point,' Ruby admitted. 'I don't think I hid my shock very well. When Maltby's had time to think about it she might very well work out that I didn't know.' She sighed. 'That means we need to say something sooner rather than later. Look, it's the fundraiser on Saturday, and I need to concentrate on that for now. With the post as it is these days, I don't think we need worry about any letters from Maltby arriving before next week. But when the fundraiser is all over, we'd better take Bobby aside and talk to her.'

As far as Ruby was concerned, the following two days couldn't be over soon enough. Spending Friday on the ward with Bobby was uncomfortable, knowing what she knew. As much as she disliked her, you would have to be an unfeeling monster not to feel pity for the poor girl. If Bobby had been open about why she was going around with red-rimmed eyes, Ruby could have offered words of comfort and let her know she wasn't alone. As it was, all she could do was try to take on as many of Bobby's tasks as possible without Sister Allen noticing.

On the morning of the singing event, she found Bobby in the nurses' sitting room, holding an unsealed letter.

'Has the post arrived?' she asked with a nod at the envelope.

Bobby gave a start, and Ruby thought she hadn't even noticed her arrival until she had spoken. 'What? Oh, no. This is a letter to my parents. I meant to drop it in the mail basket but I've got such a headache, I completely forgot.' She rested her head on her free hand, looking exhausted.

Ruby's heart went out to her. 'I'll take it for you.' It would mean losing her break because by the time she had got to the office where the nursing orderlies left their mail for censoring, she would have to return straight to the ward if she didn't want Sister Allen to put her on a charge for being late.

'Would you really do that for me?' For the first time ever, Ruby thought Bobby actually looked human, probably because she seemed too tired to try acting her usual superior self.

'Of course.' She took the envelope, unsurprised to feel its weight and thickness. Of course Bobby would only use the best quality stationery, even when paper was scarce.

Then her mind caught up with what her fingers were telling her. She looked at the envelope, half expecting to see Adam's name inked in capital letters. But she was being stupid. Bobby was hardly going to hand in a poison pen letter for censorship. As expected, the letter was addressed to a Mr and Mrs Jones in Surrey, written in Bobby's flowing handwriting.

She looked up to find Bobby staring at her. 'What's so fascinating about my home address?'

'Gosh, sorry, that was rude of me.' Ruby felt her face flaming. 'Well, I must dash if I'm to get back on the ward in time.'

She fled down the corridor but once she had rounded the corner she stopped, torn between the need to respect Bobby's privacy and the urge to remove the letter from the envelope and check for the Basildon Bond watermark. In the end it was the thought of Adam's suffering that made up her mind. With trembling fingers, she slipped the folded notepaper from the envelope, thankful that censorship regulations required personnel to put letters in the mail basket unsealed. Doing her best not to read the contents of the letter, she held it up to the window. Her gaze immediately fell upon the watermark. It was Basildon Bond.

Ruby was practically beside herself by the time she went off duty. She needed to tell someone what she suspected and so the moment she got back to Poplar Court she flew up to her room. Thankfully Holly and Meg were already there.

'All ready for the big event?' Meg asked.

Ruby's head was so full of her news it took her a moment to work out what Meg meant. 'Oh, the fundraiser. Yes, I suppose so. But listen.' And she told them what she had discovered.

'Are you telling me that Bobby's the Poison Pen?' Holly demanded when Ruby explained about the watermark.

'It all fits,' Ruby said. 'Think of all those letters she writes, saying they're to her fiancé. Only now we know her fiancé's dead, so who was she writing to? And think of all those early morning walks she's always going on about. She could be posting the letters then.'

Meg looked upset. 'I don't know. This is a big accusation, and all we've got is circumstantial evidence. There could be other people here with Basildon Bond notepaper saved from before the war.'

'What are you going to do?' Holly asked.

Ruby glanced at her watch. 'There isn't time to do anything now — we're supposed to be out carolling. But tomorrow I'm going to take Bobby aside and tackle her about it. Don't breathe a word to anyone else — as you say, I could be wrong and this is all just a coincidence.'

'You don't think you are wrong, though, do you.' This was from Meg and it was a statement, not a question.

'No. I think grief can make people do strange things, and I think this is another symptom of Bobby bottling up her feelings. I'm positive she's the Poison Pen, and I'm dreading having to speak to her about it.' She glanced at her watch again. 'Anyway, we need to leave or we'll be late.'

She pulled open the door, only to stop dead when she came face to face with Bobby. She felt sick. How long had she been standing there?

Bobby stood stock still for a moment then turned and fled down the stairs. A short while later they heard the front door slam.

'Well, that's torn it. I'd better go after her.'

Ruby had her foot on the top stair when Holly grabbed her arm. 'Leave her be. She could have gone anywhere, and you'll never find her if she doesn't want to be found. Let's go and sing and by the time we've finished she might have calmed down enough to come back to the room.'

While Ruby wasn't happy leaving a panicked Bobby to her own devices, she knew Holly was right. 'All right. Let's go.'

Chapter Twenty-Nine

Thanks to all the rehearsals, Ruby could sing her part without needing to concentrate. This was a good thing considering her head was full of the image of Bobby standing behind the door, eyes wide in her white face.

She had heard, Ruby was sure. Bobby knew that Ruby suspected she was the Poison Pen. What was she going to do? Ruby could only pray that Bobby would return to Poplar Court of her own accord and let Ruby help her.

And once she'd helped Bobby and stopped her from sending more letters, would Laurie want her back? But she shut her mind to that thought, not wanting to get her hopes up only to have them dashed if Laurie made it clear he didn't want to go out with her any more.

All the while, she was vaguely aware that the choir was receiving a warm reception. They had started in the hospital, singing a few songs in the nurses' sitting room to the assembled staff and patients. Before Ruby knew it, they were singing the closing notes of the last song to enthusiastic applause.

Recollecting herself, she cleared her throat and signalled for silence. 'Thank you,' she said. 'As you know, we're performing in aid of St Winifred's school. Their new term starts soon, and they're in desperate need of funds to replace the equipment destroyed in the bombing. Please give generously.'

While the rest of the choir moved around the room shaking their collecting tins, Ruby leaned against the wall and released a shaky breath. She'd managed to give her speech without stumbling, and that was a miracle considering her state of mind. Just two more performances to get through, then she could look for Bobby.

The performers returned with their tins considerably fuller than before and producing a very satisfying rattle. Ruby thanked them, painfully aware of Laurie's absence from the group. He had stopped coming to rehearsals after their breakup, not that she could blame him.

Next they set out for the NAAFI canteen for their second performance. This was as great a success as the first and they were holding brimming collection tins as they returned to the hospital for the final part of the evening. As it was a warm evening with no risk of rain, Ruby had arranged with the hospital staff that they would sing under the windows outside for the benefit of the patients who'd been unable to attend their first performance.

The group organised themselves on the lawn outside the hospital. It was a beautiful evening, and the sun was now setting, turning the sky gold and casting long shadows. There was a general rustling of sheet music as everyone found the words for the first song, when the WAAF beside Ruby gave a cry and pointed up. 'There's someone out on the ledge!'

Ruby looked up, and her mouth went dry with horror. A woman was perched precariously on the narrow ledge up on the rooftop. It was Bobby.

'Don't shout at her,' a nurse from the choir snapped. 'We don't want to startle her.'

'Fetch Matron!' someone else cried.

Ruby felt sick. Bobby was there because of her. It was up to her to put it right. 'I know her,' she said. 'I'm going up to talk to her.'

Without waiting to see what anyone else was doing, she ran inside and sprinted up the stairs. The hospital wasn't a tall building, only three storeys high, but high enough to make it unlikely Bobby would survive if she jumped.

'This is all my fault,' she moaned, taking the stairs two at a time. 'Please let her still be there.'

She gasped with relief when she ran out onto the roof and saw Bobby still on her perch. She was leaning back against the wall, one arm wrapped around the parapet, and Ruby took heart when she saw Bobby was clearly nervous about falling.

Much as she wanted to dash up to Bobby and grab her arm, common sense forced her to slow down and think. If she startled the girl now, she would send her tumbling off the roof. Accordingly, she edged around the roof, making sure she came into view when there were still several yards between them. Bobby was staring at the ground and gave no sign that she had noticed her.

With her heart in her mouth and holding her arms out to the sides to make herself appear as unthreatening as possible, she softly called Bobby's name.

With a violent start that set Ruby's heart pounding, Bobby turned a tear-streaked face in her direction. 'What are you doing here – come to gloat?'

'Why would I do that? I hate to see you in such pain.'

'Oh, don't pretend that you care two hoots about me. I heard you earlier. You know what I've done, and now everyone's going to know.'

'I haven't told anyone apart from Holly and Meg, and I won't tell anyone else except Adam. He deserves to know.

He'll understand, though, I'm sure. He's been through an awful time himself.'

Bobby seemed to hesitate as though contemplating climbing to safety, but her face was creased with indecision. 'What if he doesn't? What if he tells the police?'

'He won't.' It was a male voice that spoke, coming from directly behind Ruby. A voice she knew and loved.

She spun around. 'Laurie!' Had it not been totally inappropriate in the circumstances, she would have flung herself into his arms.

—

Laurie wanted nothing more than to hold Ruby in his arms and make sure she was all right but he didn't dare shift his gaze from Bobby. He edged closer, taking care not to make any sudden movements, giving himself time to catch his breath after his wild dash up the stairs. He had been looking out of the windows in the Sergeants' Mess after dinner and, on seeing the group heading for the hospital, had only belatedly remembered the fundraiser. After Ruby had split up with him, he had stopped going to singing practice. Considering she was organising the event, she wouldn't be able to leave if she didn't want to see him, and he didn't want to make her uncomfortable. However, when he had seen the choir, he had told himself that he ought to support them and so had set out to watch. He also couldn't deny that he was longing to catch a glimpse of Ruby. He had arrived just in time to see the commotion over Bobby's appearance on the roof and Ruby running to stop her. He hadn't been aware of any conscious thought but had sprinted after her.

'Adam's already told me about the letters,' he said, 'although he doesn't know who sent them. But he's always said he doesn't want the police involved. We can keep it between ourselves, I promise. Won't you climb back so we can talk about it?'

Bobby didn't budge. 'This is a trick.'

'No trick, I promise.'

He became aware of Ruby moving closer. 'Why don't we just talk for a bit,' she invited. 'You could tell us about your fiancé.'

Laurie, thinking he knew where Ruby was going, put in, 'He wouldn't want you to hurt yourself. I bet he's counting down the days until he can see you again.'

He was mystified when Ruby scowled at him and shook her head. Mystified, that was, until she said to Bobby, 'You see – Laurie doesn't know. I haven't told everyone. But I saw Penelope Maltby on Thursday, and she wanted to know how you were doing. She didn't realise that no one here knew your fiancé had died.'

Bobby gave a heaving sob, and Laurie feared she was going to jump, but thankfully she didn't release her grip on the parapet. 'I didn't want everyone to feel sorry for me so I pretended he was alive. It was easier that way.' She looked at Ruby. 'You must think I'm a coward, not facing up to the truth.'

Ruby shook her head. 'I think you're brave. You've had to go through it all alone with no one to talk to when you needed it the most. I'm sorry I wasn't more friendly. I should have tried harder. Maybe you would have felt able to confide in me.'

Laurie was horrified. How awful for poor Bobby to be grieving the whole time she had been in Starsden with no one to turn to. He had never guessed there was anything wrong. If it hadn't been for Ruby's persistence, Bobby might still be alone in her grief. His heart felt heavy with admiration and love for the remarkable young woman she was. If only they could persuade Bobby to come back, because he knew Ruby would take it as a personal failure if Bobby fell now.

Ruby moved closer to Bobby again, still not near enough to touch. Laurie, too, crept as close as he dared, weighing up his chances of catching her if she seemed about to jump.

'Tell me more about your fiancé,' she said.

Bobby wiped her eyes with the hand that wasn't clutching the wall. 'I met him when he was at Sandhurst. It was a whirlwind romance. We planned to marry after I'd finished my nursing training, only war broke out and he was sent to France with the British Expeditionary Force.'

Even in her distress, Laurie could detect the pride in her voice. 'He was proud to go. He said it was his duty.' Her face crumpled. 'But then came Dunkirk, and he was injured. He was trapped in France for days before they could get him back to England and to hospital.' She shot Laurie a glance. 'That's what happened to your brother, too. I heard. But he survived. Not like Ben. He was in hospital for weeks, in so much pain, but I thought he would be all right.' The words were pouring out now between sobs, and Laurie's blood ran cold as he heard her tale that had been so similar to Adam's yet so tragically different. 'But then he died, and I couldn't bear it that he had suffered for so long. It would have been kinder had he died right away.'

She broke down into desperate sobs, and Laurie tensed. Could he get closer without her seeing? But just when he decided he could make a move, she flung up her head and shot him an accusing glare. 'Ben died but your brother lived. Why? It's not fair!'

'No,' Ruby agreed, in a voice that would have calmed a rampaging bull. 'It's not fair. Is that why you sent him those letters?' She took another step closer to Bobby, who was sobbing so hard now that she didn't appear to notice. Laurie took a chance and also stepped forward, calculating that he was now within reach of her left arm. He let out a shaky breath, relieved he had managed to get so close without her seeming to mind.

Bobby nodded. 'I couldn't seem to stop once I started. It was my way of getting back at the world, because it seemed so wrong that Ben wasn't in it any more.'

And getting back at Adam for not dying when Ben had. Laurie was starting to understand the twisted logic that had led her to send the letters. Not, as he had assumed, from someone resentful of Adam for seemingly avoiding his duty but someone for whom Adam was a constant reminder that others had survived when her fiancé had not.

Ruby reached out a hand towards Bobby. 'Come back, Bobby. I know you don't want to hurt yourself. Let's get you inside where we can have a nice cup of tea and talk things over.'

Bobby inched around on the ledge until she was facing inwards, and Laurie felt some of his tension ease. Yet he wouldn't be able to relax completely until Bobby was well away from the drop.

He'd expected her to climb over but she stopped and sent Ruby a pleading look. 'I can't come back. It's too late. Everyone will be talking about me. I couldn't bear it.'

She turned again, and both Ruby and Laurie sprang forward, crying, 'No!'

Bobby paused. 'Why not? No one will miss me, and I can't carry on knowing people are whispering about me behind their backs.'

'I know the feeling. I really do.' Ruby was so close now that she could have closed a hand around Bobby's arm but she made no move to do so. Laurie guessed that she didn't want to do anything that might force Bobby to jump because she wouldn't have the strength to hold her up even if she caught her. She was a lot smaller than Bobby. He, on the other hand, felt confident that if he could grab her arm, he could support her weight. Unfortunately, Ruby's latest move had put herself in between him and Bobby. He took a surreptitious step sideways while Bobby's attention was on Ruby. And then another.

Ruby was still speaking. 'We all suffer humiliation at one time or another,' she continued. 'It happened to me when I was in nursing training.'

'I know. I heard you mention it once. Big deal. Someone stood you up.'

'Actually there was more to it than that, and I couldn't tell even Holly and Meg because I still feel awful when I remember it. But I don't mind telling you if you want to hear.'

'Go on.' And Laurie was encouraged to see that Bobby appeared genuinely interested. He used her distraction to inch still closer while burning with curiosity to hear what Ruby was about to reveal.

'What I never told anyone was that Dr Flint, the man who stood me up, had taken a bet with some other doctors that he could treat a nurse badly and still get her to agree to more dates. I was the lucky girl he fixed upon.' There was bitterness in her voice, and Laurie knew she was telling the truth and not just spinning a tale to make Bobby feel better. He had to remind himself that his full attention needed to remain on Bobby right now or he would have taken her in his arms and done everything in his power to persuade her that he would never hurt her. 'No doubt because I was young and gullible and oh so starry-eyed. Anyway, I had no idea that every time I was walking on air because

Dr Flint had arranged another date and assured me that this time nothing would stop him from being there, all his friends were laughing at me. Eventually one of them developed a conscience and explained. Knowing that I was the butt of a joke for the entire medical staff was more than I could take. I thought I would never get over the humiliation.' Ruby's voice shook but she squared her shoulders and looked Bobby in the eye. 'But I did get over it and look at me now. I'm happy and I've got wonderful friends that I can trust.'

'You couldn't stay at the hospital, though.'

'True, but it wasn't the humiliation that drove me to leave.'

'What was it, then?'

If this was an odd conversation to have with one person on the brink of a deadly drop, neither woman appeared to notice. Laurie took advantage of Bobby's distraction and managed to ease himself close enough to catch her. He didn't attempt to take hold of her arm, though, knowing it would be better for Bobby if she made the decision to return to safety.

'I stopped being able to trust my judgement. I questioned my every move and became afraid I would make a mistake that would cost a patient their life. I couldn't carry on nursing with that weight of dread on my mind.' Without taking her gaze from Bobby she said, 'Please come here, Bobby. I've never told anyone that before, and I've given you the power to use it against me if you chose, but I know you won't. I trust you. I feel so much better for having told someone, and I know you'll feel better if you talk through your problems with someone. Trust *me*.'

Still Bobby hesitated, and it occurred to Laurie that it was time he stopped being a spectator. Ruby had done all she could but only he could give her the final assurances she needed to get her to return to safety. 'I promise you that neither Adam nor any of our family want to make any trouble for you.'

'You won't go to the police?'

He shook his head. 'We just want to put the whole business behind us. Everyone deserves a second chance.' He said this as much for Ruby's benefit as for Bobby's, wishing she would give *him* a second chance.

Bobby nodded. 'Fine. I'll—' She moved to climb back over the parapet and her words ended in a shriek when her foot slipped off the ledge. Laurie made a lunge and grabbed her arm. The next thing he knew, he was slammed against the wall, holding Bobby's wrist in a death-grip, taking her whole weight. He heard screams from the watchers below and Ruby's strangled: 'No!' He looked down into Bobby's white, terrified face, aware of a burning pain in his shoulder, of blood roaring in his ears and the corner of the stone parapet digging cruelly into his ribs.

'Don't let go!' Bobby screamed.

'I won't.'

It felt like he was gripping Bobby for an eternity but it must have only been a second or two before one of Bobby's pedalling feet managed to find the ledge, relieving him of some of her weight. That gave him the chance to grip her with his other hand and then he hauled her over the parapet. They both collapsed to the ground.

Everything was a blur for a while. He gasped for breath as though he had just run a marathon. Inexplicably there were more people on the rooftop now: the matron of the hospital was there, as was the medical officer and another nurse. Eventually a sobbing Bobby was led away by the MO and the nurse, leaving him with Ruby and Matron.

Matron looked from one to the other. 'Good job, both of you. You should be proud of yourselves.'

And he was proud of himself. He had saved a life. He had been where he needed to be.

At that moment the weight that he had been hardly aware of most of the time fell away. He didn't need to be a fighter pilot to save lives. Bobby was still alive because he'd been exactly where he was meant to be. And if Ruby would only take him back, he would have everything he wanted in life.

He staggered to his feet and winced, clutching his shoulder.

Ruby turned troubled eyes on him. 'You're hurt!'

'I might have pulled a muscle in my shoulder but I don't think it's too bad.'

'We'd better check you out,' Matron said. 'Come to my office, both of you. Hot drinks all round, and I'll ask the MO to look at your shoulder when he's finished with Jones.'

She swept away but before he followed he turned to Ruby.

'Please. As soon as we can, let's talk. I want you back.'

Chapter Thirty

The next hour passed in a daze for Ruby. She sat in Matron's office cradling a mug of tea between her hands while Matron asked for all the details leading up to Bobby's breakdown. All the while she was aware of Laurie beside her, and the words he had spoken up on the roof whirling around her head. *I want you back.*

For the first time since the breakup, she felt hope and she longed for nothing more than time alone with him. Instead she had to endure endless questions, first from Matron, then from the MO when he appeared after seeing Bobby settled in a quiet room. At Matron's insistence, he examined Laurie's shoulder and agreed he hadn't done anything worse than pull a muscle.

'Is Bobby going to be all right?' she asked when the doctor had finished.

'I think so. I'll be sending her home to her family for a while, and I've got a colleague – an excellent psychiatrist – who lives nearby. I'm sure he'll be able to continue the fine work you started up there on the roof.'

'You certainly did a good job,' Matron said. 'You must be a valuable member of the Air Ambulance Service, and if you decide to go into nursing when the war is over, I'd be delighted to give you a recommendation.'

For Ruby, this was the highest praise and she glowed with pleasure.

'Now, I'm sure you're needing your rest, so I'll let you go.'

Ruby breathed a sigh of relief when they had finally escaped from the office. She turned to Laurie and spoke at exactly the same time as him.

'We need to talk.'

They both laughed, and Ruby felt some of her tension lift. 'Walk me back to Poplar Court?' she asked.

In reply, Laurie offered her his good arm, and she took it, feeling that she was back where she belonged. They walked out in silence, Ruby not daring to say what was on her heart until she was certain she wouldn't be overheard by any passersby in the corridor. But as soon as they were outside, their faces gilded by the dying glow of the sunset, she couldn't hold back.

'I've been such a fool,' she said. 'Can you forgive me?'

'Now I've heard what you told Bobby, I can't blame you for being so upset. It must have brought it all back every time I cancelled a date. I hate to think I reminded you of that pain. If you need my forgiveness then you have it but the fault was on my side. I should have put you first. Even Adam was angry when he heard that I'd given in to Mum's demands. I'm really sorry I ruined your weekend.'

She pulled him closer, blinking back tears. It was a huge relief to know that he understood the hurt and humiliation Dr Flint had inflicted and how it had affected her faith in herself. It gave her the courage to trust him. More than that – to trust herself and her own judgement. Laurie was the right man for her and she would never doubt it again. 'You're forgiven.' She drew a deep breath. 'I've missed you so much. Will you go out with me again?' She didn't care that women weren't supposed to ask. She just wanted him back. She glanced sideways at him in time to see a beaming smile outshine the sunset.

'I'd like nothing better.' He stopped and turned to face her, putting his hands on her shoulders. 'You called yourself a fool, but no one's been a greater idiot than me. I let you go because I thought you deserved a better man than me.'

'Why? It's always you I've wanted ever since I first saw you. No one else.'

'But I'm just an air ambulance pilot. Whenever I see a fighter pilot, I'm reminded that I'd wanted to fly Spitfires or Hurricanes. I suppose I feel like what I'm doing isn't so important, and you'd rather be with a man who's more of a hero.'

Ruby could hardly believe what she was hearing. '*You're* a hero! Bobby would be dead if you hadn't been there. And think of all the people you've saved by getting them to the right hospital for their injuries. It might not be as glamorous a job as fighter pilot, but it's just as important. I wouldn't want anyone other than you.'

Laurie didn't answer for a moment, and from the tightness at the corner of his mouth, Ruby could see he was struggling to restrain his emotions. When he spoke his voice was husky. 'It means so much to hear you say that.'

Ruby grinned. 'I'll tell you any time you need. Because it's true.' She drew a deep breath, summoning up all her courage. 'I need you to know how much I love you.' There. She'd said it. She tensed, studying his face, terrified he wouldn't say it back.

Laurie gave a whoop and lifted her off her feet before he winced and released her. 'Do you mean that? Because I love you too. So very much.' He kissed her soundly. When he broke the kiss it was to murmur in a voice that sent shivers of delight down her spine. 'And any time you need to hear it I'll say it again. Because I love you, Ruby Morris, and I'll never stop loving you.'

Ruby walked into the Three Horseshoes and smiled at her friends who were waving at her from across the snug. She felt like she hadn't stopped smiling in the three days since she and Laurie had got back together. Her friends had been delighted when she had told them, but this was the first evening they had all been able to gather and celebrate. Winnie, Laurie and Adam had arranged to come later, but Ruby was pleased to be able to spend the first part of the evening with her two closest friends.

'I had a letter from Bobby today,' she said when she sat down with her drink.

'What did she say?' Meg asked.

'It was only a short letter – she promised to write more later – but she said she had started seeing the doctor the MO recommended and she wanted to thank me and Laurie and make sure Laurie had passed her apologies to Adam.'

Holly arched her brows at Ruby. 'And was her letter written on Basildon Bond notepaper?'

'Of course!' Bobby had written more, about how much she missed her fiancé and how grateful she was to Ruby for helping her step back from the brink, both literally and figuratively. She kept that to herself, however, knowing Bobby wouldn't want her to gossip. 'But don't forget not to breathe a word about the poison pen letters to anyone else because I promised. If she got back and found everyone knew, I don't think she could bear it.'

'My lips are sealed,' Holly said.

'I promise,' Meg added.

There was a pause while they drank and then Holly said, 'What I want to know is how Adam reacted when Laurie told him.'

Meg gave Holly a playful dig in the ribs. 'You seem very interested about Adam. Is there something going on we should know about?'

'Of course I'm interested. As a friend. That's all, though. I told you. I'm staying true to Simon.'

Ruby decided to rescue her. 'Adam's fine. He was relieved when we told him about Bobby and promised not to take any action against her. He's just glad there won't be any more letters. Oh, and Laurie thinks he might be making up his mind to go back to veterinary college.'

'Wonderful!' Holly exclaimed. She raised her glass. 'I propose a toast, to Ruby, the heroine of the hour.'

They clinked their glasses, and Ruby beamed at her friends, grateful to know they were with her through thick and thin. Then, happening to glance up, she saw Laurie heading for their table, and her heart gave a bound. She raised her glass again. 'Here's to unsung heroes everywhere. And especially to Laurie, because he's *my* hero.'

Author's Note

When I first learned about the nursing orderlies of the Air Ambulance Service, I couldn't believe there weren't more books about them. Later, when I started the research for this book, I understood why – there are very few available records that mention them at all. I briefly considered going grovelling to my agent and editor to suggest I write something else but I couldn't bear to leave their story untold. Instead, I opted to move the action away from RAF Hendon (the original location of the real Air Ambulance Service) to the fictional RAF Starsden. To any readers who happen to be experts on the Air Ambulance Service, let's just say that any inaccuracies in my account are down to the different way the team worked at RAF Starsden.

I should also point out that the nursing orderlies weren't nicknamed the Flying Nightingales until they flew into Normandy after D-Day to help with the evacuation of casualties (more on that in a later book). I hope readers can forgive the anachronistic title – it was too good not to use!

I have written in other author's notes of how I've found inspiration in newspaper archives. The Poison Pen story arc in this book was also inspired by a newspaper article – the tragic story of 17-year-old Bernard Sills. The January 3 1942 edition of the *Daily Mirror* reports that he had repeatedly found white feathers on his desk at work. He finally took his own life after receiving white feathers stuck onto an anonymous postcard accusing him of cowardice. The sender's identity was unknown but believed to be a girl. The story stuck in my head for a long time, and I thought a lot about the sender. At Bernard Sills' inquest, it was revealed that he had been discharged from the army when he was discovered to be underage. That got me thinking along the lines of how a woman whose fiancé had recently been killed in action might respond to seeing a man in civvies who was apparently eligible for service. And so the character of Bobby was born!

Acknowledgements

While ideas for story lines usually come thick and fast, I often struggle with names. When it came to thinking of a good name for a dog, inspiration completely dried up. I resorted to running a competition in the Global Girls Online Book Club Facebook group, and thanks and congratulations go to Marty Stalls Frost for suggesting Bentley. As soon as I saw it, I knew it was the perfect name.

On the subject of book clubs and Facebook groups, a huge thank you to all the groups who have kindly hosted me. I've loved every single event. Also to all the book bloggers and reviewers who have taken the time to post reviews – you're amazing! A special thank-you has to go to Morton S Gray who has hosted me on her blog every time I have a book out and never fails to write a thoughtful review. All that, and she still finds time to write fabulous books!

Thank you to my brilliant editor, Emily Bedford and the whole team at Canelo. I don't know the half of how my text becomes a proper book with a beautiful cover, let alone how it ends up in stores all over the world, but I appreciate all your hard work.

Finally, to my wonderful agent, Lina Langlee – thank you for all your encouragement and support. Without you, my stories would never leave my hard drive.